Cross Switch

Cross Switch

Larry Arrowood

WOODSONG
PUBLISHING

Seymour, Indiana

Cross Switch

Woodsong Publishing
Seymour, IN 47274

www.woodsongpublishing.com

Printed in the United States of America

ISBN: 978-0-9892291-3-5

CHAPTER
ONE

The phone startled him awake.

"Is this Doctor Gary Carter?"

"Yes."

"This is Doctor Zaki Ahmed from Jerusalem, Israel. You not know me, but you referred to me by mutual acquaintance, Doctor David Stout. You know who I speak of?"

"Yes."

"Good. Let me explain my purpose for call. I am antiquities dealer and I contact you because I read about your thesis on case of DNA for Christ. I recently come across an unusual piece of wood I think is true cross upon which Christ Jesus died. I need someone of your expertise to authenticate my find."

Staring into the darkness, Gary tried to form a mental picture of this complete stranger with whom he conversed. Fat? Skinny? Short? Intelligent? Deranged? Certainly deranged. The voice droned on about the discovery and his sincere desire for Doctor Carter to partner with him.

Gary held the phone aloft.

He momentarily lapsed into a recollection of a philosophy lecture at IU. In every inconvenience there is at least a minuscule trace of opportunity. At best, it is an incredible door to possibilities. The opportunist must not only be willing to accept the inconvenience but

1

also grasp whatever straw of opportunity the inconvenience might afford. Therein lay the difficulty. Who among us could recognize opportunity?

Gary Carter, a molecular biologist by training, an archaeologist by hobby and presently an itinerant speaker on every televangelist's program that tended to sensationalize, was an opportunist by nature who gambled with fate.

Gary broke into the conversation. "If you give me exclusive examination rights to the cross, I'll be there in two weeks."

"I agree to wait for you, Doctor Carter. You will be glad you come. Wait and see, my friend."

"I'll e-mail my itinerary."

"I will see you in two weeks, Doctor Carter. *Ani veAtah neshane et haOlam!*"

"What's that?"

"I explain when you get to Israel."

The phone connection ended abruptly.

Gary's better judgment screamed that Doctor Ahmed was a con, who made a living bilking the ignorant and innocent—Gary considered himself neither. Curious? Yes, but he was not ignorant of the ways cons swindled the masses. If he spoke with associates he'd confirm an unusual amount of calls from Jerusalem, a scam as obvious as a continual going-out-of-business furniture sale. Doctor Ahmed probably has a dozen such crosses. Surely the request is a ruse, or at best Ahmed's a quack with delusions. Thinking one possesses the cross is a step away from believing one is the Christ.

Gary was not one to miss an opportunity. He smiled. What a nice publicity stunt for my book! And now I won't have to go to Columbus, Ohio.

CHAPTER
TWO

Gary scarfed down a piece of bacon. How do I tell Celeste about my trip to Israel? What did that phrase Doctor Ahmed used mean? He contemplated the bizarre request from a stranger and his even more bizarre response.

He snatched his iPhone and dialed his literary agent.

"Bob, Gary Carter here. What's the latest on a contract for my book?"

"Two verbal offers."

Gary scribbled the details. "Let's stall on acceptance."

"Because?"

"I'm heading to Israel in two weeks to verify the cross of Christ."

"Come again."

Gary rattled off an explanation.

"Sounds great!"

"Thanks for the hard work. Call me when you get something in writing. I'll keep you posted on my expedition."

Gary flipped the phone shut and glanced at Celeste standing in the open doorway.

"I love the way you smile. That's one of the million reasons I married you." He motioned for her to join him.

"Always the flatterer. Was that your agent?"

"Yes."

She undraped a towel from her head and gently dabbed her long flowing locks. "And?"

"He has two verbal offers from editors."

"Wonderful, sweetheart. I'm so happy for you. And proud." She reached out to him.

He took her hand gently and held it to his lips. "Thanks, dear."

"How long before it's on the market?"

"Hey, girl, I didn't say we accepted an offer. They've offered low advances. I think we can get more."

"But Gary—"

"Really! With all my speaking engagements, I figure they'll sell at least five hundred thousand books at say…twenty dollars each. That's…" He squinted one eye and stared into space calculating the total. "I'd say at least ten million dollars. I think they'll raise their offer. That way, they'll make sure my books don't sit in the warehouse collecting dust."

"We're not getting greedy are we, Doctor Carter?" Celeste frowned.

"Greedy? From whose perspective? Theirs or mine? I'm the one who did the research, wrote the manuscript, has the credentials and will promote the book with an exhaustive speaking tour. Why give the publisher all the gravy?"

"Maybe because of their risk."

"Am I a risk, dear?"

"Nothing personal. I'm simply thinking the offer needs to be a win-win."

"I'm the only one who'll assure myself a win. That's the real world, sweetheart. Stand up for yourself or get trampled."

"There's always the question of who's the one being trampled and who's the one doing the trampling."

"If I have to be one or the other, I'd rather be the latter." Gary pulled Celeste close and embraced her, inhaling deeply the lavender that permeated her hair.

"When did we forget that Scripture about preferring our brother, Doctor Carter? Or is that Doctor Cain?"

"Do I sound that wicked?"

"Wicked? No. Maybe a mild case of self-centeredness, though."

"Celeste Brown! I can't believe you said that. You're starting to sound more like your mother."

"Just playing the role of your conscience, dear, not your critic. And don't call me by my maiden name. Till death do us part, remember?"

"Then we're still on the same team?"

Celeste kissed him gently on the cheek but didn't answer.

He studied her facial expression. This isn't a good time to break the news about Israel.

"How did things go in California?"

"Great!" He slid a check across the table.

"Sorry I was asleep when you came home. I tried...." She stared at the check.

"It was too late for you. Nice paycheck, huh?"

"Very nice! Who called during the night?"

"Sorry about the late call. I didn't realize it woke you." His voice was raspy.

"Only momentarily."

"A colleague in Israel. Didn't realize the time here in Indiana, I suppose."

"Or else didn't care. What's up?"

"Doctor Zaki Ahmed discovered an artifact somewhere in Israel. He needs me to come to Jerusalem and authenticate his find." Gary fumbled with his napkin, folding and unfolding it a couple of times.

"Or buy it?"

"That too. Always."

"What is it?"

"The cross."

"As in Calvary's cross?"

"He thinks."

"What do you think?"

Gary shrugged.

"You going?"

"I need to ask you about that. It's during the Ohio trip." He gave Celeste an innocent I-don't-really-want-to-go-but-it's-kind-of-important look. "Do you mind?"

"It's your work. I'll be somewhat disappointed going to Ohio without you, but it's nothing a shopping trip won't cure. I know you don't enjoy vacationing in Ohio—"

"I like your mother." Gary felt more than a little indebted to his mother-in-law. She'd helped pay off his student loan as a wedding gift and helped with the down payment on their house. Of course, she wasn't above dropping subtle reminders of her generosity whenever it served a needed purpose, like the time she asked them to dog-sit her five miniature Chihuahuas while she vacationed in Florida.

"Tell her to take them to the kennel like everyone else does," he'd insisted to Celeste. "They'll do a much better job than I can. You know those dogs hate me with a passion." They made the trip to Columbus and spent the week dog-sitting.

"I wasn't suggesting you don't like mother. I realize it's the shopping you despise."

"Will Mother be upset?"

She reached across the table and touched his hand tenderly. "I'll manage without you. You don't have to go to Ohio, and you don't have to feel guilty about it, either. I'll cover with Mother for you. Anyway, she enjoys having me all to herself."

"You're the best." He grabbed a napkin from the table, wadded it into a ball, tossed it into the air and missed as he tried to catch it.

"You're as transparent as a picture window. Have you called your sidekicks?" She laughed as she picked up the napkin from the floor and walked to the trash can. "Then again, they're probably already packed."

Gary smiled sheepishly and followed her to the kitchen, carrying his unopened drink and glass of ice. "I didn't want to get their hopes up without talking to you first."

"When do you leave for Orlando?"

"Tomorrow. Another big fish." He popped the tab and poured Diet Coke into the glass of ice.

Celeste frowned as the foam rose over the top of his glass and spilled onto the countertop.

"What? I'll clean it up."

"Not the mess. It's your comment, 'Another big fish.' Is that how you feel about your clients and your presentation of the DNA marvel of God's creation, just another big fish?"

His comment was out of line. He recognized Celeste's concern and realized her disappointment. Though Gary's early life revolved around church activities, during graduate school, he distanced himself from the church. He'd never questioned God's existence, but his scalpel of faith dulled. He simply relegated God to a Sunday tradition. Conversely, Celeste kept a steady pace of personal devotion, church attendance and involvement. Gary mentally admitted a noticeable divide between them. The look on Celeste's face was obvious.

CHAPTER THREE

Celeste sat on the edge of the bed while Gary packed for his trip to Orlando. Her grin caught his attention.

"What?"

"I Believe In Miracles Ministry? Maybe they'll give you an IBIMM T-shirt for speaking."

"Don't make fun of my job. We need the income. Your BMW wasn't cheap, you know."

"I could live without a fancy car, this house, all these things," she made a sweeping motion with her hands, "and I'd still be very happy as long as I have you and the Lord."

"Hey, girl, what's with the serious tone?"

"Nothing. It's just that in two weeks you'll be leaving for Israel and now another couple days on top of that. I'll miss you."

He kissed her on the forehead and continued to the bathroom to collect his toiletries.

"Gary?"

"Yes."

"What will you do?"

"About what?" he called from the bathroom.

"With the artifact, if it really is the cross of Christ?"

"Oh, I don't know. I really haven't thought much about it. Pretty much a moot question, like what will you do with it if you find the cigar Winston Churchill smoked the day he gave his 'We'll fight them in the air, on land and at sea' speech. It's not going to happen."

"But what if?"

"Bring it home…leave it in Jerusalem…put it on eBay." Gary laughed. "I don't know. Why do you ask?"

"I was just wondering about the consequences. You know, like the arrowhead you found at Battle Ground."

"What's that got to do with the cross of Christ?"

"Just hear me out."

"Okay. You've got my attention." He returned from the bathroom.

"That arrowhead may have been from the Battle of Tippecanoe. Quite a find, if you remember. The curator said they hadn't had an arrowhead found on the grounds in five years. They wanted it to display in their museum. You wanted it for bragging rights. Remember? You kept it for yourself."

"I know, and I accidentally mixed it in with a thousand other arrowheads I've found. Now no one gets to enjoy it. So?"

"So, I'm concerned what you'll do if you should, by some wild stretch of the imagination, find the cross. If you find the actual cross of Christ, you could be a rich man, but making riches from the sacrifice of Christ doesn't seem quite right. That's my concern."

"I could always donate it to a museum."

"Just like you did the arrowhead?"

"That's a low blow." Gary tossed a pillow at her, which she caught and tossed back.

"I don't mean to be judgmental. It's just…."

"No, it's a legitimate concern. I'll give the matter consideration. After all, what if?"

CHAPTER
FOUR

Carl Swilks sat at his oversized desk that glistened from multi-layers of Pledge. With arthritic fingers that ached constantly, he wiped sweat from his receding hairline. A floor lamp, its fringed shade faded and frayed, sat behind his left shoulder and spotlighted the newspaper he held close to his eyes. His neck curved forward, forcing his chin to rest against his chest. His arched back required him to sit precariously on the edge of his chair, and he felt awkward, as if at any moment he'd slide off the seat and tumble to the floor. The lamp cast a shadow against the right wall, mimicking his awkward movements. His attention was focused on a stack of newspapers piled on the left corner of his desk. Methodically he picked up a newspaper, leafed through the pages and scanned each article. Years of research allowed him to simply scan headlines to find what he sought.

He tossed the newspaper into an overflowing cardboard box, satisfied it contained none of the information he was after. He picked up another paper from the dwindling pile and dutifully continued this routine, stopping occasionally to sip from a sweating glass of tea, long diluted from the melted ice. Late into the evening he diligently searched, holding the newspaper in an awkward position to catch the light from the reading lamp. He glanced at the clock on the mantle opposite his desk: half past ten. Laying aside the newspaper, he lifted his spectacles onto his forehead and slowly rubbed his eyes with the tips of his twisted fingers. He repositioned his eyeglasses, sighed, picked up another newspaper and returned to his search.

He had been self-employed for a long time. Too long. He planned to retire someday to warmer weather, where the climate would be a friend to his arthritic limbs. Tonight he didn't have time to think about retirement. He had utilities to pay and the mortgage was past due. He'd spent a fortune on medical bills, and even more on hiding his identity. He was still alive.

Swilks' eyes froze on a headline in the religious section. *Doctor Gary Carter to Speak on the DNA Bloodline of the Messiah.* He studied the article. Intrigued by its contents, he removed a notebook from his desk drawer and scribbled notes: *Doctor Gary Carter, renowned for research on DNA of Jewish descendants and of Jesus X.* He clumsily held the pen and winced as he pressed the tip against the paper. With labored effort, he swiveled his chair around to his computer, clasped the mouse and clicked onto the Internet. His contorted fingers painstakingly pecked at the keys. Eventually, Google appeared on the screen. He laboriously typed *Doctor Gary Carter* into the search field and pressed enter. A number of choices appeared; he clicked the first one. A picture of Carter dressed in a white doctor's jacket emerged, accompanied by an article. Swilks thoroughly read the article, picked up his pen and jotted down more notes: *Molecular biologist, graduate of Indiana University, married, no children, lives in Indianapolis. Keep an eye out for this man.* He underlined the last notation and punctuated it with an exclamation mark.

He fumbled with the telephone as he deliberately punched in the numbers. Awkwardly—as if the receiver was weighty—he pressed it to his ear.

"Reverend Tillman? Carl Swilks."

"Yes, Carl. How are you?"

"Good. Got a lead you'll be interested in."

"It's about time."

"What's that supposed to mean? I always give you preference." He dabbed his brow with a handkerchief.

"Just a minute, Carl. I have to take another call."

Swilks tossed the handkerchief onto the desk. He clumsily switched the phone to his left ear. He glanced at the grandfather's clock striking the half hour and nervously tapped his index finger on the desktop.

"I'm back. What've you got?"

"I think you'll appreciate this new lead. He's an up-and-coming phenomenon. Doctor Gary Carter, a molecular biologist turned religious speaker, moving audiences with his lectures on the DNA of Christ."

"How reliable?"

The tapping subsided. "Very reliable. Top of his class at IU. Expert in his field, especially on the proposed DNA of Christ"

"Sound's like something we might use sometime."

"I heard Benjamin Small's considering having him on his program." The tapping began again.

"If Benjamin Small's interested, it's probably because you told him about Doctor Carter. I'll give the proposition some thought. You got a number?"

"Sure do." He quickly thumbed through his notebook and found the number. "I wasn't the one who told Reverend Small about Carter, but if Small's interested, you better act fast before—"

"Thanks for the tip. Would you mind calling at a decent hour the next time?"

The connection went dead. Swilks stared at the receiver before slamming it onto the phone cradle.

Swilks grimaced from the intense pressure in his chest and swiveled his chair around from the computer, accidentally knocking his phone off the desk. He swore loudly, fumbling for his bottle of pills in his shirt pocket. He worked the lid open and popped a pill.

CHAPTER

FIVE

G ary exited the car curbside at the Indianapolis International
Airport. Celeste smiled and waved good-bye as he lugged his
suitcase and the corrugated box that contained his double helix to
the nearest kiosk. He handed his ticket to the attending skycap.

"What's in the box, Doctor Carter?"

"The secret to happiness."

"No drugs allowed, my man." He laughed.

"Would you believe a cardboard cutout of the DNA of Jesus
Christ?"

"What can wash away my sins, nothin' but the blood. Man after
my own heart. Hallelujah! Where we be travelin', my man? Heav-
en?" He laughed again.

"Orlando."

"Close, but not quite. Two pieces of luggage?"

"Yes, thank you."

"I've got you down for two bags straight through to Orlando.
Your Delta flight is number eight twenty-two and will be departing
at Gate B-eight." He handed Gary a boarding pass.

"Thank you, sir." Gary handed a crisp ten-dollar bill to the skycap, who thanked him, deftly slipped the bill inside his pocket and
placed the luggage onto the conveyor belt.

"You have a nice day, Doctor Carter. Come back and see me real soon. Thank you for flying Delta."

Gary hastened to his gate. The boarding call had already started. He slipped into line and followed the slow-moving crowd down the ramp and onto the plane. He handed the attendant his suit jacket, stepped to seat 1B and immediately buried his face in a *Smithsonian* magazine. He'd purposefully bought the magazine to read an article, *The Pharaoh Returns*, that piqued his curiosity. *"After thirty-three hundred years, young King Tutankhamen will have his day in court. Hopefully the age old mystery of the boy-king's death will someday be solved by modern technology. Was he murdered? Did he die from a wound in a hunting accident?"*

Gary hoped to see the upcoming tour of the display of fifty funerary objects from young Tut's tomb. He was especially interested in the fact wooden artifacts had survived. Gary looked out the window at the puffy clouds floating effortlessly across the baby blue sky that faded into a hazy June horizon. If a wooden shabti can survive thirty-three hundred years and still be intact, why not the cross? It's a similar climate, too. Then again, it was gilded and preserved in an airtight chamber. The cross didn't have such preferential treatment. Gary's emotions about finding the cross fluctuated from a dim ray of hope to elation and mental flagellation for even considering such a preposterous idea.

The flight proved uneventful; the article exhilarating. He watched out the window as the huge wing dipped toward the Magic Kingdom to make a final approach.

Brother Benjamin Small's personal chauffeur drove Gary to his hotel——Courtyard Orlando, downtown.

"Pick you up at seven tonight, sir."

"Thank you." Gary offered a twenty dollar bill.

The chauffeur waved it aside. Gary awkwardly slipped the bill back into his pocket. What a Midwestern cheapskate I am! He surreptitiously surveyed the chauffeur's appearance: spit-shined shoes, flawless black suit adorned with a red cummerbund and bronzed skin. His tall frame looked more like a bodyguard than a cabbie. His speech betrayed education and social graces. How does the IRS view a not-for-profit organization with a private limo thirty feet long, complete with a private chauffeur who's probably multi-lingual?

"I didn't get your name."

"Thomas, sir. Jamel Thomas."

"Thank you, Mr. Thomas."

"You're welcome, Doctor Carter. I'll see you at seven."

At the studio that evening, Reverend Benjamin Small's assistant, Cal Ripley, greeted Gary warmly and proceeded with details of the program. Gary was impressed by Cal's down-to-earth style: blue jeans, Florida shirt, sandals and no socks. An hour later he stared into the TV cameras to the cheers of a live audience as Brother Benjamin introduced him.

"His doctoral dissertation on *The Preservation of the Kohanim Bloodline Throughout the Jewish Diaspora and the Presumed Uniqueness of Christ's DNA* hasn't earned the raving reviews it deserves among the world of academia, but it has gotten the attention of Christendom. Our speaker mesmerizes fundamentalist audiences across America. He explains in layman's terminology the complex scientific jargon of the existence of man. Please put your hands together and help me welcome to our program Doctor Gary Carter. Welcome, Doctor Carter."

"Thank you, Reverend Small. Glad to be here."

Reverend Small waited for the applause to fade. "You're trained as a molecular biologist, schooled in evolution, yet you're a proponent of creationism."

"That's right."

"Would you elaborate?"

"Darwin's vision of relatives swinging from trees was distorted by biased reasoning. We readily admit Mr. Darwin had limited resources, but that is a poor excuse for his unscientific assumptions. Due to the antiquated microscopes he used, he never saw inside a single cell. He only saw blobs of protoplasm with a dark spot identifying the nucleus—even though mankind has about seventy-five trillion of those little fellows that make up his body. Darwin had no way of realizing a single human cell, about one-thousandth the size of a period, has a DNA strand of over three billion base pairs. He couldn't comprehend it takes ten million atoms to build a single cell. When Mr. Darwin rejected the Psalmist's proclamation, 'I am fearfully and wonderfully made,' he became blind to the more than seventy-five trillion cells in a human body that carry the fingerprints of the creator."

"So you think he was blinded by a bias against creationism and by the antiquated research technology?"

"I think so."

Amens punctuated the room. Feathers from hats, scattered across the audience, resembled peacocks strutting across the field, as heads nodded approvingly.

"How is research different now?"

"He couldn't see the synchronized cells working together like the hundreds of service operations of cities such as New York, Los Angeles or Orlando. Mr. Darwin had no clue about the complexity of the cell: a nucleus that houses the DNA, a control center, a waste removal program, a microscopic city in full production, ever reproducing itself. Apart from his rejection of creationism, he may have done the best he could without modern tools, genetic research and the Hubble space telescope, but Darwin now looks like a kid tearing apart his plastic Batmobile and thinking he's an engineering expert for NASA's Shuttle Discovery."

The audience erupted in laughter that exploded into a thunderous applause.

Gary smiled, held up his hands in a modest gesture of thanks and waited for the clapping to cease. "Man wasn't an accident, or a lucky toss of the dice. Though similar in DNA structure to other creatures, he didn't mutate from the animal world of chimpanzees and gorillas and evolve over millions of years into the delicate human being he is now, who can think, speak, create and see the need to brush his teeth and comb his hair. And fall in love. No. Man is the intricate design of a master planner who controls the universe. Man is the design of the God of the Holy Bible."

The response of the audience exhilarated Gary.

"What about theistic evolution?"

"God didn't set the evolutionary process in place and then step aside for millions of years to allow the process to work on its own, eventually evolving into humankind. God created everything with His spoken word, just like the Genesis account proclaims."

"What about similarities in design. Doesn't that point toward evolution?"

"Any similarities in design are proof of a singular designer."

More applause.

"You're the expert on DNA, and you've speculated about the DNA of Christ in your dissertation. Would you explain your premise?"

"Yes. Christ's DNA carried the message of immortality. That's why Jesus could say, 'I am the resurrection, and the life: he that believeth in me, though he were dead, yet shall he live: And whosoever liveth and believeth in me shall never die.' Jesus, the God-man, carried a God strand of DNA that would appear picture perfect in the world of microbiology under the lens of electron microscopes and examined with laser tweezers. He was the only perfect man since the creation. That's how Paul could say, 'With His own shed blood Christ purchased the church.' That's how a flawed humanity can be considered perfect in Christ Jesus. We have perfection within through Christ's indwelling Spirit."

Gary made the DNA technical information, that lulled the O.J. Simpson jurors to sleep, come alive with spiritual applications. The crowd stood to its feet, clapping; some lifted their hands. The audience loved the lecture.

Gary scanned the faces of the audience. Deep down he wasn't as sincere as he tried to appear. He had some regrets about the lecture circuit in the Christian community instead of applying himself to research, but his bills kept coming due, and financially profitable speaking engagements kept coming.

"I understand, Doctor Carter, you're leaving on a very adventurous trip in a few days."

"Well, yes, I'm going to Jerusalem for a few days."

"In search of the cross, I understand."

"Not actually in search. An antiquities dealer has found the cross, or rather a cross."

"You've been asked to inspect the cross because it's presumed to be the cross of Christ, and you, being a molecular biologist, could possibly prove scientifically this particular cross is the actual cross upon which Christ died."

Benjamin Small wasn't a small man. Gary guessed him to be well over six feet tall, and he had a way of using all his intimidating inches to his advantage. He leaned toward Gary when asking questions and reclined his frame in a smug way to make an indisputable statement, or await a response.

"Well, that's a mighty big assumption at this point."

"Your thesis in graduate work postulated the idea if we could find the cross, and if there were traces of Christ's blood upon it, we could authenticate it as being the cross of Christ by doing DNA analysis. Would you mind telling this fine Christian audience, in layman's terms, of course, how Christ's blood could be authenticated even though we have no databank from which to compare?"

Reverend Small's use of technical terms impressed Gary. Reverend Small seemed impressed himself.

"It's all hypothetical at this stage." Gary felt the urge to disprove what was presumptuous teaching on his part in the past. He suddenly realized his graduate theory was about to be put to the test. Not by the doubting Thomases of academia, but by the zealous Christian community.

"You are going to Jerusalem?"

"Yes."

"To examine a cross?"

"Yes."

"Why?"

"The owner feels very strongly it's the actual cross of Christ."

"Why?"

"I don't know."

"You're willing to go and test it? Isn't that because there's a possibility it is the cross that Christ bore on His back along the Via Delarosa to Golgotha?" Reverend Small leaned toward Gary and pressed for a yes.

Gary made a good living on the speaking circuit promoting the very thing he was now tempted to argue against. He'd admitted he was going to check on a cross, but he wasn't going to admit his primary reason for going to Jerusalem was to avoid a two-week shopping spree and break away from the routine of canned lectures.

"A cross has been found. It's old, quite old, I'm sure. My contact sent me a photograph of the cross. It matches the description given by historians, like Josephus, a contemporary of that day, who well understood the Roman style of execution by crucifixion. However, you could say I'm not going to prove it's the cross of Christ so much as to prove it isn't Christ's cross."

"Why the negative approach?

"The Roman Church already claims to have the cross, or at least parts of it, even claiming the nails that held Christ to the cross. Traditionally, the cross disappeared right after the Crucifixion, but Constantine's mother, Helena, thought there might be a chance of finding it. She discovered a secret vigilance committee, no doubt Jewish, had disassembled the cross, heaved it into a well and covered it with stones to hide it from Christ's followers. I suppose they did that to prevent any veneration to a supposed impostor. The Jews had their mezuzah to remind them of the Holy Scripture, but they didn't want others kissing a cross in remembrance of Christ—kind of like eliminating the competition, I assume. Well, this one Jewish fellow, ironically by the name of Judas, showed Helena a well where the cross was hidden. When the debris was removed, eureka, the cross was at the bottom of the well. She sent part of it back to her son, left part of the cross in Jerusalem and sent splinters of it as gifts all over the known world. Even a portion of it became encased in a statue of Constantine."

"That's all legend. No actual proof, right?"

"In my research, it's certainly legend. Eusebius, Bishop of Caesarea in Palestine, and called by some the father of early church history, recorded Helena's trip to Palestine. He recorded the many good deeds she did and the various churches and shrines she was responsible for building but never mentioned the finding of the cross. Being the bishop in Palestine at the time of Helena's supposed discovery around three hundred years after the Crucifixion, he would've certainly recorded such a momentous event. Don't you think?"

"One would think so. I've visited Jerusalem several times. In Jerusalem every year, on different dates for the Latins and Greeks, they have a celebration for the finding of the cross—they call this The Invention of the Holy Cross. There are all kinds of legends and speculations—by the Latin Church, the Greek Church, even the Russians and French have their hands in the pot. I read one legend where King Baldwin of Jerusalem gave a fragment of the cross to the Templars, who in turn presented it to St. Louis of France. The fragment is still preserved in Paris. So, while you're researching the cross, Doctor Carter, you might as well visit Turin and the Holy Shroud. Don't forget the Holy Grail in England either."

Brother Benjamin's knowledge impressed Gary. The audience clapped enthusiastically at his comments, a reminder that Brother Benjamin was the star of the show.

"Even with all the giving away of fragments, tradition has it the cross never grew smaller. All that sounds phony to me."

This was the first indication to Gary of Brother Benjamin's inclinations.

"Who found the cross you're going to authenticate?"

"We're keeping that confidential. Let's just say my colleague was educated at the university in Jerusalem with a degree in archaeology and religion. He's already done a carbon test, and it's definitely a first-century cross. He wants me to do a DNA test."

"Why you? No offense, Doctor Carter, but why not someone already in Jerusalem?"

"I'm the expert."

"But modest." The audience laughed. "I'm not an expert on DNA, Doctor Carter, but I'm aware you'd have to have some human evidence to test in order to prove it was Christ that hung on the cross."

"My contact thinks he does."

"Like what?"

"Blood."

"Whose blood?"

"The victim's."

"How can that be? After two thousand years it's inconceivable blood stains would remain on unprotected wood."

"My contact thinks differently."

"Why?"

"The cross was made from a pine tree. My contact has traced its source to be native of Judea. Being a pine tree, it seeped sap where the nails were driven, in three places, indicative of the Roman crucifixion, coating the areas where the hands were nailed to the horizontal crossbeam and where the feet were nailed to the perpendicular beam. He speculates under the hardened sap is preserved the blood of Christ."

The audience stood and clapped.

"That's pretty incredible, the possibilities, Doctor Carter. Of course, we dare not get our hopes too high."

"At first I thought it was a lark. More recently, I've concluded it's worthy of research. I'm rather excited about our excursion."

"If you fail to disprove it's Christ's cross, you leave much room for speculation within the Christian community."

"Of course…"

"So, we'll prayerfully await the outcome of your trip. Thank you, Doctor Gary Carter, for being on our program and for being so candid with our interview. Of course, when you return, we'll want to have you on our program again. Maybe even with the blessed cross of Christ."

"That would be great." Gary smiled.

"If you don't mind, I want to pray for you that the Lord will guide you and bless you in your endeavor to prove one of the greatest mysteries of the ages: What happened to the cross?"

Gary bowed his head as Brother Benjamin took both of Gary's hands and cupped them in his own enormous hands and prayed. The prayer sounded sincere enough—perhaps too sincere for Gary's own attitude toward the Jerusalem trip. *Does my face reflect insincerity?* Guilt throbbed in his chest, and he was glad the prayer was short.

"There you have it, ladies and gentlemen, Saints of the Most High God, the latest breaking news in the Christian world. After two millenniums, it's possible we'll have access to that old rugged cross." Reverend Small lowered his voice in a reverent tone as he looked directly into the camera.

A royal blue curtain parted on stage, directly behind them, and revealed the seventy-five-voice program choir, dressed in matching white robes highlighted with a crimson cross. They sang *The Old Rugged Cross*. An accompanying orchestra—the men were dressed in black tuxedos, white shirts and red ties and the women wore black glistening evening gowns highlighted by red scarves—held out the final note as the audience arose to their feet and clapped.

Gary saw the camera zoom on his face. *I hope Celeste isn't watching.*

CHAPTER
SIX

Celeste bounded from her BMW and embraced Gary. "Missed you, sweetheart. How did it go?"

"Okay. Did you happen to see the program?"

"No. I'm sorry. Did I miss something important?"

"No. I was just wondering since it was live. Hey, how about some spending money for your trip?"

Gary reached into his pocket and pulled out his love offering—a check for twenty thousand dollars. He held it at arm's length for Celeste to see, but far enough away from her so she couldn't grab it. It was a game he liked to play—just to tease her. In the end, he always signed the checks and gave them to her to deposit in their joint account.

"Not a bad paycheck." Celeste smiled as he held the check closer. "My place or St. Elmo's for dinner?"

"St. Elmo's sounds wonderful. I never get tired of that place. It's where you changed my life, you know."

"I hope there are no regrets."

He recalled in vivid detail the night he proposed. They sat at a corner table at St. Elmo's on Valentine's Day. A vase of red roses adorned the table.

"Thank you for the roses. They're lovely."

"More so sitting beside you than they were in the florist shop."

She blushed. "You shouldn't have spent so much, and the meal is way too expensive."

"Anything for you, dear, to the half of my kingdom."

Celeste smiled but didn't reply. He reached across the table and gently caressed her hand. Soft light from the flickering candle spotlighted Celeste's charming yet modest smile. Her beauty radiated innocence; her demeanor exuded an unpretentious quality Gary adored about her.

"Would you like a refill on your drinks?" a waiter asked.

"Yes, please," Gary said.

Chatting, laughter and the clinking of tableware echoed from the wood paneled walls of the dining room. It was a happy place, and Gary was the happiest man present.

The waiter, in phantom fashion, returned with Diet Cokes and moved on to the next table. Gary breathed deeply, reached into a pocket of his sports jacket and pulled out a small golden box adorned with a red bow. He set it on the table beside the flowers. He looked into Celeste's eyes for a reaction; the usual unassuming gleam in her eyes reflected the candlelight.

"Thanks for a lovely meal. This place is so…so elegantly casual."

"I'm glad you like it. I like pleasing you."

"How sweet."

"Celeste, I'd like to spend the rest of my life pleasing you?"

"I'm surprised…amazed. You've only known me a few months."

"Long enough to know I want to spend the rest of my life with you."

"Is that a proposal?"

"Yes."

He untied the red bow, opened the small box and nervously took out a silver ring, studded with a single diamond. He reached for her hand. She withdrew it. Gary sat stunned, unable to speak.

"Gary, I, too, would want to please you with my life, but there's something about me…and you…that could make both of us…uncomfortable…even unhappy."

"What?" He spoke louder than he intended. Celeste didn't answer. "What?" he pleaded softly.

"My entire life has been focused on church work. That's why I'm in college now. I'm considering mission work as a nurse. Your life, please forgive me for being judgmental, but your life seems so focused around…secular goals. I may not be the right person for your future."

"You are the right person for me."

"How can you be sure?"

He didn't answer. He sat in silence as she stared into his sky-blue eyes with a pained expression on her face. He could tell she cared about him, but she refused his proposal.

"Not now, Gary. Let's give ourselves some time to see where life takes us. A few months, perhaps, please?"

At first Gary was angry, but after some tough introspection, she was right. His goals for life, and his faith in God, were two separate entities. One didn't facilitate the other. Their parting that night was painful but amicable. They didn't see or speak to each other for a few weeks.

For days, an icy silence calloused Gary's heart that even the memory of Celeste's warm smile didn't thaw. He contemplated ways to hurt her as she'd hurt him. Though he knew he loved her, and she expressed she deeply cared for him, he battled with an ego bigger than he cared to admit. After much soul searching, he realized she was right in being honest with him. So he sought to embrace science through the eyes of his Christian faith. When the two came into conflict, he attempted to stand on the side of his faith. This caused him some discomfort in the classroom, but Celeste warmed to his change of thinking. Pleasing her meant far more than pleasing colleagues. To further gain favor in her eyes, he hit upon an idea for his doctoral dissertation.

"Absolutely not," his professor vehemently opposed the idea. "A thesis on the DNA of Christ is too juvenile…too Bob Jonesy to be accepted as IU graduate work."

Gary insisted, pointing out his premise that if there was a Christ—an Incarnation—and if Christ's DNA could be evaluated, the strand of the double helix would be absolutely perfect; free from any abnormalities or mutations. By expanding the subject to include a study of the Jewish priestly caste—the descendants of the *kohanim*, who had a chromosome so distinct they were unique among all other groups—Gary won the prof's reluctant approval; his project, reflecting a renewed faith, won Celeste's hand in marriage.

Security walked their way. "Best be loading, or else we'll be walking home. Oh, by the way, I forgot to check the other envelope Jamel gave me at the airport."

"Who's Jamel?"

"Reverend Small's personal chauffeur."

He handed the envelope to her as she climbed into the passenger seat. He maneuvered his luggage into the small trunk, closed the lid gently and eased behind the wheel. Celeste sat silently. The opened envelope lay in her lap.

"What is it, dear?"

"Another check."

"Great! Probably for expenses. How much?

"A five with five zeros behind it."

"What?" He snatched the check from Celeste.

"You must have done a good job, dear."

"It's not for the lecture." Gary sighed and handed the check back to Celeste. "We both know that. It's some kind of bribe money."

"For what?"

"The cross. What else could it be? Reverend Small definitely showed interest in my Israel trip."

"You can't accept it."

"I know."

Gary eased the BMW onto I-70 toward downtown Indianapolis and whipped into the far left lane. A black sedan with tinted windows, that had followed them out of the airport parking lot, maneuvered into the same lane—a few car lengths back. Gary accelerated, passed a car and worked his way back into the right lane; the sedan turned on its right blinker but allowed a semi to pass on its right. Gary glanced into the rearview mirror. The sedan had dropped back. He relaxed his grip on the steering wheel.

"Is something wrong?" Celeste still clutched the check.

"I could have sworn a car was following us, but I was wrong. Kind of jumpy, aren't I."

"No explanation at all for this check?" Celeste held it up as if checking for a watermark.

"No. Any note with it?"

"Nothing but the check."

"I have a suspicion Reverend Small's trying to manipulate a purchase of Admed's discovery."

Gary turned onto the Illinois/McCarty Street exit and took the Illinois Street ramp towards St. Elmo's. Celeste leaned her head against the headrest; she held Gary's free hand. The check lay in her lap.

Gary braked for a red light. The black sedan screeched to a stop beside him. The passenger door flew open and a masked assailant leaped out, dressed in black, including leather gloves. He flashed a handgun. Without warning, he smashed his forearm into the driver's window and yelled a muffled command. Gary grimaced. Celeste screamed for him to go, but a line of traffic streamed across in front of them. Gary considered turning right, but it was one-way into on-coming traffic. The gunman yanked on the locked door and aimed the pistol at Gary's head. Gary's mind raced. A robbery in down-town Indy in broad daylight?

"What do you want?" Gary screamed at the assailant. He snatched the check from Celeste's lap and pressed the down button for the window.

"Get out," the masked man shouted, his guttural voice heavy with accent.

Gary thrust the check in the man's face. "You can have it."

The attacker slapped at the check with his free hand, refusing to accept it. "Get out, Doctor Carter, before I kill you."

Gary gripped the steering wheel. He knows my name! It's not a robbery. A kidnapping? It's me he wants. Not Celeste. I can protect Celeste, but if he wants me to go with him, it has to be for other reasons or else he'd have shot me already. Gary fought the urge to floor the accelerator into the congested intersection.

"Obey my command," the attacker snarled.

Where's that accent from? His blood boiled. What's the chromosome for stubborn?

The light turned green. Gary grabbed the door handle, yanked upwards and slammed the door against the gunman, knocking him backwards.

The gunman recovered and grabbed at him through the window; Gary pressed the up button and the window tightened on the attacker's gloved hand; he refused to let loose of the window. Gary accelerated toward a break in traffic and steered toward the opening.

The gunman sprinted alongside the car. Gary jerked the steering wheel as he swerved dangerously close to cars along the curbside. The attacker's head slammed against the window and ripped off the mask. Celeste screamed and braced her hands against the dashboard. The attacker's face was hideous, his skin scarred, paper-thin and drawn taut, the effects of having been terribly burned. A blurry gray eye peered out through an uneven slit; the other eye was massed over completely. Jagged teeth, rotten and stained, jutted from his mouth and dug into cracked parched lips. An indiscrete opening of disfigured flesh protruded from where a nose had once existed. Scars covered his entire head. The attacker snarled in rage and clawed at the window with his free hand. Gary pressed the window button to open and accelerated, giving the intruder the chance to free himself of the car. He held on instead. He relentlessly grabbed at Gary through the open window while he clung to the door with his other hand. Gary fought off the attack with his left hand as he frantically tried to steer the car with his right.

A siren blared in the distance. Gary refused to stop. Celeste's panic-stricken voice shrieked out useless orders and pleas. A car swerved to miss the Beemer, too late. Gary's left-front headlight smashed into the car's front bumper. The car caught the attacker with its rear bumper and ripped him loose from the car. In the rearview mirror Gary saw him tumble along the pavement. He drove another half-block before he slammed on the brakes and the car slid to a stop. His heart pounded in his chest.

He glanced at Celeste's colorless complexion and reached across the car to console her. Holding her trembling hands, he peered through the rear-view mirror. The attacker had vanished.

A curious and noisy crowd gathered. A policeman approached, carrying the dark mask and a glove, wading through the hypothesizing crowd that surrounded the car. Against the backdrop of commotion and curiosity, the cruiser lights flashed noiselessly. Gary sat in stunned silence, except for his heavy breathing. His body shook violently from an adrenaline rush of fear and anger. Celeste, her face buried in her hands, cried softly. The five hundred thousand dollar check lay at her feet.

"You two okay?" a voice called through the open window.

"I think so." Gary looked up into the badge of the IPD officer. He glanced at Celeste who shook her head affirmatively but didn't speak.

"Can you get out of the car, sir?" The officer spoke gently, yet commandingly.

"I hope so."

The officer opened the door and Gary stepped out onto wobbly legs.

"Whoa! Best sit back down, sir. A medical unit is on its way."

"Where is it?"

"The ambulance is just a few blocks away, sir. Just try and relax."

"No, not the ambulance. The fiend."

"The what, sir?"

"The attacker…that thing…the monster...whatever was trying to get inside our car." Gary placed his arm across Celeste's shoulders and pulled her gently toward him. She showed no response to his comforting embrace.

"Sir, have you been drinking?"

"I'll take over from here." A man in plain clothes stepped up to the car and flashed his badge.

"Glad you're here, sir. Best do a breathalyzer," he spoke quietly but loud enough Gary heard.

CHAPTER SEVEN

They sat across the desk from Detective Dan Mink at the Indianapolis Police Department. Celeste fiddled with a wadded up tissue, occasionally dabbing the corners of her eyes. Gary gently caressed her hand.

"Eyewitnesses collaborate your account, Doctor Carter. No matter how bizarre it sounds. You didn't see the attacker running away from the car after you stopped? Or get into another car?"

"No, sir." Gary shook his head. After the response of the initial police officer, he didn't dare tell Officer Mink what he really thought about the Tut-like face, with demonic strength, grabbing at him through the window.

"We're checking all area hospitals for emergency care. He'll have to turn up sooner or later, unless he's lying dead somewhere. Officers are still checking the surrounding area for clues. We'll stay on it."

"Thanks. What about the mask and glove? Any clues?"

"We found a mask which we can now assume belonged to the attacker. Did you see him with or without the mask?

"Both. He was masked at the beginning of the attack, but it got ripped off."

"So you can identify him?"

"Maybe."

"We'll need a sketch artist. Any unusual features?"

Detective Mink scribbled in a notepad. Gary glanced at Celeste. He could tell she wanted him to come clean, to tell the full account of the inhuman creature clinging to their car. Gary mouthed an emphatic "no." Celeste's lips tightened and her forehead creased. She disagreed. He was resolute in his decision to remain silent about the attacker's bizarre appearance.

"I only got a glimpse. Everything happened so quickly."

"Anything you can remember will be helpful: color of hair, teeth, scars."

"Like I said, it happened so quickly. Did anyone else happen to see the attacker?"

"Pretty much the same…everything happened quickly. Every eyewitness has a different perspective…some quite unbelievable."

Celeste tossed Gary another facial command, which he ignored.

The detective handed him a piece of paper. "I'm sorry, but under the circumstances, I have to cite you for crossing the middle line and hitting the approaching car. The car suffered some damage, so you'll need to report it to your insurance company."

"Sure. Not a problem." Gary gave no resistance.

"It wasn't Gary's fault…"

"I'm sorry, Mrs. Carter, but when you cross the center line and sideswipe a car, it's always your fault."

"But under the circumstances…"

"Under any circumstances."

"We understand, sir." Anything else from us?" Gary stood.

Celeste gave him another I-can't-believe-you're-taking-this look.

"Also, I must ask if both you and Mrs. Carter had your seat belts on."

"Yes." Celeste made a distorted face that reflected her frustration at being a punching bag for his insinuating questions. Gary was glad the officer's attention remained glued to the notepad and therefore didn't see Celeste's facial expressions.

"Good."

"Will that be all, Detective?" Gary extended a helpful hand to Celeste, who stood without his assistance.

"Yes. You're free to go. We'll run a check on the glove and mask the officers found. It might surprise you to know what we can find out with modern technology and all. Used to be we relied on eye-witnesses and fingerprints. Nowadays we have modern techniques like DNA fingerprinting and such. You wouldn't believe some of the things that can be found out from crime scene investigation in the lab. Just the other day I heard they identified a person by his spit left from licking an envelope fifty years ago."

"Really?"

"Like I said, it might surprise you what modern technology can do."

"Maybe so, sir. I'd appreciate you letting me know of any new developments." Gary handed the detective a business card.

Officer Mink studied the card for a moment. "Molecular biol-ogist? I'll be...what a coincidence. I have egg on my face, Doctor Carter. We may be calling you for some assistance."

"Be glad to assist any way I can, sir. Feel free to call."

"Ah, Doctor Carter, there was one more oddity to this rather bizarre event." The officer hesitated.

"What's that, sir?"

"One of the officers found this." He took a Ziploc bag from his pocket and handed it to Gary, who stared at its contents.

"A ring? Where was it found?"

"Inside a finger of the glove we found."

Gary turned the plastic bag over in his hand, looking at the ring from different angles. He held the bag so Celeste could see the ring. She showed bewilderment. The golden ring revealed a sculptured cross, superimposed over a skull, embedded in an amber stone.

"By any chance does this mean anything to you, Doctor Car-ter?"

"Not really. I've never seen anything quite like it. I've seen a skull and crossbones, of course, but never a skull and cross."

"Didn't really think it had any meaning to you but just thought I'd ask. Thanks for your cooperation. I don't really have anything else at this time. You're free to go, unless you have anything to ask me."

"No. I don't think so."

31

Celeste hastened from the building. Gary caught up with her in the parking lot.

"Why didn't you tell him?"

"For starters, he'd throw me in the slammer in a straitjacket. It's more than that. The attacker was real, but not human. Since real but not human, then he, or it, had to be some kind of spirit…a demon of some sort. Policemen aren't exorcists. I doubt guns and handcuffs have much effect on evil spirits."

They drove along the Indy streets in silence. Celeste crossed her arms and drew them over her upper body, as if chilled. Gary adjusted the thermostat.

"Why us?" Celeste broke the silence.

"I'm not sure. You okay?"

"As well as can be expected after being attacked by a Gadarene descendant."

"A what?" Gary frowned at her.

"You know, the guy from Gadara in the Bible…lived among the tombs…tore and cut himself…super strength and all that stuff."

"He looked old enough to be from Bible days." Gary turned the BMW into their drive and pressed the garage door opener; a dozen floodlights illuminated their driveway—still wet from the evening sprinkler system that watered the manicured yard and the colorful flowers bordering the driveway. A neighbor, emptying his trash, waved from across a trimmed hedge; Gary waved back. He maneuvered the car into the three-bay garage and cut the engine. They sat for a long moment in silence, his hands grasping the steering wheel. Celeste's head leaned against the headrest, her eyes closed. He reached across the console and gently squeezed her hand; it was cold and trembling.

CHAPTER
EIGHT

Taking advantage of the Memorial Day weekend, Gary relaxed in his study. In the corner, a radio transmitted the muffled roar of the Indy 500, blending in with the droning noise of a neighbor's mower. The pungent scent of the freshly mowed grass arrested his senses. He leafed through a photo album of his wedding as he distractedly listened to Mike King describe the play-by-play action of the big race. Life had been good to him—a great wife, excellent income and this beautiful home. He contemplated a job change, viewing his occupation as being worthless as far as productivity, but he had grown accustomed to the intoxicating applause and dependent on the hefty paychecks. He kept thinking his gig would peter out any day, and he'd move on to more meaningful causes, but the calls for him to speak kept coming in. Supply and demand made for a great business.

All had been smooth sailing since graduate school. He certainly hadn't counted upon the recent turn of events. He worried for Celeste's safety. "How do I explain asking anyone to check in on Celeste while I'm away to make sure the skulled goon hasn't returned?" His audible thoughts shocked him.

Gary had discussed calling off the trip to Israel, but Celeste felt strongly he should pursue the project. Plus, she'd be in Ohio, so he didn't need to worry for her safety. He had invited college buddies

Rick Hogg and Jack Metz to accompany him to Israel. He wondered if he should tell them about the recent strange incident by the attacker but concluded they wouldn't believe him. He'd always been good for a practical joke during college days. They wouldn't fall for such an outlandish story. At times the attack seemed to have been only a surreal nightmare, but he carried some bruises on his left arm, and he had the testimony of a shaken Celeste as an eyewitness, to verify the ordeal really happened.

Gary studied the certified check from Benjamin Small's ministry, contemplatively turning it over and over in his hands. He counted for the umpteenth time the zeros behind the five and finally placed the check back inside his desk drawer. He tapped ten digits on his iPhone and hesitantly touched send.

"Thank you for calling I Believe In Miracles Ministry. How may I direct your call?"

"Reverend Small, please."

"May I tell him who's calling?"

"Doctor Gary Carter."

"One moment, Doctor Carter."

After a five-minute wait, a familiar voice interrupted the soft music. "Sorry to keep you waiting. How are you, Doctor Carter?"

"Fine...and you?"

"Fantastic. What can I do for you?"

"Uh...I need to speak with you about the additional check."

"It didn't bounce did it?" He laughed.

"No, sir. I haven't tried to cash it. It's not that. I'm more than a little confused about the amount, and I'm not sure what the additional check is for."

"A gift, Doctor Carter. A gift to your ministry."

"My ministry?"

"The one God has called you to perform—finding the cross of Christ. I want to help you not only find it, but I want to help bring it to the States. I mean to be considered a benefactor of the cross, to help the cross find a proper home. Should circumstances arise that the cross goes up for sale, I'd like IBIMM to be considered as the future owner. You can call the check my good faith money if you like. I'll double it when you deliver the cross to me."

"I'm not sure about the authenticity..."

"Doctor Carter, with your reputation and expertise, all you have to do is purchase and deliver that cross to me. I'll convince the people it's the real thing."

"Half a million..."

"I said double upon delivery."

"A million dollars for something unauthenticated is a lot of money, sir."

"You authenticate it and I'll raise my price to five million. If you can't authenticate it, just keep your research silent and I'll still give you the million for the cross as is."

"Reverend, how could I ethically keep silent if I know otherwise?"

"Doctor Carter, it's simply a business deal. Like Christopher Columbus' bones the Dominicans and Spaniards both assert they have. Neither is in a hurry to disprove the other's claim, for in trying to do so, they might find out the bones they possess aren't Columbus' either. So, they keep a great public relations campaign going, and people keep coming to their shrines, just in case it is the real thing. I'm asking you to prove the authenticity of the cross, if you can, but certainly stop short of disproving its genuineness. I'm willing to pay you well for your work and, of course, for the cross. Cash the check and we'll work out the details when you return from Israel with the cross. We got a deal?"

"Well, if I don't have to decide right now, I suppose we can work together on the project." Gary sighed.

"Thank you, Doctor Carter. I look forward to hearing from you soon."

The phone clicked and Gary held it for a long moment, wishing he could discuss the issue further. He thumbed absentmindedly through a stack of mail. One piece caught his attention. He didn't recognize the name of the return address, but he knew what esquire at the end of a name meant. For that reason, he hated to open the embossed envelope.

"Who else is wanting a piece of the pie?"

The letter was from a lawyer that represented Reverend John Tillman. Gary wasn't surprised. He slowly read through the numerous "pursuant to, therefore, and whereas" clauses until he came to the bottom line—Reverend Tillman was demanding Gary give him first chance at purchasing the cross. A copy of a speaking contractual agreement, signed by Gary, was enclosed. He read and reread the small print of the contract. "How could I have been such a pig head?" He tossed the contract onto the desk.

Tillman had beaten Small by a few days in having Gary appear on his program. Small tried to buy him; Tillman had outfoxed him. Tillman both impressed and disturbed Gary. He proudly walked Gary through the multimillion-dollar facility that housed state-of-the-art technology. Tillman's attention to detail would have made him a good scientist, but on a scientist's salary he could not have afforded the luxuries that surrounded him. An oriental rug adorned the yellowish-brown teak flooring of Tillman's massive office. He purchased the rug in Afghanistan on a mission of peace; he found the hardwood in an antique shop in Bombay. Purportedly, the wood was from a ship sailed by Admiral Sir Edward Rice Owen during the heyday of the East India Company, or else it was from the company's famous building on Leadenhall Street. The salesman wasn't definite about which story was true, but either one made a great impression on Reverend Tillman. He spared no expense to have the finest technicians aboard. The recording studio, a showcase fit for royalty, featured purple draperies, gilded picture frames, with porcelain and marble statues everywhere. Tillman owned his own satellite and made a lucrative living airing a host of Christian programs other than his own. He beamed his personal program into every widow's living room daily, and twice daily the first few days of the month, when retirement checks arrived.

The Tillman gospel was unfamiliar to Gary; it greatly contrasted the gospel message on which he'd cut his teeth. That childhood message focused on Calvary, grace, repentance and salvation. Tillman's was a message of what "he" was doing for the kingdom, and it was all made possible because of his faithful partners. Further, it was what "he" could do if a few thousand more partners stood beside him with a minimum donation of one thousand dollars each, and more if God moved on their hearts. "God will bless you for blessing me." He spoke with such sincerity Gary felt guilty about the hefty paycheck Tillman gave him.

In his talks throughout the Christian community, Gary was stunned by how many people ordered the DVDs of his presentations.

Even more so he was shocked at how many people purchased vials of holy water and small sacks of sacred sand from various TV personalities he'd become associated with. Seeing firsthand this commercialization of Christianity bothered him, especially when a TV minister sometimes summarized the lecture he gave and used his educational credentials to peddle some religious trinket to finance his program and a home in Florida and California and Maine. Still, Gary justified his participation in such ministries; he wasn't saying anything untrue. His lectures were mere speculations about the DNA of Christ. He was paid well for lecturing—as shown by the latest reviews of religious broadcasting—but he wasn't responsible for any unethical antics by the producers. He tithed to his local church and gave to various charities. He had a house mortgage and three vehicles to pay for—not to mention financing Celeste's upcoming shopping trip.

Gary pondered his predicament of a multiple of hands vying for a piece of the pie. Jack's father was sponsoring the trip with the assumption it gave him first chance to purchase the cross, if it should prove to be the true cross of Christ. Now Tillman's claim, by way of a signed contract, gave him first chance at buying the cross. To further complicate matters, Brother Benjamin had given half a million dollars in earnest money, sight unseen, true or fake, for the cross—with a promise that could top out at five million. Stoking the flames to the drama, an unidentified demonic force seemed to have determined to have the cross by any means necessary.

Considering his options brought some relief. Jack's father was too presumptuous. He might be disappointed but he would get over it. Tillman's contract seemed to read first chance "if" and "when" Gary sold the cross. The option would terminate after five years. Further, it seemed the cross had to be authentic before Tillman wanted it. Both clauses could be an out for him. He could wait until Tillman's option expired and then sell the cross for a much higher price if he put it on the auction block. Still, he wasn't convinced he'd want to sell the cross. Brother Benjamin certainly seemed the most promising, for he'd given a substantial amount up front with a promise of much more. Perhaps Gary could lease the cross to Brother Benjamin for a period of time, at least five years, and then sell it to him for who knows how much, if he proved the cross to be authentic. Until then, whatever was left over of the half million—after he purchased the cross from Zaki—could be applied to lease payments. In the meantime, what about the cloak and dagger danger that owning the cross placed Celeste into? He wasn't sure he was up to another carjacking attempt.

A simple e-mail to Jerusalem could put an end to the drama—at least Gary's role. If he proved the cross to be authentic, the discovery could plaster his face on the front cover of every archaeology magazine. He might even outdo young King Tut in the *Smithsonian*. Every major news network worldwide would call for an interview. But the danger seemed too costly. How could he put Celeste in such danger?

Gary logged onto the Internet and typed an e-mail.

Doctor Ahmed,

Thank you for the opportunity to authenticate the cross, but I must decline the invitation...

He hesitated. If he failed to pursue the project, he could go down in history as the one who stopped short of the mother lode in archaeology research. He considered the article he'd recently read in the *Smithsonian*. Ironically, in the discovery of King Tut's tomb, an American archaeologist, Theodore Davis, hung up his shovel just a few feet away from the greatest archaeological find ever. Eight years later, Howard Carter, a British archaeologist, literally struck gold when he found the boy-king's tomb. The coffin lid alone was solid gold and weighed almost two hundred fifty pounds. Before Howard Carter finished with the dig, he'd cataloged over five thousand items. To think the tomb was actually found by a water-boy digging a hole in which to place his water jar! The lad accidentally exposed the first step leading down to more than a dozen steps and ultimately to the sealed doorway of an obscured thirty-three hundred years of the past—almost perfectly preserved—waiting for someone to discover.

Celeste would be safe at her mother's, perhaps safer than at their home. She would enjoy shopping, visiting old friends and helping her mom around the house. He would be home in two weeks; she'd hardly miss him..

He hit delete and re-typed his message. Excitement stirred. He couldn't allow this opportunity to pass without giving it his best shot. He'd go to Jerusalem and either authenticate the cross as being that of Christ or quell the excitement and questions that existed over the supposition. To authenticate the cross would distinguish him as a popular figure in molecular science and, perhaps, if he played his cards right, make him a wealthy man. Still, failure might very well end his tenure as a lecturer, for the crowd seemed to love the sensational rather than facts. Gary knew he couldn't stoop to bring back a fake cross, no matter how much Reverend Small was willing to pay. It was a chance he had to take. Sink or swim, he was taking the plunge.

He continued to type:

Doctor Ahmed,

All arrangements have been made. Attached is our itinerary. Kindest regards,

G. Carter

He clicked the send icon.

An unseasonable cool breeze blew through the open window of his study. A gust of wind rattled a newspaper resting on a chair. He stared into the unusual darkness caused by the heavy overcast sky that had drifted into the Midwest. He glanced at the street below. A dark-colored sedan drove by slowly, lights off. He wondered until it turned the corner. He closed the window.

The sound of clinking glass came from the kitchen and he went downstairs to see what Celeste was doing. He slipped into the kitchen as she unloaded crystal glasses from the dishwasher and gently tapped her on the shoulder. She screamed as she turned around, glass drawn. He threw up protective hands and laughed.

"Please, Gary. Don't scare me like that."

"Sorry, dear."

He placed his arm around her waist and drew her rigid body close. "With your permission, dear, I'm going to Jerusalem."

"Many more tricks like that and you won't."

"Here's the game plan. You drive me to Cincinnati on your way to Columbus. If you stay with your mother until I return, you can pick me up on your way home from Columbus. That way you won't have to spend any nights alone here."

"Why all of a sudden are you concerned about me being alone in our house? That's never been an issue before as you've traveled around the country."

"Oh, just a precaution. One can never be too careful."

"It's the…attack…the thing, isn't it?"

"Well, let's just say I'd feel better knowing you weren't home alone."

"I appreciate your concern."

"I love you. I couldn't stand…I'll miss you more than you know while I'm away."

"Do you love me more than your call to adventure?"

"That's a cruel shot. Just for that, I ought to go with you to your mother's."

"Right. Kicking and fussing all the way to and from the malls. Not a chance, Gary Carter. The thrill of adventure has stolen your heart, and I'll never get it back."

"Then go with me to Israel."

"And miss a shopping trip with Mother? She'd never forgive me."

"So?"

"So? Easy for you to say."

The ding of the doorbell interrupted their bantering. Gary stiffened as he glanced at his watch. "Wonder who that is at this time of evening?"

"Maybe a good neighbor." Celeste shook off his question with a frown. "We do have some very nice neighbors, you know."

"Sorry. I'm just a bit jumpy." He brushed past Celeste to answer the door.

He eased into the living room and cautiously pulled back the window curtain ever so slightly. The black sedan was parked along the curb. He tiptoed quietly toward the door. Through the beveled glass a figure, dressed in dark clothing, stood erect, face distorted by the oblique glass. He slipped an umbrella from a brass container sitting by the door, clutched the handle and unlatched the door. He slowly turned the doorknob and hesitantly pulled open the door until the safety chain caught. From the slight opening, a familiar voice pleasantly surprised him.

"Sorry, Gary, to drop in unexpectedly, but I was in the neighborhood and have something I want to share with you."

Gary breathed out long and slowly.

"Who is it?" Celeste called from the kitchen.

"Pastor Johnson." He swung the door wide. "Come in." He sheepishly replaced the umbrella into the holder.

"Pardon me for intruding without calling ahead. I was in the area and thought I'd stop by. Have something on my mind. Got time to talk?"

Celeste stepped into the living room. "Coffee, Pastor? Maybe some dessert?"

"Coffee sounds wonderful. It's a bit chilly outside for June. Strange turn of weather. No dessert, please. Trying to cut back. Thanks anyway."

"A little cream, lots of sugar?"

"You remember. So much for trying to cut back, huh?" Pastor Johnson laughed.

"Be right back." Celeste disappeared into the kitchen.

"So how's the church building project coming? I've been a might preoccupied and haven't been around much lately."

"I understand. It's coming along very well. We're into the interior work. Drywall is going up in a couple weeks. Things should move along rather quickly from here."

"Glad to hear that. I look forward to seeing the finished sanctuary. I must confess, I've felt some nostalgia regarding the old sanctuary."

"You and a couple hundred others." Pastor Johnson smiled.

"A couple hundred others what?" Celeste returned from the kitchen with a tray in hand.

"Folks going to miss the old sanctuary," Pastor Johnson said.

"Oh, that. I was afraid you were talking about absenteeism." She grinned as she tossed Gary a glance.

"She knows where to gig me, Pastor."

"I believe she does." The pastor laughed.

"I'm not missing on purpose. That should count for something."

"I'm sorry. I shouldn't have spoken so accusingly." Celeste handed Gary a cup of coffee.

As the three savored the coffee, they talked about the weather, Celeste's upcoming trip and a half dozen other inconsequential items.

Pastor Johnson finally set his coffee cup down and rubbed his hands together like a pitcher warming up a new ball. He looked directly at Gary. "There's something I find very intriguing I'd like to share with you." The seriousness intensified in the creases around his eyes and forehead.

"Sure. Feel free to share whatever you want. I…we…both highly value your input."

"Celeste told me about the bizarre encounter you had with an attacker…an apparition. Whatever it was caused me to do a lot of thinking about Bible examples of the spirit world—both good and evil. First, we should acknowledge there is a spiritual realm of which we know little about, primarily because we have little encounter with it, though the Bible certainly documents such. Take, for example, the Scripture found in Ephesians: 'For we wrestle not against flesh and blood, but against principalities, against powers, against the rulers of the darkness of this world, against spiritual wickedness in high places.' Still, we readily see the Scripture limits details regarding the spirit world. Perhaps God wants us to dwell little on the devil and spend more time focusing upon heaven and Christ's goodness and greatness."

"You're saying the Bible is God's biography, not the devil's," Gary said.

"Absolutely." Pastor Johnson reached into his pocket and retrieved a folded piece of paper. "I jotted down some notes on the subject. The term devil is only mentioned sixty-one times in Scripture. God is mentioned over four thousand times. Satan is only mentioned fifty-six times. On the other hand, the name of God incarnate, Jesus—the most personal name we know for God—is mentioned more than nine hundred times. While Lucifer is mentioned once, references to God as Lord are mentioned more than seven thousand times. Even considering my calculations may have allowed a couple lower case 'lords' and 'gods' to have slipped accidentally into my accounting, the numbers overwhelmingly show where our focus should remain."

"We shouldn't be afraid, should we, Pastor?" Celeste looked at Gary.

"No, just prayerful. 'Be sober, be vigilant; because your adversary the devil, as a roaring lion, walketh about, seeking whom he may devour.' The Scripture gives us enough directives we don't have to walk blindly, nor fearfully. Still, we shouldn't live carelessly, heedlessly going about our daily routines with little prayer and personal devotion to Christ. Satan does attack, especially those whom the Scripture describes as slumbering. We need to realize that just as much as Christ is good, the devil is evil. Take for example, it's inconceivable one could be so wicked as to enjoy the murder of the innocent unborn child, or to abuse infants, but Satan does, even promotes it among some cultures."

"One can only ask why? It makes no sense to destroy the helpless," Celeste said.

"I've thought about that, and I have an opinion. The first commandment to mankind recorded in Scripture was to 'be fruitful, and multiply, and replenish the earth.' Satan has tried to prevent that command from being carried out, perhaps because he himself can't reproduce. He can only seduce others to his cause. So he promotes that which is in opposition to God's instructions: infanticide, abortion and homosexuality."

He folded the paper and replaced it inside his coat pocket.

The room echoed the silence of the pastor's pause. As his eyelids closed—a habit not uncommon to the pastor when counseling, and one of those characteristics lovingly talked about among his parishioners—Gary tossed Celeste a perplexed glance and received a reciprocal expression.

"Let's talk about the cross. Could I read from your Bible?"

"Sure." Gary quickly picked up the Bible from the coffee table and handed it to Pastor Johnson, who thumbed through the pages.

"Here it is. 'And when they were come unto a place called Golgotha, that is to say, a place of a skull, they gave him vinegar to drink mingled with gall: and when he had tasted thereof, he wouldn't drink....'"

Celeste wiped a tear. "I'm sorry. You'll have to overlook my emotions. I'm a woman, you know. The story of my Savior's death grips my heart."

Gary shifted in his seat and offered Celeste a consoling smile. She smiled back blushingly.

"Indeed, it is a touching message," Pastor Johnson said. "I don't mean to make you uncomfortable."

"Not at all. To the contrary, I love to hear the story. It's truly the world's greatest love story. Pardon me for interrupting. Please go on."

"The gospel terms Calvary and Golgotha are interchangeable." The pastor paused again as he shifted from reading Scripture to interpreting Scripture.

Celeste reached for Gary's hand and held it tightly.

Gary sensed her reaction was a combination of loving interest in the gospel story but also an awakened trepidation from the recent wacky encounter on the street in downtown Indy.

The pastor continued, "Golgotha is the Aramaic term for the place of the crucifixion. It simply means *skull*. Calvary, as is used in Luke's account, is the English translation from the Latin root '*calva*' which means 'the scalp without hair,' or again, 'skull.' I believe these accounts of Scripture are significant to your encounter with what evidently is an evil spirit."

"The thing was skull-like," Celeste exclaimed.

"The skull-faced person attacked you just days after you became involved with the cross search. The crucifixion was at a place called 'skull.' Isn't' it conceivable the evil spirit was in charge of this place…in charge of causing humans to be treated in such an inhumane way as to be crucified on a cross…a slow and agonizing death that sometimes took days, exposed naked to passersby, the elements and ravenous buzzards? What creation of God, other than a rebellious angel turned demonic, or someone possessed by their spirits, could be given over to such debauchery as to contrive and carry out such a depraved punishment?"

"Especially in the case of Christ," Celeste said.

"The crucifixion was a favored tactic of the Romans to instill fear, and it was the sentence demanded for thousands. Whether modern Rome admits it or not, history speaks loud and clear that ancient

Rome, in all its supposed civilization, was a depraved and diabolical society." Pastor Johnson paused and took a sip of coffee.

"Is the coffee okay?"

"Delicious. Thank you, Celeste."

"Rome protected her empire," Gary said.

"Yes. Still, Christ's crucifixion was more than Rome's concern for the stability of her empire. Christ's death went far beyond Rome's interest. Isn't it possible the most horrid crucifixion of all times would have some semblance of Satan's sadistic hand in it? When talk surfaces the actual cross of Christ may be identified, isn't it feasible Satan is interested?"

"I think so," Gary said. "Are we in harm's way, Pastor?"

"This is more than a summer's archaeological trip. This is a trip to authenticate the object of God's mysterious plan from eternity, 'the lamb slain from the foundation of the world.' You've entered into the lingering battle of the ages. It's the battle between good and evil. The good book tells us to not be afraid, for 'greater is He that is in you, than he that is in the world.' We must build a hedge of God's protection around you with our prayers as you endeavor to follow Christ's leading. My promise to you is daily prayer until you fulfill God's purpose."

"Thank you, Pastor."

"Yes, thank you," Celeste said.

"Well, I'd best be going. I've taken enough of your time."

As Pastor Johnson stepped toward the door, he turned. "Isn't it ironic that a tree—the tree from which mankind disobediently ate—was a part of the demise of the perfect creation, and a tree took part in that same creation's redemption? Perhaps the cross was to be Satan's biggest trophy since the tree of knowledge in the garden was partaken of. It would have looked grand in the spirit-world's trophy case, like Samson's locks or Judas' rope. The cross eluded their anthology of relics."

The pastor turned and walked briskly to his car. Gary and Celeste stood in the doorway, hand in hand, as he pulled away.

"In another place, and another time, that man could have been Nathan the prophet delivering God's proclamation of David's judgment," Gary said.

"Or Moses proclaiming 'Let my people go.'"

CHAPTER
NINE

Reverend Benjamin Small sat at his kidney-shaped desk in silence, his eyes closed, his elbows resting on the arms of his leather chair. Light from a coral-decorated, exotic fish tank cast a shadow of his huge frame on the wall behind the desk. The hum of the motor pumping oxygen into the aquarium created a tranquil atmosphere, but Benjamin wasn't at peace. He was troubled. Tillman was boasting of an archaeological artifact he was "in the process of acquiring." Doctor Carter had seemed rather cool in their recent phone conversation. He was having second thoughts about giving him the check. Perhaps he'd been too impulsive and presumptive in his ploy to acquire ownership of the cross. Then again, Doctor Carter hadn't even seen the cross and so was in no real position to make a decision as to what he would do with it. Still, he was apprehensive about his investment. Carter hadn't cashed the check. He could cancel it, but that might cause a gossip stir, which could cost more money to squelch. He opened his eyes, picked up the phone and dialed the number of an old friend. The clock showed midnight.

"Hello," a coarse voice echoed in the receiver.

"Is this Smoke?"

"Yea. Who's asking?"

"Ben Small here." A long silence followed. "You there, Smoke?"

"Been a long time, Rev." Smoke spoke with a harsh drawl and a tinge of aloofness. "Thought maybe you'd forgotten your old room-mate."

"I don't forget friends. Been busy, though."

Heavy breathing pervaded the awkward silence. "I assume this ain't no social call. What's on your mind, Rev?"

"You busy these days?"

"Maybe, maybe not. I'm listening, though."

"Got a job I need done. Can we meet?"

"My place or yours?"

"Yours."

"Anytime you can make it. I'm going nowhere soon."

"I'll be there tomorrow. Can I reach you at this number, say noonish?"

"I'll be here."

"Call you tomorrow."

"G'night, Rev."

"Good night, Smoke."

Small placed the phone into its cradle. He'd first met Smoke in a tiny cell they shared in prison. Brian Smoke—his real name was Brian Williams—had enormous hands and numerous battle scars. Small spent many an evening listening while Smoke told his story. While a teen, a caring benefactor, who saw his need and potential, rescued him from a gang of thugs and spent countless hours sparring with him in a worn canvass ring at an inner-city boys club. Smoke survived adolescence, struggled through high school and enrolled at a local college, where he found fulfillment on the boxing team. That's where he got his nickname—Smoke. He always smoked his opponents with his lightning speed and overpowering strength.

A youthful marriage ended in divorce and left Smoke with a chip on his shoulder he harbored too long and too often. Drugs and alcohol became his escape; they also became his prison. In a moment of jealous rage, he killed his ex-wife's boyfriend and received a hefty prison sentence for it.

Benjamin Small's story was similar, but in prison he and Smoke took different paths. Smoke spent his spare time pumping iron and pounding faces of opponents in and out of the ring. Small spent his time reading the Bible and attending chapel. After Small's prison release, he used his knowledge of Scripture and his inspiring testimony of deliverance from drugs and alcohol to develop a small following in Orlando. His commanding frame and baritone voice soon made him a favorite on free local Christian television. Early on in satellite Christian broadcasting, he found his niche—and a prosperous livelihood. For a while, he stayed in touch with Smoke, writing him on occasion and accepted collect calls.

Smoke's release from prison came several years after Small's. Smoke moved to Orlando and worked as a custodian for IBIMM. Eventually, he moved back to Miami. They called occasionally. Smoke existed by doing odd jobs—enough to pay the rent and buy a few cans of food—and hung out at a juvenile prevention center for inner-city boys, where he offered instruction to the boys as they sparred in a makeshift ring. The calls between Small and Smoke became fewer. This late night call was the first they'd spoken in a few years.

The call was difficult for Small. Now Smoke's gonna have to save the preacher man. What strange bedfellows we make!

CHAPTER
TEN

The black limo circled the block before it pulled alongside the curb and stopped. A light drizzle formed beads of water that snaked their way down the tinted windows and merged into larger pools near the bottom. The rain reflected the lights of the bustling business district. Small exited the limo. He stepped over a puddle to protect his pointed-toed, alligator boots. The white suit, dark sunglasses and Panama hat, decorated with a black band, concealed his identity somewhat. He caught the attention of a couple winos sitting in a stairwell out of the rain. He looked left and right and leisurely strode toward the small neon-lighted diner. The limo pulled away. The winos watched as the taillights disappeared around the corner but turned their attention to the unfamiliar figure heading for the local grill. He tipped his hat and handed them a couple bills.

"God bless you, sir," one of them said.

The red, neon sign reading "Big Al's Barbecue and Grill," with the letters "Gr" unlit in Grill, flashed incessantly. A faded, hand-painted barbecue sandwich with fries smothered in ketchup and flanked with an overflowing Coke glass, leftover from the fifties, adorned the picture window. Underneath the painting, the words *Miami's Best Barbecue Diner* were unconvincing. The signage mirrored the obsolete image of a long-haired, freehand painter, a paintbrush between his teeth and another in his hand, working out his next meal.

An annoying bell jingled and heads turned his direction as Small stepped inside the diner. He removed his sunglasses and appraised the analytical stares of the dozen customers, deftly wiping the rain from his hat with a silk handkerchief he took from the front pocket of his suit coat. He made his way to a corner booth where he stopped and stared into the cold, yet familiar, face of Brian "Smoke" Williams. Their eyes met for a long moment of uncertainty forged by a neglected friendship. Smoke broke the ice with a dawdling smile, revealing a gold front tooth. He motioned an invitation to be seated. Each reached across the table and clasped a lingering, almost competitive, hand.

"Glad to see you, Smoke."

"Likewise, Rev."

A waitress quickly approached the table to take their orders. The other customers turned their attention back to their greasy fries and the sports page.

CHAPTER
ELEVEN

"What's going on?" Celeste's heart leaped at the sight.

"I'm not sure," Gary responded.

Celeste was developing an aversion for policemen and cruisers.

Three police cars, lights flashing, were in front of their house. As Gary turned into their driveway, an officer stepped in front of the car and motioned him to stop. He approached the driver's side, his thumbs tucked inside his gun belt.

"Afternoon, sir. It's Doctor Carter, isn't it?" He had an unusually southern drawl for north of the Ohio River.

"Yes. Afternoon, Officer."

"Officer Scott, sir." He tipped his hat at Celeste. "Ma'am."

"Something wrong, I presume." Gary opened the door and slowly exited.

"Sorry, Doctor, but someone broke into your house. A neighbor reported some suspicious activity. I'm assuming your alarm system isn't connected to a security company."

"Never thought we'd need it."

Celeste exited the car and walked briskly to the front door without speaking. Another officer opened the door for her. "I'm Officer Mullins. Are you Mrs. Carter?"

"Yes."

"Sorry you've had to return home to this. The side door was ajar, so we took the liberty of doing a walk-through. The house looks fine. No obvious vandalism, but we'll need you to help us do a more thorough investigation. I think our sirens may have chased them off before they took anything." The officer was unusually tall and instinctively ducked as he entered the doorway. A horrible scar marked his face from his right eyebrow to the earlobe.

Celeste couldn't help but wonder if it was a wound in the line of duty, a barroom brawl or perhaps a childhood accident.

"I can't believe they'd break in during broad daylight." She shook her head.

"You been to church?"

"Yes."

"That may be the explanation. The thief probably knows your routine. Maybe cased the neighborhood before making a move. Good thing your neighbor called."

"Yes, we're blessed with good neighbors." Gary entered the house, followed by a plainclothes detective—checkered shirt, fat tie and jeans.

"What's the scoop, Mullins?" The detective took immediate charge.

"Break-in, sir. Jimmied the side door. Our sirens apparently scared 'em off, though. Nothin' seems disturbed."

"Call in a technician. We'd best do some dusting for prints."

"Yes, sir." Mullins disappeared through the door, ducking again.

"Doctor Carter, I need you and the wife...I'm assuming you're Mrs. Carter."

"Yes."

"Detective Connors." He smiled pleasantly and extended his hand.

"Sorry I can't say I'm pleased to meet you, Detective Connors." Celeste distractedly shook his hand.

"I understand. I'll need you and Doctor Carter to walk with me through the house but don't touch anything." He spoke in a kinder-garten-type instructional manner.

Celeste absentmindedly wandered across the living room and stared out the window. A few neighbors stood chatting. Theirs was a quiet neighborhood and the police did routine drive-bys but seldom had to be called. Freshly cut roses adorned an ornate end table resting atop an ancient rendition of the world. She slowly inhaled the fragrance, savoring the aroma and gently caressed a velvety leaf, longing for the return of serenity she once relished. Lately life seemed to spin out of control. She returned to the entourage slowly walking through the house, room by room. They walked past an undisturbed china hutch loaded with cobalt Northwood carnival glass, including Celeste's favorite pattern: peacock at the fountain. A Fenton butterfly and berry table set looked untouched. It was her cherished possession from her father. A bronze statue of Christ healing the blind man—sculptured by Mark Hopkins—which Gary had purchased in Gatlinburg, Tennessee, sat underneath a signed artist's proof by Greg Olsen of Christ lamenting over Jerusalem. Gary's gun rack containing a prized Remington Keene Indian Rifle was still locked, with no signs of tampering. Nothing seemed amiss in the entire first level. They ascended the spiral, oak stairway to the second level and walked slowly along the hallway, mentally taking inventory. Gary stopped in his tracks as he entered his office.

"What is it Gary?" She placed a hand on his shoulder.

"My computer! My Mac is missing." The top desk drawer, where he kept his laptop, was partially open. "Everything else seems in place."

"Don't touch anything." The detective slowly opened the desk drawer with the end of an ink pen and peered inside. "Anything else missing in here?"

"No. Just my computer."

"How valuable?"

"Mid to upper range PowerBook. A little pricey, twenty-five hundred, but less than a dozen items the thief, or thieves, walked by in the open to find my computer in a closed drawer."

"That's strange they'd leave so much more. Ah, what was in the computer?" Connors circled the room slowly.

"Typical stuff—correspondence, some research, my doctoral dissertation. I always keep backups, though. Not a great loss."

"Perhaps research they wanted."

"The thesis is public record at the university library."

"Where do you keep your backups?"

"The safe." Gary walked to the far wall, pushed aside a chair and opened a hinged picture of the Indy skyline. Behind the picture, built into and flush with the wall, was a combination safe. Gary reached to unlock the safe.

"Don't..."

"Touch anything." Gary withdrew his hand and stood aside.

"Get me some gloves."

An attendant accommodated the request.

Connors snatched the gloves from the attendant's hand and handed them to Gary, who donned the gloves, thumbed the spindle and slowly turned it left, right, left and clicked the handle. The safe opened. Gary reached inside and retrieved a stack of plastic cases containing discs. He handed them toward Detective Connors, who retrieved a handkerchief from his hip pocket and delicately placed the contents from the safe onto Gary's desk.

"Everything seems to be here, sir." Gary surveyed the cases.

"What might they be looking for, Doctor Carter?" Detective Connors studied the titles of each of the disks.

"I don't know."

"Can I take these with me?" Connors held up the stack of disks. "We may find something on the disks that could explain why they stole the computer. Lab boys will be arriving shortly to dust for prints. Like I said before, you and the wife try not to touch anything until they've finished. I'll stay in touch. We'll be here till the technicians arrive if you remember anything of significance."

"What about the check, Gary?"

"What check?" Connors wheeled around.

"Gary had a check for...for a large sum in his desk."

"I deposited it in our account."

"How much was the check, may I ask?"

"Half a million."

Connors' eyebrows rose slightly. "The purpose of the check?"

Gary hesitated. "Down payment on an archaeological find."

"What? A treasure ship?

"A cross."

Connors turned his head sideways and stared at Gary. Without responding, he handed Gary a business card and abruptly turned and left the room. His assistant followed close behind.

"We'll be in touch, Doctor Carter," Connors called over his shoulder. He hesitated momentarily in the foyer to speak with the arriving crime technicians.

Celeste and Gary stood at the top of the stairway, watching. She hugged him gently. He rested his chin on top of her head and pulled her close.

"They're seeking information about the cross, aren't they? Maybe someone wants my correspondence with Ahmed. But who?"

"I think you're right."

They stood for a long moment in a silent embrace. Car doors slammed and engines started up.

"Let's leave tonight," Celeste whispered. "Most everything is packed except our personal stuff. Let's pack up and get out of town as soon as the police are finished with their inspection."

CHAPTER
TWELVE

Gary rendezvoused with college buddies, Jack Metz and Rick Hogg, at the Greater Cincinnati Airport. They'd traveled together on several expeditions but nothing of this magnitude. The short flight to O'Hara was uneventful and Gary's adrenaline had crashed by the time they arrived in Chicago for their connection to Tel Aviv.

Jack reclined in his seat, stroking the leather armrests. "First class, Rick? Whatever happened to your college days frugality?"

"Not my money, It's Metz' inheritance." They both laughed. "He said the budget was bottomless—evidently his dad needs a tax write-off. ACE Hardware isn't just the place to shop; it's the place to make lots of money."

"And Metz is making sure he can nap comfortably. Where is Metz?"

"Went for a magazine. Never in a hurry."

The smell of coffee permeated the cabin. An array of languages filled the coach section, separated by a wall with hinged curtains at each of the doors of the double aisles. People scrambled to stuff their luggage into overhead compartments and corral their children into the correct seat.

"Excuse me." A rather large man in a black, baggy suit with a full-face salt-and-pepper beard and a black fedora cocked sideways stood beside Gary studying his ticket.

The fringes of his tallith flowed from underneath his suit jacket. He emanated a strange scent—not necessarily unpleasant, but rather an unusual odor to which Gary was unaccustomed.

"I will be sitting beside you, sir. I am Yosef Arav." His booming voice and heavy accent demanded attention. He extended his hand. "Call me Joseph."

"Gary Carter." They shook hands.

"Can I help you with your bags, sir?" A flight attendant asked.

"No, thank you." He held tightly to his duffel bag. "I can manage quite well." He stuffed the oversized bag into the overhead compartment.

Jack appeared in the doorway, carrying a rolled-up magazine. Grinning.

"Pillows anyone?" The attendant was back.

Joseph snatched a pillow from her and thanked her with a nod of his head.

"Yes, please," Gary said.

"And something to drink." Jack took the window seat beside Rick. "Since my dad paid for it, we'd best enjoy every advantage." He laughed.

"What would you like, sir?"

"Coke's fine," Jack said.

The attendant, congenial to a fault, served Jack a Coke and weaved her way by the boarding passengers as she pleasantly took orders from others in first-class.

The casual manner and conversation of the pilots through the open door of the cockpit intrigued Gary. How do pilots remain so calm minutes before they maneuver eight hundred thousand pounds of steel, aluminum and plastic loaded with four hundred passengers and their luggage—not to mention explosive fuel—down a runway at breakneck speed and somehow manage a liftoff? That's with a landing still to come. What's in Joseph's duffel bag? Is he Jewish? Arabic? Do terrorists wear prayer shawls? Gary's world demanded patience, not nerves of steel; it called for persistence rather than speed. Lately he needed more courage than usual. Who was the masked bandit? Where did he come from? Where did he go? Who broke into our house? Why? As the plane prepared for takeoff, these questions raced the runway of his mind. Was the break-in to steal information about this trip? If so, the thief was probably the same person that tried to hijack them but, then again, a couple wealthy televangelists were pretty hot on the trail of the cross. The attacker didn't want the check? But was it the check the robber sought? Why didn't Joseph allow the attendant to help with his luggage?

The roar of the turbo engines distracted his rambling thoughts. The plane climbed rapidly and banked, revealing Chicago's skyline and the bluish waters of Lake Michigan. The sight was impressive. A dozen colorful sails dotted the glistening water. Their tacking maneuvers sliced the endless rows of whitecaps as their sails maximized the wind. A zigzagging pattern of white wakes snaked behind them. He assumed some of the boats were fishing boats trolling in search of a freshwater catch of the day, and some were pleasure seekers enjoying a day off work. Merchant ships lined the numerous docks; both the ships and the docks were stacked high with rusty-red metal containers. The Windy City was one of the most visited cities of the States. It was the drop-off of the cargo of semi-rigs, cargo that would be loaded on ships built to navigate the Saint Lawrence Seaway. From the sky it was an endless sea of man's creativity and hard labor—and only a hundred and fifty years old; it seemed much older in comparison to other cities its equal.

Celeste was on her way to Ohio. He already missed her. She'd be safe at her mother's place. That thought comforted him.

Joseph opened a book. Gary glanced at the pages: an English Bible. Is he a believer or a seeker? Gary subdued the temptation to paraphrase Philip the evangelist in the Bible, who witnessed to the truth-seeking Ethiopian and later baptized him into the Christian faith. Understandest what thou readest? It sounded too preachy.

"So what is your profession?" He couldn't control his inquisitive nature.

"Rabbi."

"Why is a rabbi reading the Christian Bible?"

"It was Jewish long before it was Christian." The rabbi's quick response surprised Gary—he wished he hadn't inquired. Still, he was glad Joseph was a rabbi and not a terrorist.

"Only the Old Testament was Jewish."

"Who wrote the New Testament?"

"The apostles mostly...Luke the physician and Mark, who weren't apostles, and, of course, Paul, who called himself an apostle but some don't think he can be numbered among the twelve." Gary braced himself for the rabbi's retort.

"Right." The rabbi slowly flipped through the pages. Gary waited for him to continue his statement. He didn't.

"What do you mean by right?"

"I mean you are right about the Jewish men who wrote the New Testament, but you are wrong about it not being Jewish. Most of them were Jewish, so it is a Jewish book."

Gary's face flushed. He didn't quite know where to take the conversation. It seemed so easy for Philip the evangelist. *Maybe I should wait for a more opportune time.* He was in too deep to back down. "You're right the New Testament was written by Jewish authors, but the New Testament clearly identifies Jesus as the Messiah whom the Jewish faith rejected, even caused Him to be crucified."

"Right." The rabbi stopped thumbing the pages. Gary assumed he searched for a particular Scripture as he traced the page with his finger. Gary waited.

The rabbi read slowly. "'I say the truth in Christ, I lie not, my conscience also bearing me witness in the Holy Ghost, That I have great heaviness and continual sorrow in my heart. For I could wish that myself were accursed from Christ for my brethren, my kinsmen according to the flesh: Who are Israelites; to whom pertaineth the adoption, and the glory, and the covenants, and the giving of the law, and the service of God, and the promises; Whose are the fathers, and of whom as concerning the flesh Christ came, who is over all, God blessed for ever. Amen.'"

He paused and laid his Bible aside. "I am a late answer to Paul's prayer of almost two thousand years ago. I am a rabbi by profession. I am a Christian by experience. By your knowledge of the Holy Scripture, and your inquiries, am I correct in assuming you are likewise a Christian, and therefore my spiritual brother?"

"Yes." That was the only thing he could think to say.

"You wonder how a rabbi could also be a Christian? Yes? The same way a teacher can be a Christian. That is what I am, a teacher of the Torah to the youth of my ancestry, but like Nicodemus, I am a believer in the New Covenant as the way into God's Kingdom. All the while I pray for the opportunity to share this new faith with my kinsmen. What is your profession, may I ask?"

"Molecular biologist, though I've been on a lengthy sabbatical. Never really started actually. I'm doing some lecture tours, and more recently I've become involved in archaeology."

"That is why you go to Israel?"

"Right." Gary thought about leaving the rabbi hanging there as he'd done him, with a singular answer, but he was more than a little interested in any knowledge the rabbi might impart regarding Israel, so he kept the conversation alive. "Do you live in Israel?"

"*Jerushalayim...Atah Mevin Ivrit*? Do you understand?

"*Rak me'at*...very little."

"Little is better than nothing! I will teach you more. "

"Thank you. *Rav Todot!*"

"You are most welcome. Back to your question of where I live. Jerusalem is my home, though I was not born there. My parents immigrated there shortly after the declaration of Israel as a nation—after the British pulled out. I was five years old at the time."

"That makes you about...sixty-two...three?"

"You know your history well."

Gary was glad he finally said something that impressed the rabbi. "Where were you born?"

"Chicago. That is why I return to visit. I still have relatives who live there."

"Why did you move to Jerusalem?" Gary felt himself digressing from having just impressed the rabbi to being nosey.

"I had no say in the matter. Remember, I was only five."

Gary had digressed, but the rabbi no longer spoke with any hint of condescension in either his words or the tone of his voice.

"I should've said why did your parents—"

"Yes. I was about to answer that for I knew what you meant. It is okay to ask questions, so long as you do not always expect intelligent answers. Ha! Ha! Ha! Right?"

"Right." *He actually has a sense of humor underneath that black suit and behind that bushy beard.*

"My father was a professor in the Hebrew University in Chicago. When Israel became a nation, God placed it upon his heart to return to the land of promise to teach the Torah. You are familiar with the Shema, our basic doctrine?

"Yes. Hear, oh Israel, the Lord our God, the Lord, is one."

"And Moshe, or Moses, instructed us to teach our children and they their children. My father wanted to obey the Torah. He felt he could best do it by teaching. That is how I ended up in Jerusalem and a rabbi."

"That doesn't explain how you became a Christian."

"True. That part is more complicated."

"We have a long flight."

"Enough time, perhaps—"

"Coffee anyone?" the attendant interrupted the conversation.

Perhaps the rabbi knows Zaki Ahmed. Do Jews and Arabs mix socially if they're Christians?

The sun dropped from the sky, burning its way into the western horizon. The engines hummed as the jet swooshed toward the approaching night. Gary wanted to learn more from the rabbi, but he was extremely tired. He felt himself drifting.

The buzz of voices in the cabin startled him awake. The rabbi was gone. The glow in the eastern horizon surprised him. He'd slept through the night. His shirt collar showed signs of drool. He maneuvered slowly, stretching the soreness from his back.

His watch showed it was ten. He calculated it to be six in the morning. Got to reset my watch. Celeste is just going to bed. The aroma of brewing coffee didn't agree with his nauseous stomach.

"Mornin', Carter. Thought you'd never wake." Rick spoke too cheerfully.

Jack still slept; his magazine lay across his chest.

"Oh the drag of jet lag." Gary held his head tightly between both hands.

"You okay, Mr. Carter?" The attendant held a tray of coffee.

"Nothing a Diet Coke won't cure."

"Right away." She smiled and left.

The coach was abuzz. Parents dressed small children from pajamas to daywear.

The door to the restroom opened and the rabbi squeezed out. Silhouetted in the open doorway of the restroom, his size seemed amplified.

"Shalom," he said pleasantly.

"Shalom." Gary combed his fingers through his hair.

"I trust you slept well."

"Slept, yes. Well? That's questionable." Gary rubbed the back of his neck.

"We are almost to the land of *Avraham Avinu*...Abraham our Father." He clutched his Bible to his chest and spoke softly. Poetically, reverently it seemed, in Hebrew.

Gary listened intently; he assumed the rabbi quoted from the Old Testament.

Joseph switched to English. "The LORD loveth the gates of Zion more than all the dwellings of Jacob. Glorious things are spoken of thee, O city of God. I was glad when they said unto me, 'Let us go into the house of the LORD.' Our feet shall stand within thy gates, O *Yerushalayim*. *Yerushalayim* is builded as a city that is compact together...Pray for the peace of *Yerushalayim*: they shall prosper that love thee. Peace be within thy walls, and prosperity within thy palaces...Great is the LORD, and greatly to be praised in the city of our God, in the mountain of his holiness. Beautiful for situation, the joy of the whole earth, is mount Zion, on the sides of the north, the city of the great King. God is known in her palaces for a refuge...As we have heard, so have we seen in the city of the LORD of hosts, in the city of our God: God will establish it for ever...For this God is our God for ever and ever: He will be our guide even unto death."

The plane banked gently over the sky blue Mediterranean.

Joseph pointed. "That is the coastline of Israel. There is Tel Aviv, situated northwest of Ben Gurion."

Gary's adrenaline rushed like when he descended into the Indy airport after being gone too long from home. He felt an immediate kindred spirit to a land he'd never set foot on; he felt a kinship to a man who eight hours earlier was a total stranger.

"You will dine with me and my family, yes?"

"I'd be delighted. Give me your number and I'll call after I get settled and find out my schedule."

"I did not find out why you are in Jerusalem." He handed Gary his business card.

"I've come to test a recently discovered cross, believed by a Doctor Zaki Ahmed to be the actual cross of Christ. Do you by chance know Doctor Ahmed?"

"Doctor Ahmed calls in Indiana Jones! Ha, ha! Ha, ha! Ha, ha!"

Gary enjoyed the humor but felt somewhat embarrassed.

"You're making fun of me."

"No, my brother, I am not making fun. Forgive me. I tease a little, but Zaki Ahmed teases you a lot."

"Then you know Doctor Ahmed?"

"Yes. Most Christians in Jerusalem know Ahmed. He is trying to prove the Christian faith with things, objects. If he finds an ancient dagger, he imagines it to be the one the big fisherman used to cut off the ear of the high priest's servant. He searches for the upper room where the Spirit first fell upon believers. He is forever making outlandish claims, like the group of archaeologists who found the ossuary of James and assume him to be the brother of Christ. It toured your country recently, no?"

"Yes."

"The guards are forever chasing him away from digs around the temple area. So he now thinks he has found the cross of Christ?"

"Yes."

"The cross doesn't need to be found. It is in here." Joseph thumped his chest. "I hope I have not harmed your trip by my strong opinions. I do not mean to speak against Doctor Ahmed; he is my Christian brother and basically he is a good man, maybe a bit eccentric, but he is a good man. You will like him, and he will show you a good tour of the Holy Land. *Chabdeihu vechoshdeihu*…as you say in English, take him with a grain of salt."

Gary instantly felt sick to his stomach, and it was more than jet lag!

CHAPTER THIRTEEN

Celeste traveled northeast on I-71. She had dropped off Gary at the Greater Cincinnati Airport and spent the day shopping at Rookwood Mall, then a night at the Hilton. She tapped her fingers against the steering wheel in time with the music of *Philips Craig and Dean,* a CD she picked up at Rookwood. She was on vacation, with no schedule to keep, and she looked forward to seeing her mother. She hadn't told Gary she was spending the night in Cincinnati; that might have caused him concern. She'd be in Columbus shortly.

Endless rows of corn, wheat and soybeans created a sea of green on the southern Ohio landscape. How do farmers create such straight and symmetrical furrows? Her grandfather Brown had been a small-time farmer, mostly for a hobby. She spent many summers in Chillicothe, south of Columbus, weeding green beans and picking bugs off tomato plants. After all those years, the foul odor hovering the Scioto Valley reeked in her mind, an odor created by the pulp-producing paper mill—her only negative memory about her grandparents' farm.

Under normal circumstances, the black sedan that tailed her would have brought no alarm. It slowly dawned, that the vehicle had followed her for miles. Did it trail me from the hotel? It remained behind her no matter what speed she drove. She glanced compulsively into the mirror. Stay calm. "Calm?" I've every reason to be suspicious. A mile marker flashed by: thirty miles from Columbus. She reached into her purse and retrieved her cell phone. Holding the phone gave her security. She toyed with familiar numbers. By now Gary is in Israel and a call to him is senseless. Most of my close friends are in Indiana. I don't want to needlessly alarm Mother. She dropped her phone into her purse. Are my car doors locked? She pressed the lock button, twice. No one can harm me. Think positive thoughts.

Her grandparents took her to the Tecumseh outdoor drama for her twelfth birthday. Her eyes stung from the pungent smoke of gunpowder in the climatic ending. She received autographs of the painted warriors who lined the stage after the performance, actors who moments before seemed so real, screaming and wielding tomahawks, bows and rifles as they attacked the forces led by General William Harrison. The drama on Sugarloaf Mountain that cool summer evening, the reenactment of a battlefield strewn with the dead and wounded, piqued her emotions and created an interest in nursing. She felt anger toward Tecumseh's brother, Tenskwatawa, also called The Prophet, over the senseless carnage. He rallied the warriors into a premature battle that dashed all hopes of the Indians brokering a peaceful treaty to their benefit. The Prophet's grotesquely painted face was forever etched in her mind. For years she saw him in dreams that frightened her. His image morphed into that of the skull-faced attacker.

Why am I thinking these horrible things?

She gripped the steering wheel and glanced in the mirror; the sedan was nowhere in sight. Where did it go? In her periphery, a car approached. Reluctantly, she glanced to her left. A red Corvette, top down, driven by a young man with wavy black hair that riffled in the breeze, smiled at her; she smiled back. She relaxed her grasp of the steering wheel. Mother will be excited to see me.

CHAPTER
FOURTEEN

They crammed into a rental car, its dimensions about that of an oversized golf cart. Jack drove, and Rick rode shotgun, gripping a map and rattling off directions. Gary squirmed in the back seat, sandwiched against the window by three suitcases.

"To think we offered the rabbi a lift—", Gary said.

"Which he sensibly declined." Jack grinned at him in the mirror.

"Thank goodness," Gary said. He stared out the window. *Was the rabbi's description of Doctor Ahmed true? Are we on a wild goose chase?*

Their decision to rent a car instead of using public transportation was simple: the Tel Aviv central station was one of the largest in the world, and the words "bus" and "bombs" seemed too synonymous in Israel. The railways sounded just as crowded. Jack didn't mind driving. His adventurous spirit soared behind the wheel. Rick's analytical mind would guide them to Jerusalem. Once they arrived in Jerusalem, Doctor Ahmed would direct them.

They turned onto the main road connecting Ben Gurion International with Jerusalem. Gary had read the ancient history of this road—the prophets who traversed it and the armies it facilitated: the victorious and the conquered. Tel Aviv and ancient Jaffa lay northwest of Ben Gurion about a twenty-minute drive. Jaffa was one of the

66

world's oldest continuing cities. The Prophet Jonah boarded a ship at Jaffa bound for Tarshish, the farthest known port from ancient Nineveh, which Jonah desperately wanted to avoid. On two occasions, shipments of wood—Cedars from Lebanon made into rafts—landed at the treacherous Jaffa port to be used in the construction of the first and second temples at Jerusalem. The Apostle Peter was a guest in a home in Jaffa when he had the vision that opened the door for the gospel to be carried to the Gentile world. Locals called the modern city of Tel Aviv "The Big Orange," after New York's "Big Apple." Tel Aviv was nonexistent until about 1880, when residents started two settlements as an alternative to the expensive living in Jaffa. Established as a city in 1909, Tel Aviv eventually swallowed up ancient Jaffa. Until recently, Tel Aviv was the capital of Israel and still remained the cultural capital, boasting several museums and priceless pieces of art. Counting the surrounding communities, it was home for two and a half million people.

Gary leaned his head against the seat, closed his eyes and let his mind wander the ancient paths of this historical seaport community. Quite naturally he journeyed eastward to the beloved city of Jerusalem, situated less than an hour away by car.

Jerusalem, the City of Peace! How ironic the city of peace, home to the three major monotheistic religions of the world, doesn't enjoy harmony! Pray for the peace of Jerusalem is a prayer that needs answered. Conquered forty times. Numerous times destroyed by the conquerors. Beloved by many but bothersome to some. The ancient citadel is God's gift to a particular people who at times prove unworthy of the city and of her God.

The bumper-to-bumper traffic slowed their approach to the outskirts of Jerusalem. Gary envisioned the Crusaders, armor reflecting the hot Judean sun, marching in broken and scattered columns along this very road. The Genoese—whose galleys had sneaked past the Fatimid patrol boats along the coastline and landed at Jaffa—dismantled their ships and salvaged the larger beams to build war machines to breach the walls of Jerusalem. They torched the remains of the ships—eliminating the option of retreat—and trudged along this road bearing the heavy sodden timber upon their backs. Any hope of returning home dissipated like the smoke billowing from the flames. The Crusaders, though journey weary, experienced intense excitement as they strode along this road in anticipation of seeing the Holy City for the first time. Each step along this famed highway gave them renewed energy. The ancient Templar Knights, with flowing white robes emblazoned with red crosses, rode guard for the Christian pilgrims who'd landed at one of the coastal ports. They trudged along this very route, excited about seeing the city of Christ's death—and resurrection. Fast forward almost a century, expressionless post-war Jewish immigrants journeyed this path. Fathers laden with single duffel bags, and mothers clinging to the hands of their children, disembarked ships in hopes this Promised Land offered more than the heartache they left behind. There were no welcoming committees, and they soon cringed from the horrendous sounds of battle. They scurried for shelter among the rocks from the impact of exploding bombs dropped from the warplanes of impassioned pilots who already claimed ownership to this land. The Arabs were determined to prevent the busloads of Jewish emigrants from making the final miles to Jerusalem, where they would join up with Zionists who held a section of the sacred city by a two-thousand-year-old hope of threadbare optimism.

A sign read, Jerusalem, 20 km, and surprisingly, in English, 12 mi.

The rental car couldn't keep pace. A passenger bus roared past and cut in front of them. Diesel fumes left them coughing. A line of vehicles formed behind, horns blaring for them to pull over and let others pass.

"Next light turn onto King David Street." Rick rearranged the fold of the map.

"Let's hope it's not a one way the wrong way." Gary said.

"It's a two way."

"How can you be so sure?"

"You need to learn how to read a map."

"I can make it a one way our way if we need to." Jack grinned mischievously, looking back at Gary through the rear-view mirror. He braked hard for a crossing pedestrian. A dozen horns blared and a few words were exchanged as the pedestrian rushed across the street to a waiting cab. The green light changed to red, but a few cars forced their way through the intersection any way—which produced another burst of horns and verbal exchanges—blocking the intersection entirely. Jack gripped the wheel as if the starting gate was about to spring open. The light changed, the traffic flowed again and Jack's demeanor returned to an uncharacteristic sullenness as the rental car sputtered to take off.

Gary chuckled. "Not quite like your classic back home. What model is it?"

"A V-8, four speed, '63 Sting Ray convertible that goes from zero to one hundred in sixteen and a half second."

"There's the motel." Rick pointed toward a towering golden building punctuated with palm trees.

Jack eased the car into the drive at Twenty-three King David Street. The old city, with it multiple towers and ancient buildings, emerged in the background.

"After the Twenty-third Psalm?" Jack asked.

"Sounds right. King David Hotel, named after the king who wrote the Twenty-third Psalm, and the hotel's located at Twenty-three King David Street," Rick explained.

"We'd better ask someone who knows before we spread our ignorance back in the States," Gary said.

"*Shalom aleichem*," a concierge greeted them.

Jack butchered a response that sounded more like salami than shalom.

"*Aleichem shalom*," Rick said.

"Welcome to King David." The concierge's uniform looked fine enough for a king's guard. He radiated professionalism and kindness. "My name is Joseph and I will assist you with any needs you have while at King David. Are all of you checking in?"

"Yes," Gary answered.

"*Rak rega bevakasha*. One moment please. *Shaalosh*," Joseph called to his assistants.

"The young men are pleased to take care of your luggage." Three bellhops rushed to retrieve their luggage. "*Bo iti*...come with me. I will assure you a speedy check-in to the finest rooms in all of *Yerushalayim*, the city of God."

CHAPTER
FIFTEEN

They looked the part of tourists: monogrammed shirts, sunglasses and expressions of being momentarily lost. Rick studied the map as they wove their way through the narrow, cobblestone streets of the Arab section of old Jerusalem. Gary snapped pictures, occasionally glancing at Jack who continually lagged as he purchased another trinket to add to his stuffed shopping bag.

"How much farther?" Gary asked, glancing at the map, which seemed useless to him since the directions were in Hebrew. An "x" marked the location of the antiquities shop owned by Ahmed. The desk clerk had located it for them.

Rick stopped at every street corner and calculated their location. "We should be close by now."

"You said that five blocks back."

"Six."

"You're holding the map upside down."

"Hold it in the direction you're going: upside down when going south, right side up when going east and left side up when going west. Only hold the map north side up if you're going north." Rick was a stickler for procedures.

"But I like to know which way is north at all times."

"North is whichever way the 'N' arrow is pointing if you hold the map correctly and walk in the direction indicated by the map."

"Why not just use MapQuest?"

"Too simple. Real explorers need a challenge. You surprise me, Gary. I thought you had a more adventurous spirit."

"I still like convenience. Why not use a GPS? You're stuck in a time warp." Gary laughed.

"A GPS is expensive, not to mention the batteries. I'm tight with my money. Remember?"

"How can I forget?"

"This map was free."

"Also in a language we can't read." Gary snapped a close up of Rick.

"Where's Jack?" Rick studied the crowd.

"You worry about directions and I'll worry about Jack. He stopped off at another trinket shop." Gary motioned with his hands and called to Jack, "We'll wait on you at the next corner."

"I'll catch up. Don't worry about me."

"What do we tell his wife when we return to the States without him?" Rick asked.

"He died happy...bartering!"

"He's a bold sort." Rick shook his head.

They stopped at an outdoor shop and waited for Jack to catch up. It was too long a wait and the aggressive clerk cornered them. "For you today, my friends, very special gift."

"*Kama ze ole?*" Gary read from a translation book.

"For you, my American friend, very good deal!"

"How much?"

"Twenty American dollar."

"Too much."

Jack caught up and continued the bartering. He pulled an identical item from his shopping bag. "Five dollars." He got the clerk down to five dollars before confessing he had no interest in a duplicate gift.

The clerk wasn't discouraged. He pulled another box of trinkets from under the counter and started over, but he seemed to view Gary as a more likely customer. "For you, my friend. For your wife and child. You like?"

"I don't have a child. I look for a cross...the cross of Christ. *Yesh lecha crucifix?* Have you heard about anyone finding the cross of

Christ?" Gary drew an outline in the air. The clerk exhibited a silver plated menorah and a brass coated mezuzah.

"No! I look for the cross of Christ."

A smile replaced the question mark in the clerk's expression. He disappeared through a side door but quickly returned with a small cross, carved out of olive wood, with a leather string for around the neck. Gary tried to explain it was too small, but the clerk shook his head, evidently not able to comprehend why Gary wanted a larger cross.

"Ahmed's place should be just ahead." Rick studied the map.

"It gets farther away every block," Gary said.

They laughed. The clerk seemed annoyed.

Once away from the aggressive clerk they paused to take in the sights and sounds of Jerusalem. It was a sweltering ninety-eight degrees, with no breeze. They wiped gritty dust from their faces with handkerchiefs drenched in sweat, and they lingered under the only tree within blocks. A vendor offered them a warm coke without ice. They declined.

Gary inhaled the myriad smells from the stalls of the street vendors. It reminded him of the farmers market in downtown Indianapolis. He and Celeste visited often on Wednesdays when merchants sold fruits, vegetables, meats and assorted cheeses. He could smell the baked goods with their unique spices and herbs. The Indy market was seasonal from May to October when fresh foods were at their peak. The excitement at the market was quite exhilarating compared to a Walmart experience. The older city of Jerusalem was a continuous adventure, but he suddenly yearned for a relaxing evening with Celeste.

A young boy tugged at his arm, interrupting his thoughts.

"*Bevakasha.* Excuse, please. One American dollar."

Gary assumed he was a beggar.

He pointed toward his haggard donkey where a Polaroid camera rested on a worn blanket tossed across the donkey's back. "Picture? You Christian?"

"Yes, we're Christians."

"Take picture with donkey Mary rode. One American dollar."

They laughed heartily and huddled as the skinny lad focused the Polaroid, hesitated and coaxed Jack onto the donkey. His shoes scraped the ground as he sat astride the swayed back donkey, which brayed its disapproval.

"You're gonna break the poor things back," Rick said.

"Don't blame me. Blame her owner."

"Cheese." The lad coached them. As the image appeared he smiled his approval and handed the photo to Jack.

"Two dollar."

"But you said one."

"One for photograph and one for use of donkey."

Jack lost the argument. They continued on their way, the lad following, hoping for two more photo shoots. The donkey decided he had enough action and braced his feet against the cobblestones. The lad pulled and coaxed in vain.

Old men sat along the sidewalks in small groups puffing the pungent smoke from their glass hookahs, engaged in conversation. An argument erupted. Gary didn't understand the language, but he interpreted their passion and tried to identify their tête-à-tête. Was it claims of bargains? Political persuasions? Languages differ, but fervor is universal. He recognized reprimands to children sneaking grapes and dates from the fruit tables. Arab wives, hiding behind layered garments of traditions and facades of submission, barked out orders to their husbands, who hastened to fulfill their demands. Working mothers schooled their children while on the job. Gary observed a world unchanged for centuries but altered by honking horns as drivers snaked their vehicles along old Jerusalem's crowded streets. This was where he found exhilaration, where his creative juices flowed instinctively, among a civilization of antiquity.

"Look! That's it." Rick pointed at a shop across the street.

Scrawled over the doorway of a replica of the hundreds of shops they'd just passed was the name *Ahmed House of Antiquities*.

"Where's Metz?" Rick asked.

Gary pointed to a booth a block back where Jack sat on a wooden soda case and leaned on the countertop of a vendor whose arms flayed like the straw man in *The Wizard of Oz*. Gary whistled and pointed across the street toward Ahmed's shop. Jack waved for them to go.

The two weaved their way across the crowded street and stepped through the opened doorway. Gary removed his sunglasses and hesitated as his eyes adjusted to the dim lighting. How weird and yet wonderful to stand here! For a moment he appreciated his decision to abandon a career as a molecular biologist. He could be cooped in a lab, chained to a microscope, but here he stood in the midst of adventure. His Daniel Boone spirit had almost been corralled by a career in a lab. Why endure the long hours of tedious and boring work bent over a microscope exploding sperm into eggs in an attempt to modify the future when you can be free to chase antiquity. He had considered teaching but was discouraged by the financial competitive edge the pharmaceutical conglomerates had over the graduate school laboratory. Those companies had millions of dollars to pump into a project that would make them a billion. The lab at the IU School of Medicine operated from a restricted college budget and a few grants that petered out before the research concluded. Any significant discoveries were readily shared with the world of academia and soon assimilated into the research of private companies whose lawyers worked around the clock on new patents and protecting old ones. He appreciated Eli Lilly's generous philanthropic efforts to research schools, but he was glad to be out of the classroom and into adventure.

His wandering mind returned as his eyes adjusted to the dimly lit room. The emerging sight shocked him. The room looked like the aftermath of a Kansas tornado, its contents topsy-turvy. A middle-aged man sat on a three-legged stool—the only furniture right side up. His raven black hair revealed streaks of matted blood. He held a cloth to his battered face, but feigned a smile and touched his right hand to his forehead in the traditional gesture of welcome.

"*Salaam.*" The Arab greeting varied from the Hebrew.

"*Ata medaber Anglit?*" Gary responded haltingly, hoping the stranger understood Hebrew.

"Yes, I speak English. I would very much want to stand and welcome you to my humble shop, but I am not well, you see."

"Am I correct in assuming you are Doctor Zaki Ahmed?"

"Yes. You are Doctor Gary Carter?"

"Yes. What has happened?" Gary moved toward Zaki.

"I was made a visit by some dreadfully bad people, this very morning. As you see, they make a mess of my shop. Is this a friend you bring?"

"Yes. Professor Richard Hogg, University of Cincinnati." Gary acknowledged Rick as he turned in a circle and surveyed the wreckage of the shop. Rick knelt beside Zaki and examined his wound.

"*Salaam*, Professor Hogg."

"And peace to you, Doctor Ahmed, something which seems to allude you at the moment. This is a nasty cut." Rick took the cloth from Zaki's hand and wiped at the blood. "It could use some stitches."

"Stitches? I am not familiar—"

"Sew...suture...needle." Rick gestured as if sewing.

"Ah, yes, surgery. I will see."

"What happened?" Gary asked.

"Three men with black hats over their faces, no...how do you say hats over face?"

"Hoods?"

"Yes, hoods. They come in and demand I show them the cross of Christ. I am surprised they know about my find. They also seem to know I wait for you and they seem in a rush to make sure they are gone before you come. How did they know about our private meeting?" Zaki's expression revealed his disappointment that confidences had been betrayed.

"I'm not positive, but I think I know." Gary placed a comforting hand upon Zaki's shoulder. "I didn't break your confidence, but a number of strange things have happened to me since my decision to come to Israel."

"Like what? Rick asked.

"I'll share when we have more time." He averted eye contact with Rick. "Did they steal your cross?"

"Yes."

"I'm sorry they're a step in front of us."

"No, Doctor Carter, they are still behind us."

"They have the cross—"

"They have a cross, but not the cross of the Christ." Zaki managed a slight smile, but flinched in pain. "The real cross of Christ I save for you, just like I make promise. By the time they discover the cross they take is fake, you will have authenticated real cross of Christ, and cross will be on journey to America where you protect from evil men."

75

"What do you mean they don't have the real cross? You have another cross? Here?"

"I do not keep cross of Christ here in my shop. Does one keep Mona Lisa in art shop? No, no, no! You keep Mona Lisa in museum where guards protect her from thieves."

"So you have the cross in a museum? Here in Jerusalem?"

"No, my friend. Museum is only expression of speech. I have it in secret place. I show you tomorrow. Today, I take you to finest restaurant in Jerusalem to eat authentic cuisine of my fathers and to talk of exactimundo crux of Christos."

They smiled at Zaki's mélange of languages.

A commotion ensued outside the shop. Zaki leaped to his feet but fell back onto the stool, grimacing in pain and holding the side of his head. Gary grabbed for a makeshift weapon just as Jack burst through the doorway. Half a dozen merchants waited outside, arms loaded with trinkets, proclaiming their best deal, "Mr. Jack, just for you today, our American friend." Jack's grin faded as he adjusted to the scene huddled in the room.

CHAPTER
SIXTEEN

The day finally arrived. It had been a long time coming. Goleth, perched atop a rock, watched with keen interest the unfolding events in the valley below. The relentless sun bore down. Beads of sweat dotted his brow. He squinted to observe movement in the heat waves dancing in the distance. Uncoiling a tattered turban from his head, he craftily erected a makeshift tent to shield his eyes from the glare of the sun. Settling into a more comfortable position, he fiddled with a leather parchment tucked inside the frayed belt around the waist of his caftan; he pondered its written contents.

An agama lizard ventured from a fissure in the rock below. Its oversized yellow head and long tail, with bluish torso, identified it as a dominant male. A gaped mouth revealed teeth of varying sizes. Its head and chest bobbed up and down in a defensive stance, challenging the intruder who had invaded its territory, stolen the higher ground and now soaked up the morning sun essential for its life. The odd little critter amused Goleth for a while, but he eventually picked up a pebble and flung it at the lizard, which darted back into hiding.

A pair of honey buzzards flew an arching pattern that descended toward the mount where Goleth sat, then gained altitude over the expansive eastern valley. Their winter foraging for food in this warmer climate was ending, and soon they would migrate back to their breeding ground in the northland. He glanced from the buzzards to the lizard peering out from the crack in the rock. His primary attention focused on the scene unfolding a hundred yards beyond his perch, where a couple of soldiers, in full regalia, stood expectantly overlooking the valley. Even from the distance, he could easily identify them.

A shadow passed over Goleth; he welcomed the temporary reprieve from the blistering sun.

His orders were specific: witness the death and bring back the trophy as sufficient proof. It was a pleasurable assignment, for he loathed life and delighted in executions, especially the more gory. He didn't fully understand why, but the sight of death, especially by torture, gave him a temporary high that boiled his emotions hot with gratification and morphed his brain into spasms of grotesque pleasure. Low guttural sounds escaped his lips in short rasping bursts as he glanced with amusement at the circling buzzards. An insidious grin divulged his sinister imagination.

Perhaps easy dinner for you scavengers tonight.

It seemed only yesterday the event happened, but two thousand years had slipped by, waiting, wondering and searching. After all these years, news of the cross had surfaced. His loyalty will finally be vindicated. Zatar will be pleased.

CHAPTER
SEVENTEEN

Heads turned as a towering brass door squeaked open, and a colossal figure silhouetted the doorway. Scraping of metal against the stone floor ricocheted off the walls as a delegation, clustered around a marble table, pushed back bronze chairs and stood in unison to welcome their leader.

"Zatar. Zatar. Zatar." The chanting began as a low rumble, which escalated in cadence and volume as the figure entered the room. The crescendo echoed throughout the castle fortress as Zatar raised his hands in an acceptance of their greeting.

Flickering candles from multiple brass containers—mounted on the walls and suspended from the ceiling—cast eerie shadows throughout the hall. The acrid smell of smoke stung the nostrils of the assembly and hung heavily throughout the room occupied by strangely clad individuals. Goblets, emptied of foul smelling wine, cluttered the tabletop and lay scattered along the cobblestone floor.

Zatar swaggered into the room, flanked by assistants. He walked briskly across the floor and ascended a marble platform overlooking the assembly; his assistants stood guard a few feet behind and to either side of him. His fiery eyes briefly scanned the assembly with a clairvoyance that caused the strongest among them to shudder with trepidation. Without speaking, he settled into his marble throne, and in one swift movement he motioned for the others to be seated.

From the rear wall, Goleth, as rigid as a statue, and flanked by his timid entourage, remained standing. Zatar looked in their direction.

"Yes?" His resonant voice echoed throughout the great room.

"May we approach the throne, your majesty?" A black mask covered Goleth's entire head, with slits for his eyes, nose and mouth.

"From where are you and what is your business at this assembly?" Zatar leaned forward to get a better look at this small band of intruders, his laser-like eyes penetrating the smoke-filled hall.

"We are from Jerusalem, but much wandering has sent us to many places. We are the sons of the skull, keepers of the cross, your majesty. I am Goleth."

At the announcement, c hairs shuffled against the floor as the entire assembly turned to assess this small group hugging the back wall. Whispers echoed throughout the room.

Zatar sprang from his throne and pointed an accusing finger. "Goleth? Yes, I remember. You are more like an absconder than a guardian. I commissioned you to claim the cross for me, and then you were to guard it, but you failed. I have not seen nor heard from you for two millenniums. I assumed you had been cast into the pit with Legions"

"No, I have been busy, and I have never abandoned my commission."

"I do not see the cross you were to bring to me. How do you guard something you do not possess? You have failed me. How dare you show your face in my presence empty-handed! But then again, I do not see your face behind that ridiculous mask."

Goleth awkwardly adjusted the mask. "I have news, Your Majesty. Very good news."

"Good news? What good news is there that a traitor like yourself could possibly bring?"

"There are reports of the cross having been discovered, Your Majesty. Please, may we approach to share our better fortune of these last few days?"

"You may approach." Zatar's reproachful stance faded into scarcely veiled antipathy as he straightened the flowing sleeves of his black robe and sat down.

The cultish clan apprehensively scampered toward the throne but stopped a few feet short. Goleth inched forward and knelt at the feet of Zatar. The others fell prostrate. Silent. They waited.

"Uh'uh." Zatar cleared his throat.

Goleth hated what he must now do. Without rising, he stretched forward, lifted his mask slightly and kissed the sculptured ring on the outstretched hand of Zatar.

"You may rise and share with us this good fortune you speak of."

CHAPTER
EIGHTEEN

Zatar listened, his suspicions obvious, as Goleth reported the mystery of two millenniums. He challenged the story as ambiguous, and he demanded details. With each challenge, Goleth felt emboldened. He did not deserve for Zatar to treat him with such contempt. He had completed his commission, be it ever so lengthy an accomplishment. Or at least he was about to finish it.

Zatar sipped from a brass mug. "You may continue.

"The calloused executioner commenced his assigned task while the officer in charge, still atop his prancing mount, read aloud the crimes of the condemned. Soldiers flung the three prisoners backward upon crudely assembled crosses and roughly constrained them while the executioner wielded an iron mallet that pummeled pointed spikes through the hands and feet and into the crossbeams."

Zatar remained sullen.

"Their bodies jerked spasmodically, and they screamed long and hard in anguish." Goleth's pace intensified as he shared details. He had never told this story before. By the recent discovery he had earned the right.

"Were you close enough to see his facial expressions?" Zatar's question surprised him.

"Yes."

"And?" Zatar's impatience was obvious.

"He grimaced, biting so hard on his lips he drew blood."

"Did he beg for mercy?"

"Not for himself."

"How long did it take him to die?"

"Death by crucifixion always takes hours. His was no exception."

"Good."

Goleth sensed camaraderie.

"Were their witnesses besides yourself?"

Why would he ask that? Does he not believe my story? "Seldom do observers, even the most curious, stay until the end, but the spectators seemed in no hurry to leave this crucifixion."

"Good!"

Zatar is pleased. I must share more.

"The hourglass trickled slowly, as if stifled by the coagulating blood oozing from the wounds of the condemned, staining the rocks beneath their feet. Other than the soldiers, only a handful of the piteous lingered, huddled near the one we hate. He seemed to speak to them, in an awkward way, as if he needed the use of his hands for emphasis." Goleth laughed but subdued it quickly.

"What did he say?" Zatar leaned toward him.

Goleth seized upon the moment to gain favor. The right words could restore him to his rightful position. He could leapfrog all his comrades who had enjoyed Zatar's favor the past two thousand years while he wandered in solitude and shame.

"He said 'I thirst.' He asked for a drink of water."

"You did not give it to him?"

"No, of course not. One of his own near the cross spoke to the guards, at first demandingly, but finally in a pleading way."

"A drink of water? How ironic! Was not he the one who told the story of a tortured man asking for a drip of water to be placed on his tongue? The tale has come back to haunt him. Ha, ha. Did he get water?"

"One of the soldiers impaled a sponge on the point of a rod and soaked it with vinegar poured from a leather pouch. He pressed the dripping sponge against his parched lips. When he realized it was not water, he clenched his lips and turned his head away. The soldier continued to cajole him with the sponge of bitter vinegar but finally, tiring, lowered the rod and rejoined his comrades who laughed at the taunting."

"Good." A faint smile broke forth on Zatar's face. He seemed pleased with Goleth's report. "Then what happened?"

"We waited. Amidst the groans of pain and death, we waited. One of the guards paced back and forth in front of the crosses clutching his javelin, as if expecting an imminent attack. The others huddled a few feet away, playing a traditional game of wager for the seamless garment of the Galilean. Always the soldiers were near their javelins. How ironic the soldiers needed their javelins to guard three helpless men suspended on crosses by nails through their hands and feet." A subdued chuckle escaped Goleth's lips, a precursor to laughter, but Zatar was not laughing.

"Enough of this nonsense," Zatar screamed, leaping to his feet. "Why do I need to hear about the ancient javelin of the Romans? I am interested only in the present. Where is the cross? Why have you not brought it to me these two thousand years?"

"I was getting to that, Your Majesty. I wanted to explain—"

"I do not want excuses; I want the cross! Guards, remove this imbecile from my presence."

CHAPTER NINETEEN

G ary awakened from a nap feeling drugged and disoriented. "Drink plenty of water and exercise to prevent jet lag," a friend had advised. He had done neither. He dialed Rick's room. No answer. He tried Jack's room to no avail. Memories flashed of the failed car-jacking by the fiendish goon. Where are Rick and Jack? American's are targets of foreign kidnappers. His concerns escalated when he noticed a piece of paper pushed underneath his door. A single word scribbled on the paper confused him.

"*Canyon*? What does *canyon* mean?"

He grabbed his translation book and thumbed through its pages. He stopped at a page and ran his index finger down the list of words until he came to the one he sought.

"*Canyon*...they're shopping."

Celeste loves shopping. He was glad she was with her mother. Should I call her? He glanced at his watch and realized she'd be asleep this hour of the day. He'd call her later. He intertwined his fingers, stretched them backward until his knuckles cracked, then rubbed at the tenseness in his neck. How long have I slept? A hot shower, or maybe cold, will do me good. The phone interrupted his plans.

"Hello."

"Doctor Carter?" The voice sounded familiar.

"Yes."

"John Tillman, Christian Broadcasters' Association. How's it going?"

"Good, Reverend Tillman. What a surprise! And how are you?"

"Great! Call me John, Doctor Carter. Reverend is too formal for friends. Don't you agree?"

"Sure."

"I'm really glad I caught you. I'm actually in Israel, myself. Right now I'm spending a few days at this nice resort down by the Red Sea. It's a little pricy but worth it. Good to get away for a few days and relax. Know what I mean?"

"Sure, Reverend...uh, John. What's up?"

"Thought maybe we could get together when I get back to Jerusalem. Maybe do a documentary about the cross. We could visit the holy sites together. I could narrate and have you do your lecture about the DNA of Christ. We could do that at Mt. Calvary. Seems like the most appropriate place. Don't you think?"

"Probably so—"

"So you're in?"

"I'd have to check my itinerary."

"By the way, have you seen the cross?"

"Not exactly."

"What exactly does 'not exactly' mean?"

"Well, it means I'm here and the cross is here somewhere and I'll be meeting with my contact..." Gary caught himself in mid sentence and suddenly wanted to misdirect Reverend Tillman. "I've told you all along this whole thing was speculation, didn't I?"

"And I've told you I'm interested in your work, Doctor Carter."

"Gary, call me Gary."

"Right. Maybe my camera crew could accompany you and film you actually locating the cross. I could do some narration while you work with the cross in the background."

"Ah, I don't think that would work."

"Why not? I think it would be spectacular."

"Well, my contact may not appreciate being exploited—"

"I can send someone over and talk with him. I'm sure he'll understand."

"Send them over where?" Gary jumped on the last sentence.

"Over to…at his…wherever you tell us we can find him."

In split-second rerun Gary rehearsed the last few days' events. House burglary…itinerary, addresses, phone numbers and names stolen…Zaki Ahmed's shop location…his refusal to cooperate… the beating, ransacked shop and theft of what they thought was the cross. Tillman knows where I'm staying? Is all this a coincidence? Is he in on the robbery of my computer and now Zaki's shop? Has he already discovered the stolen cross is a fake? Or am I just being overly suspicious? Perhaps paranoia has set in. Get a grip. Tillman may just want to aggrandize his ministry with an official-looking documentary from Israel. Gary knew he couldn't be certain about Tillman's actions or intentions, and a tinge of guilt surfaced over his suspicions of Tillman. Tillman's insistent request corralled his marauding thoughts.

"What do you think? Why not let me help you with the cross project?"

"Let me talk to my contact first. Where're you staying when you return to Jerusalem?"

"Crown Plaza. Be there in a couple days."

"Okay. It may be a few days." Gary stalled for time.

"I'll wait. I'm a pretty persistent man."

Is that a veiled threat? "I haven't even seen the cross, let alone authenticate it."

"Did your sweet wife come with you?"

Why does he want to know? "No. She's visiting in Columbus, Ohio, for a few days." He immediately regretted telling Celeste's whereabouts.

"I've some friends in Columbus. Didn't Columbus have a string of shootings…someone killed, I think. I probably shouldn't have mentioned the shootings. I wouldn't want you to worry about Celeste. That's her name, isn't it? She'll be fine at her mother's, I'm sure."

Gary didn't answer. He could hear himself breathing. I didn't tell Tillman Celeste's name nor that she is at her mother's. He wanted to scream at Tillman and return the threat, but he knew he must remain calm. His suspicions were all speculative—baseless other than his imagination. Still, it wasn't speculation that Tillman had all this information. What was he up to? Think, Carter. You're in a battle of wits with a religious fanatic—though ever so subtle. Celeste's safety is at stake.

"You there, Gary?"

"Yes. I'll let you know when I get the cross. Some others want it also, but I'm sure I can work with you. You feel free to go back to the States. My goal is to get the cross stateside—though customs will be the challenge—and then I'll work on the details of a deal for you. What do you think?"

After a seemingly long pause, Tillman cleared his throat. "I think I'll stick around. I'll be in touch."

The line went dead just as someone knocked on the door. Gary stiffened. He tiptoed across the room and peeked through the telescope opening in the door. A stranger, with a youthful face and typical Middle Eastern beard, faced the door—expressionless and nondescript. A guest at the wrong door? A worker for the hotel? A friend? Or enemy? What does he want?

"Who's there?"

"I am a friend of Zaki Ahmed. He sent me to pick you up for dinner. Your line was busy, so I just came on up. Your friends, Mr. Rick and Mr. Jack, are waiting in the hotel foyer." Gary exhaled slowly and started to unlock the door. The phone rang again. He hesitated, staring at the receiver and wondering about the person waiting outside his door. Perhaps that's Rabbi Joseph calling. He promised to call.

"Just a minute." He walked across the room and picked up the telephone.

"Hello."

"Doctor Carter, please."

"Speaking."

"This is the front desk clerk. I have a message for you from Doctor Zaki Ahmed."

"Yes?" Gary glanced at the door.

"He phoned for you, but your line was busy. He left a message to inform you that with his deepest apologies he is not up to dinner tonight, and he will meet you and your friends at eight tomorrow morning. He said for you to plan for your meeting with him to last all day."

"Thank you, sir." Gary slowly replaced the receiver. He stared at the door. There was another knock.

CHAPTER
TWENTY

Gary walked slowly to the door. "Go away, sir, or else I'll be obliged to call the police."

"Carter?" a familiar voice called back. "What in the world's going on in there?"

"Hogg?" Gary's voice trembled with relief.

"And Metz," another voice called out. "What've you been drinking?"

Gary swung the door open and managed a feeble smile. "You guys ready for dinner?"

They settled on King David's La Regence for their evening meal. The richly decorated interiors, the beautiful view, and the garden terrace were impressive side benefits to the creative menu elaborately served by attentive waiters.

Gary tried to be upbeat, but he had little appetite."

"What's wrong?" Rick asked.

"I should've told you earlier."

"Told us what?" Jack asked. His ever-present grin somewhat camouflaged his true emotions.

Gary pushed his food around his plate as he shared the encounter with the stranger at his door.

"Probably coincidental, don't you think?" Rick said.

"Perhaps. There's more." Gary pushed his plate back.

89

"Like what?" Jack asked.

"It began back in the States a few days before we left. I've hesitated in telling you because..." Gary looked around the room. "I doubted you'd believe it."

He shared the details of the events of the past two weeks—the televangelists' interest in the cross, the masked monster, the break-in, the robbery of his computer and Tillman's recent suspicious call.

Their waiter interrupted the conversation as he served dessert.

Gary explained he suspicioned these events were interrelated to the roughing up of Zaki and the robbery of what the thieves thought was the cross of the Crucifixion. He expressed his personal concerns for Celeste and how the events affected her emotionally.

"So what, if anything, can we do?" Jack scraped the last of his crème brûlèe. "Should we call the whole thing off and catch the next flight home?"

"Perhaps."

"I don't think so, but we must take this very seriously, Rick said. "It's more than a spoof. Too many real-life events have happened for this to be a hoax. I'm beginning to think someone believes more than we do the actual cross has been found, and they want the cross at any cost, maybe more than we do."

Gary rubbed the back of his neck. "So, we must become proactive, not just reactionary like I've been the past couple weeks."

Rick continued, "Whoever took the cross from Ahmed's shop surely doesn't know the cross is a fake. So we've at least got them off our case for a while, maybe time for us to come up with a plan. Don't you think?"

"I've thought about that." Gary looked from one to the other and then around the room. He lowered his voice to a whisper. "If the person who stole my computer is the same one who robbed Doctor Ahmed, they may have already found out it's a fake. They may very well be pursuing us right now, assuming we have the real cross."

"How could they know so soon the cross they stole is fake?" Jack asked.

"Ahmed e-mailed me the description of the cross and why he felt it was the actual cross of Christ. If they have access to that information, which I'm beginning to think they have, surely they will compare the cross with that information, don't you think?"

"Yes," Rick said.

"Ahmed could not duplicate the fake cross with the real. In their haste at Ahmed's shop, the thieves may not have noticed, but once away from the shop, they may have inspected closer, and by now they realize the cross they stole is just another ancient piece. They will come again searching for the authentic cross." Gary scribbled on a napkin, underlining certain words for emphasis.

"You're right. The thieves are still out there, and they're no longer celebrating. They're angry by now and probably burnt the cross with an effigy of Ahmed, or you, on it," Rick said.

"We should warn Ahmed," Gary said.

"No need. He already knows."

They turned toward the voice of a lone figure sitting with his back to them. A white headdress, held in place by a black rope circlet, flowed across his shoulders.

CHAPTER
TWENTY-ONE

"Salaam, my three friends from America."

"Doctor Ahmed?" Gary asked.

"Yes. Forgive me for my, how do you say, incog…"

"Incognito," Rick finished the word for him.

"Yes, my incognito. I realize, just as you, our enemies will soon discover they stole a replica of the cross, and they will return. That is why I canceled our dinner arrangements. I did not wish to endanger your lives, so I went into hiding and eventually came here secretly, hoping to meet you. Though I am disappointed I could not take you to my favorite restaurant, I meet you over dinner anyway. Yes?"

"Yes. Pull up your chair and join us," Gary said.

"Thank you, my friends." The light from the table candle illuminated his battered forehead. His left eye was swollen partially shut. He had followed Rick's advice and had the wound treated with stitches.

"We're glad you're safe, Doctor Ahmed." Gary said. The others nodded their agreement.

"Thank you, my friends. It is time we stop formality. You stop calling me doctor and call me Zaki."

"It isn't safe for you to go home. They will find you. Your family would not be safe. Do you have a family?" Gary asked.

"Once." Zaki bowed his head. His face reflected sadness.

"I'm sorry," Gary said. "You don't need to explain...unless you wish."

"I do not mind speaking about my family, though it does bring pain, the kind to which a physician cannot attend. I had very wonderful wife and two beautiful children. They were my life. Now they are gone, and I am fortunate to have life. My work helps me...sorry, I can't quite find the right word."

"Cope?" Rick said.

"Yes, that is the word, I believe. My work distracts me from my loneliness, so I cope better without distressed situation all the time."

"May I ask what happened to your family?" Gary asked.

"Yes, but is a sad story. A terrorist blew himself up at the Mahane Yehuda Market in West Jerusalem. My wife, Sarah, and my two sons, Ibrahiim and Amal, went to that market because it has wonderful fruit. They wanted watermelon for dinner. They were killed in blast. It was so very ironic, for name Amal means *hope*. My Amal, my hope, was dead. I could not believe news when they come and tell me. 'How could a merciful God let this happen?' I ask myself over and over." Zaki paused.

Gary instinctively touched Zaki's sun-bronzed hands that rested upon the white table linen. "We are so sorry."

"Thank you. You are kind. For days I wander through streets of Jerusalem in daze. I question how two monotheistic religions that both profess to have same God—the God of *Avraham*—could hate one another so. The terrorists who kill my family look like children of *Avraham,* but they are deceptive. They dress in ultra-Orthodox garbs to blend into crowd, but they carried hate, not love for God, in their hearts. They carry explosives and nails packed into briefcases. With such hate for one another, I conclude neither the followers of Allah, nor followers of Yahweh, truly follow the God of Scripture. They follow only traditions of men—traditions filled with hate and revenge—since ancient time when Ishmael and Isaac were unable to cohabit same tent of their father, or even same land of our fathers."

Zaki's voice quivered with emotion as he tried to continue.

"We're sorry, Doctor Ahmed...Zaki, so very sorry," Gary said.

Zaki slowly lifted his face. The flickering candlelight amplified the creases on his brow. His strained face softened as he gently tapped his chest over his heart.

"All is not bad, my friends. That is how I became Christian. The Scripture of Christian faith defines God of Torah and God of Koran much better than some Judaism followers and some Islam followers define Him."

No one responded.

"You seem confused by my comment."

"Surprised," Gary said.

"Let me explain. A neighbor who is Arab, but also Christian, point out Christian verse: 'He that loveth not knoweth not God; for God is love.' My neighbor said, 'The Christian faith is the faith of our fathers made perfect through a perfect sacrifice for our sins in the God/man, Yeshua.' He explained to me messianic message found in writings of prophet Isaiah: 'Surely he hath borne our griefs and carried our sorrows: yet we did esteem him stricken, smitten of God, and afflicted. But he was wounded for our transgressions, he was bruised for our iniquities...' My neighbor explain how God of *Avraham* humbled himself to be born of virgin, Mary. The Christ-child, born as an innocent babe, became perfect sacrifice for mankind's sins." Zaki paused as a waiter removed the dessert dishes.

"Something more to drink?" the waiter asked.

They all declined.

Zaki continued, "At first I do not believe another monotheistic faith associated with Father *Avraham* would be any different than what I already witness. The crusades and inquisitions attest to that. I read in our newspaper of fighting still going on between Protestants and Catholics in Ireland. But I know all who profess Islam are not true to Koran, so I go with him to his Christian service and am surprised. I find Jews and Arabs in same room worshiping same God. Are they fighting one another? No! They have much love for one another. 'How can this be?' I ask. They direct me to Christ of Scripture. No, it is more than that. They love me and I see Christ of Scripture in them. That is when I search the Scriptures of Christianity and study the teaching of Christ and of his apostles and I become a believer. Since then I use my profession—archaeology—to try and prove to others the Christian faith is true faith of Scripture. That is why I am so pleased to find cross of the Christ. Perhaps I can help others to believe in Christ."

Zaki bowed his head when he finished his bittersweet story.

"Perhaps you can," Gary said. "Perhaps it will be a great witness. I'm glad we've come to be a part. Tonight you'll stay with us in the hotel. Tomorrow you can show us the cross."

CHAPTER
TWENTY-TWO

G oleth remained prostrate before the throne. "Please, Your Majesty. Allow me to continue. I beg you. You will not be disappointed."

"You may continue, but at the risk of peril from your own mouth."

Goleth stood, emboldened. "The one on the center cross, *Yeshua*—"

"I do not like that name. Do not speak that name in my presence."

"He, the Galilean, shifted his body and painfully pulled himself upward on the cross. Between gasps for air, he spoke to someone in the crowd. An emotional scene erupted among those at the base of the cross. One young man draped his arms around an elderly woman, pulled her away from the scene and directed her down the slope of the mount. The Galilean lifted himself aloft again, as if gazing after them, and then he slumped. His sagging position caused his breathing to come in short, wheezing gasps. He pulled himself upward and cried out in one long exhalation, and then collapsed against the full weight of the nails, silent. His head abruptly drooped sideways, leaving his chin resting awkwardly against his chest. A quilt of quiet grief blanketed the assembly like no one knew what to do.

The Jewish leaders complained about a desecration of their Sabbath. The soldiers sufficed them by shattering the legs femurs of two of the condemned. An argument ensued as to whether or not to break the Galilean's legs; one pointed out he was already dead. The soldier quickly silenced his comrades as he stepped forward, and in one quick motion, thrust his javelin deep into the upper left side of the motionless body. Blood and water gushed forth, splattering onto the rocks. The lamenting cluster at his feet howled their disbelief. The soldier quickly withdrew a few paces, his melancholic expression explaining he was only following orders, fulfilling his duty as a legionnaire. His was not a sadistic act."

"Very good."

"There was something else."

"What was that?"

"The midday blackness." Goleth voice trailed off. He momentarily relived the impressionable event that burned in his memory.

"Speak up, you imbecile. What did you say?"

"The blackness."

"What do you mean by the blackness?"

"Without warning, it rushed in from the western sea like an unmanageable monster slashing and hammering out a pathway towards its enemy. I had seen its likes before in the ancient past. A squall appeared out of nowhere and created havoc in its wake, moving methodically as if controlled by some unseen force. By the time that storm—with its accompanying phenomena—ended, a vast sea of slaves streamed out of Egypt headed northeast. Egypt never recovered to her former glory and we have never regained—"

"Forget Egypt. I have long ago lost interest in that squalid country. What about the darkness in Jerusalem?"

"It was…frightening. I sought cover in a crevice as a cloud of dust and darkness, followed by a downpour of rain and hail, cascaded across the hilltop, threatening to consume all in its path, including me." Goleth paused.

"And?" Zatar anxiously tapped his boot against the stone floor.

"It was uncanny weather for Jerusalem, one the scribes recorded in historical accounts of their ancient city. The storm was more than a spring thunderstorm skipping across the skies. It was a ragging reaction from the heavens above followed by a catastrophic outburst from the earth beneath. It was an earthquake like I have never—"

"Ridiculous. It was a naturally occurring earthquake, nothing more."

"Whatever passed through the region that day scuttled the crowd's curiosity, and they dispersed from the hillside, scampering back inside the walled city. No, I do not think it was a common storm. It was too timely…too reactive…it was another force beyond our own. And the earthquake came moments after—"

"Earthquakes happen all the time. It was a coincidence that it happened during his death." Zatar motioned with his hand to dismiss the subject of the earthquake. "Then what happened?"

"After a long while, one of the mourners turned numbly from the cross and staggered down the rocky trail. The others followed, one by one, leaving a singular woman who hesitated in departing. They called her Mary"

"That would be his mother?" Zatar smiled.

"No. His mother was already gone, with the disciple called John."

"If it was not Mary, his mother, then it was Mary the devoted one." Zatar spoke as if he'd been there.

Goleth seemed surprised.

"She once belonged to us. Wretched woman." Zatar cursed and spat upon the floor.

Goleth continued, slowly, as if reliving the scene. "She, Mary, reached out with a trembling hand and devotedly dabbed the blood from his feet. She pressed her fingers to her lips and again to his feet, gently. She wiped her eyes with the back of her hand and brushed back a lock of raven-colored hair that had fallen across her pallid face. She lingered still, then irresolutely turned from the cross and left. Only the soldiers and the condemned remained."

"Did you leave also?" The contempt in Zatar's voice challenged Goleth's allegiance.

"No. I kept my distance and continued to observe. 'It will not be long now and the soldiers will remove his dead body. Then I will have my prize."

"My prize," Zatar shouted."

"That is what I meant, your prize I was sent to retrieve. Two men, bracing themselves against the wind, hastily made their way up the hillside. Their flowing, black and white robes, with fringed phylacteries, identified them as the elite among the religious of Judea. They used their ridiculous prayer shawls, to shield themselves from the pelting sand that stung their eyes and penetrated their nostrils.

"Jerusalem had been busy all week with pilgrims coming for the holy event of Passover, and it had been in an uproar since the dawning of this morning leading to the Passover that would begin at sundown. The storm had settled the people down, sending them hurrying for cover. Perhaps these two men wished for the storm to settle down so they could accomplish their task of benevolence, for I perceived they came for the body of the Galilean. I watched as one handed the sentry a scrolled parchment, which he carefully examined before he stepped aside for them to accomplish their task."

"You did not intervene?"

"Their actions seemed no harm to my plan, for I wanted only the cross. They could have his bruised and lifeless body. I waited as they hastily ascended a makeshift ladder propped against the cross and reverently removed the one many locals worshiped as Messiah. They wrapped his naked body in a shroud. The gentle way they handled the body would cause one to think he was a dear friend or beloved relative. They hoisted the shrouded body onto their shoulders and descended the hill. Spots of crimson blood soaked through the shroud and stained their garments. The wind died down, and the soldiers took their time removing the remaining bodies." Goleth paused, as if the story was finished.

"What happened next?"

"I watched while the guards tossed the bodies across the backs of two mules. They gathered their tools and weapons and leisurely descended the hill, letting the animals set the pace. I scrambled toward the three vacant crosses and had almost dislodged the center one when a lone figure ascended the hill and came straight toward me. His broad frame bulged impressively underneath his loose fitting robe. We rendezvoused at the summit of Golgotha, the center cross between us.

"He did not speak but clinched the base of the beam like a fighter preventing his opponent's blows, and with a gut wrenching bellow he yanked the cross out of the ground. He hefted it across his shoulders and turned toward the path down the hill."

"You stood there and allowed him to have my trophy. You have failed me, Goleth. I cannot believe you would show your face after such failure," Zatar screamed as he leaped to his feet.

"Please, Zatar. I have not failed. You must allow me to share the good news."

"I am not convinced you have good news. You had the cross in your hands and let it get away. Why did you not stop him?"

"I did, by jumping in front of him and blocking his path."

"He still got away and it was not your fault? I can finish the story for you. You need tell me no more."

"Please, Zatar. Another moment of your time."

"One minute."

Zatar's bodyguards stepped closer.

"He brushed past me and started again toward the path descending Golgotha. Without hesitating, he called to me, 'You have two more crosses from which to choose.'"

"'No'", I screamed to him. "'This cross belongs to my master. It is the spoil of the victor and the shame of the vanquished. He has sent me to collect the prize.'"

"He stopped abruptly and turned to face me. 'You cannot have it,' he said. I grabbed onto the end of the cross and lugged it backward. He clung to the cross still balanced atop his shoulders. Then he spoke directly to me. 'Today the enemy enthroned my Lord upon this cross in mockery and malice. In ridicule and pain they crowned Him with thorns and scoffed at Him as they placed a reed for a scepter in His bruised hand. They will not taunt Him further by displaying this cross as a victory relic. I will conceal it forever from His enemies.'

"'If you care as much as you say, where were you earlier when he hung on this cross dying?' I taunted him."

"'True, I have denied my Lord thrice already today, but I will not deny my Master again by cowardice in giving up the object of His death.'"

"'Who is this master you speak of? Is he not now lying cold and alone, shrouded by death and entombed in stone?' I mocked him."

"He would not release his grip on the cross. I did not know what to do. I had not anticipated this action, his resolve or his strength. I reluctantly released my grip. I could only watch as he staggered down the hill, bearing the cross on his shoulders. I followed him but he eluded me."

"You have come to tell me this?" Zatar screamed. "To reveal your failure in retrieving the cross for me? Am I supposed to accept your story of failure and let you go guiltless? You are even more stupid than I imagined."

"No, Your Majesty. I have good news for a bad beginning. The cross has resurfaced and is in the care of easy prey. We will have it for you this time."

Goleth knelt on one knee and bowed, signaling the end of his presentation.

Zatar rubbed his chin contemplatively. "After nearly twenty centuries I may have my trophy? How can I be sure?"

"We searched the world for it, my lord. We found it in Jerusalem. I have dispatched associates to retrieve it."

A heinous grin broke forth on Zatar's face. "I had nearly given up." He stood and stepped down from the throne. He paced in front of the assembly, pounding his fist into his open palm. He paused, wheeled on his heels and pointed accusingly at Goleth. "You do not have it yet. I will believe it when I see you walk through that door with the cross on your shoulder."

"I will bear it for you, my master."

"Perhaps I can offer some helpful advice?"

"Of course, Your Majesty."

"Have you not heard of the angel of light?"

"You mean the angel announcing the birth of *Yeshua*?"

"Do not use that terminology in my presence!" Zatar struck Goleth across the face. The mask flew off face and skidded across the floor.

Goleth quickly veiled his face with his cloak.

Zatar continued without an apology. "I do not speak of others. I speak of my own. I speak of deception, cunning devices and craftiness. Perhaps you should acquire the cross by a more cunning means, like Constantine's acquisition of the church through infiltration and assimilation, instead of a Genghis Khan's routing-of-the-enemy approach. Become an angel of light, stop wearing that disgusting mask and men will be drawn to you like astrologers to the stars."

"You shall have the cross. I vow it with my life."

"You are already dead to me. When you did not return after the Crucifixion I crossed your name from the list of my loyal subjects. And you now come to me hidden behind that foolish mask."

"Please do not mock me."

"Mock you! You mock me by coming into my presence without the cross. Why do you wear that outlandish disguise?"

"To hide the scars."

"Scars? From what? Certainly not battle scars."

"Oh, but they are, Your Majesty. From guarding the tomb of the Galilean."

"Why guard the tomb of a dead man?"

"I thought the one who stole the cross would return."

"So how did you get the burns? From falling asleep too close to the fire?"

"It was at the tomb, early in the morning. It happened so suddenly. First, another quaking. The guards fled in terror. I rushed toward the tomb, but a blinding flash stopped me. A radiance more brilliant than the noonday sun burst forth from the tomb. My clothes were ablaze...my body badly burned. I wear the mask to cover the wounds... wounds I received doing my duty."

Goleth removed the cloak draping his face.

Zatar laughed. Goleth started to speak.

"Enough!" Zatar waved his hand to silence him. "I am not interested in your pitiful story of defeat. It is victory I want and demand. Retrieve the cross and bring it to me, or else, you may find yourself hanging from your own cross."

CHAPTER
TWENTY-THREE

Celeste sat in a restaurant overlooking the main floor of Lazarus Department Store in the Northgate Mall. The break was a reprieve for her aching feet. She had spent the day shopping. She shopped for nothing in particular. "Just browsing," she told helpful clerks. The only items she purchased were a couple shirts for Gary. Sitting alone it suddenly dawned how much she missed him.

She lifted a cup to her lips and sipped hot tea, savoring the aroma of orange pekoe. That's when she noticed him; actually, she'd seen him before, strolling the aisles, or standing behind a clothes rack. She'd seen him in another store. This was the first time she considered he was always within sight of her—for hours now. Her hands trembled from an adrenaline rush and she quickly set the cup down—too hard. The clink of the china brought stares from the nearby table.

"Sorry."

They gave her subdued smiles. She reciprocated, nervously. Slowly she looked across the mall floor again. He averted her gaze and picked up an item from off a rack. She cradled the cup with trembling hands and stared at the table linen. *Where have I seen him? Why is he...stalking me?* She hesitated to consider that word, stalk. *Relax. He can't do anything to me in a crowded restaurant in the middle of the day. The masked bandit attacked in the middle of the day on a busy street.* Her heart ached for Gary.

"Anything else, ma'am?" The waiter startled her.

She wanted to grab him by the arm and point toward the man below and scream, *Yes, make that man quit following me*, but she restrained her emotions. "No, thank you. Do you mind me occupying this booth for a little longer?"

"Long as you like, ma'am. Crowd's dying down till dinner." The waiter smiled. "Would you need to tell a caring ear what's bothering you?"

"Oh, nothing. I'm fine." She managed a smile.

"Okay, but I'll be here if you need anything. Care for a refill on your tea?"

"Yes, thank you."

"Coming up, ma'am." The waiter hustled back to the counter to retrieve the teapot.

Trying to appear unintentional, she scanned the mall. He was gone. She sighed and began a slow and methodical rhythm of breaths. "In…hold…out slowly."

"What's that, ma'am?"

"Nothing." Celeste laughed. "Just talking to myself. I'm okay. Really."

"I'm here till closing time."

"Thanks."

She longed for the security Gary gave her, and she suddenly felt weak. Vulnerable. Afraid. She fumbled in her purse and retrieved her cell phone. She clicked onto his number but considered the time difference from Columbus to Jerusalem and quickly calculated he was sleeping. It was unfair to disturb him and, even more, it was unfair to cause him worry over her fragile female emotions running amok. There was nothing he could do for her except fret; that wouldn't help her situation. She closed her cell phone and placed it on the table. *What should I do? Why is a stranger shadowing me? What does he want? Where is he now?* She scanned the mall, hoping he was gone for good. To her dismay he sat three tables away, his back toward her table, as if studying the menu.

Celeste's heart raced. She fought impulsive thoughts and didn't know what abruptly possessed her, nor did she care. She snatched up her cell phone, stomped to the stranger's table and stared down at him. He continued to hide his face behind the menu.

"Excuse me," she said.

He lowered the menu and cleared his voice. "May I help you, ma'am?"

Her body trembled and she assumed her voice would also. *Enough is enough. Fight fire with fire, no matter if only ashes are left. One should go down charging the enemy, not running away.* "How does it feel, Mr. whatever your name is?" The man appeared shocked.

"I'm not sure—"

"I take it you don't like it." The few customers in the restaurant stared at the unfolding drama. "We'll see how you like this." She flipped open her cell case, punched in 9-1-1 and pressed send.

"What are you doing?" he asked in a subdued volume but a forceful manner.

"What does it look like? I'm reporting you."

"Oh, no. You don't need to do that."

"You don't like it, huh? You should've thought of that before you started stalking me."

"I'm not stalking you, Mrs. Carter. I'm protecting you."

"So you know my name. You're...protecting me? From who? Did I miss something?"

"Yes." The stranger took charge. "Your husband, Doctor Gary Carter, that is your husband's name isn't it?"

"Yes. Gary—"

"Doctor Carter hired me before he left for his trip to Israel."

"So that's why I thought you looked familiar." Celeste snapped her cell case shut. She suddenly felt silly.

"Probably. Officer Scott Davis. Part-time deputy sheriff."

"Carmel, Indiana, no doubt?"

"Right."

Celeste reached out her hand as a peace gesture; he shook it with a sigh.

"Were you at the investigation of our break-in?"

"Yes, ma'am." He seemed pleased she recognized him. "That's when I met your husband. He called and asked me to do some moonlighting, so here I am."

Mixed emotions of gratitude and surprise washed through her. *Gary was considerate, but why does he feel I need protection?* "Why did Gary hire you?"

"Doctor Carter really didn't explain. Just said it was precautionary and to not trouble you with it. Probably has to do with the break-in. You caught me guarding you, so my cover is blown and—"

Celeste's phone rang.

"Hello."

"This is the Columbus dispatcher for nine-one-one. We just received a call from this number, but the line went dead. Are you the one who called?"

"Ah, yes, but everything is okay. I'm sorry to have bothered you."

"May I have your name?"

"Celeste Carter, but you really—" She gave Officer Davis an I'm-really-sorry-about-this expression. He remained pokerfaced.

"Where are you calling from?"

"I'm at a restaurant at the Lazarus Department Store in the Northgate Mall, but really, I'm okay."

"Would you mind holding that position for a few moments until we have an officer verify?" Celeste could hear conversation in the background punctuated by radio static. She assumed they were attempting to locate her. "We have an officer in that mall right now, ma'am. I must ask you to remain there."

"Really, ma'am, I'm…"

A police officer approached.

"I hope you have proper identification, Officer Davis." She smiled as she closed her cell case. "We have company coming for dinner."

CHAPTER
TWENTY-FOUR

Celeste handed Officer Davis a check. "This is for your trouble. Thank you very much for guarding me, but I'll be okay without you following me down every aisle in every women's clothing store in Columbus. Not an exciting assignment, huh?"

"I didn't mind, ma'am, but I don't feel right taking this. I feel like I'm walking off the job, and I've never walked off a job in my life."

"You're not walking off the job. If Gary says anything, I'll simply explain I fired you."

"I've never been fired before either, ma'am."

"You have now."

His jaw dropped.

"Not really." She smiled. "You've done your job well. Thank you."

"Anything I can do before I head back to Indy, ma'am?"

Celeste studied her nails. "Yes. Follow me to my mother's place, let me pack and then drop me off at the airport. I'm going to Israel."

"That's the least I can do for you, Mrs. Carter."

*****

He parked behind her vehicle after she pulled into her mother's drive. He watched as she stepped from the car and walked to the door. He waited until her mother answered the knock and let her inside the house before he pulled out his cell phone and punched in a series of numbers.

"Scott Davis here."

He kept an eye on the front door of the house.

"You'll be well pleased. She's decided to go to Israel. I'm dropping her off at the airport in a few minutes."

He smiled as he snapped his cell phone shut.

Easiest five thousand I've ever made. And paid twice for the same job.

CHAPTER
TWENTY-FIVE

They arose before dawn and sat at breakfast as the first hint of light streaked across the horizon.

"We journey to the western shore of the Sea of Galilee to the city of Tiberias. It is a favorite city of Israel, the most popular resort for the northern population. Many people take their holiday there." With the excitement of a child anticipating a field trip, Zaki briefed them on the day's activities

"That's where the cross is stored?" Gary asked.

"Yes."

"How far?" Rick asked.

"About one hundred fifty kilometers."

"How far is that in miles?" Jack asked groggily.

"Ninety miles, plus," Rick answered.

"Yes, about ninety-five miles," Zaki said. "Tiberias has rich history. It was built by Herod Antipas, the son of Herod the Great, the one who first tried to kill the Christ child. He named it Tiberias in honor of the Roman Emperor Tiberius—a rather obvious way to earn favor. Do you not agree?"

"Maybe a little presumptuous," Gary said.

"Brown-noser," Jack added.

"I am not familiar with that term, brown-noser." Zaki frowned.

"Ingratiating, self-seeking," Jack said.

"A fawning parasite," Rick said.

"Yes, I understand now. Brown-noser. It is a funny term." Zaki laughed. "Ah, let me get back to my story of Tiberias."

"Please." Gary sighed.

"In Hebrew Tiberias is called *Teverya*. In Arabic we say *Abari-yyah*. It has been under control of Romans, Jews, Arabs and for a while Crusaders. When Antipas first built Tiberias, Jewish people refused to settle there because of a cemetery that made it unclean to them. Antipas forced the Jews of Galilee to move into his city. Over time Tiberias became an important city for learning and for the arts. When the Jews were expelled from Jerusalem around one hundred thirty-five AD, many settled in Tiberias, making it a major Jewish religious center. It is believed by some that Jewish Mishnah—oral teaching of Jews, which eventually formed first part of Talmud—was first put into print at Tiberias. It was also last meeting place for Sanhedrin. Enough talk about Tiberias. Let us go and see with our own eyes."

They crowded into the rental car. Jack drove and Zaki rode shotgun, calling out directions. Gary and Rick crammed in the backseat, their elbows boxed as they bumped along, and their chins rested against their knees. The air-conditioning worked poorly so they rolled down the windows to get fresh air. The June sun beat down mercilessly. Gary's straw hat revealed a growing band of sweat. Jack constantly pulled off his Cincinnati Red's cap and wiped his brow with the topside of the hat. Rick's curly hair was a sweaty mess from the wind rushing through the open windows. Zaki didn't seem to mind the heat. He talked ceaselessly to the them, to pedestrians and to the occupants of the other cars—one hand hugging the dash and the other gesturing wildly—as they weaved their way around mopeds and an occasional donkey pulling a cart. A constant line of traffic flowed both north and south.

Jack tapped the steering wheel in time with a Jewish song blaring from the radio. He swayed back and forth until the mini-car rocked somewhat dangerously. "If I were a rich man, da, da, da, da, da, da, da, da ,da," Jack bellowed in his baritone.

A melancholic mood had griped Gary. He missed Celeste. He reluctantly joined in the frolic, clapping his hands over his head and keeping rhythm with his shoulders. Rick, usually analytical and subdued, surprised him as he nodded his head in pace with the music and joined in the singing. The atmosphere resembled Gary's postulation of a gypsy wedding party.

"What would you do if you were rich, Zaki?" Gary yelled.

"If I were rich, I would go to America and live with my new friends." He turned and smiled at Gary.

"If you've found the actual cross, you might as well pack your bags. You'll be rich."

"What would you do, Mr. Metz, if you were to suddenly be rich?" Zaki asked.

"I'd have UPS overnight my Corvette to Israel and have this piece of junk scrapped."

"No. I change my mind." Zaki held up his hand for their attention. "I will move my new friends to Israel and as you say in fairy tales, 'we live happily ever after.'"

"You'd have to talk to our wives about that," Gary said.

Jack honked the horn and swerved to miss a mangy dog crossing the street.

They waved at pedestrians who gazed after them as their crowded car sputtered into Tiberias, the music at earsplitting level. Their frivolity resembled kids at a monkey pavilion.

"Turn right at next street," Zaki instructed Jack, who slowed and turned on his blinker. Zaki killed the radio. The sense of D-day suddenly silenced them.

"We make one pass by the house without stopping. Third house...on the left. Act non...what is that word?"

"Nonchalantly?" Rick helped.

"Yes, that is word I mean. You make a great Thesaur..."

"Thesaurus," Rick said."

"That is the house. One never knows for sure when he is being followed, so we act like we are passing by."

Jack braked to a crawl.

"All seems well, my friends." Zaki sighed. "We will go back now and you will see with own eyes cross of Christ.

They circled the block and stopped. The sandstone house appeared modest compared to the houses around it. Its red-tiled roof showed need of repair. Clumps of grass grew about the sandy yard.

"Welcome to my home away from Jerusalem." Keys jingled as Zaki fumbled with the key ring trying to find the right one. "This is house I purchased after my wife and children were killed. It was my place of healing." He slid the key into the lock. "It is not much, so I was able to afford it." Zaki opened the door slowly and stepped aside, motioning them to enter.

Their footsteps echoed off the bare walls as they stepped across the tile. Surprisingly, the house felt cooler than the sweltering temperature outside. The design was simple: a great room with adjoining bedroom and bathroom. A pair of slatted doors between the bedroom and bath remained shut. The textured walls were a drab brown, the varnished woodwork darkened by age. The few windows were shuttered. Sparse furniture gave the dwelling a larger feel than its actual size: a leather sofa and matching arm-chair, a built-in bookshelf—lined with books from floor to ceiling—and a small kitchen table with four chairs. The appliances were a dated yellow. A skylight illuminated a worn Persian rug in the center of the room. Stale air mingled with the scent of burnt candles that had bonded to the table.

"Please sit, my friends." Zaki stepped into the kitchen area. He filled a teakettle with tap water, placed it on the front burner and turned a knob. Gas hissed but didn't ignite. He struck a match and reached it toward the burner. The gas lit with an explosion that caused Zaki to jerk his hand away. The blast extinguished the match. He adjusted the flame. From a drawer he selected tea bags, untangled the stringed tabs and placed one in each of four teacups.

"Americans like tea mild, no?"

No one disagreed.

"And cold," Jack said.

"Strange."

"Is there any ice in Israel," Jack asked. He wiped sweat from his forehead. They laughed.

Zaki served the tea.

Between sips, Zaki talked, slowly and studiedly. "After the death of my wife and children, I retreated to this house to grieve. My newfound Christian faith took care of my sins, but did not cure my loneliness and pain. Time has done that some. In this house I sought...death...to join them in heaven. I prayed to die. Instead of death, I find strength to live. Strange how God allows prayers he denies to answer requests you do not ask."

Jack shifted in his seat. Gary gave him a consoling "patience please" glance.

"I am sorry, my friends, to bore you with my past—"

"No, go on, please," Gary interrupted his apology.

"You are kind. All of you...very kind. Another moment perhaps I will finish. A few years ago, while digging on the north shore of Galilee, I discovered some mounds. I assume they are foundations of an ancient community. Archaeologists dug there some but show more interest in places like Megiddo and Qumran. There never seems to be enough funds to adequately search ancient sights so most only search for the big find. Archeologists' funds end sometimes abruptly, maybe political strings are pulled, I know not. For whatever reason, this area was left alone for years. As I continue to make trips there, I discover little, except some pottery from a garbage site and some foundations, but garbage and foundations represent past civilization. I decide to focus my search in this area alone. I devote every hour I can spare to my new project. After a few years, what do I find?"

Jack and Rick looked at Gary. No one answered.

"What do I find?"

"The cross," Jack said.

"Not yet, Mr. Metz. First, I find the area is ancient ruin. Night and day I dig through layers of sand. I discover a stone-covered ceiling of ancient cellar. I very carefully remove a stone that revealed the opening and peer into darkness. My eyes adjust to darkness and I climb down into ancient tomb-like cellar. I switch on my pocket light and scan the contents of room: fragments of pottery, broken furniture and yes, Mr. Metz, cross of the Christ leans against the wall. I read inscription of the titulus and my heart began to live...to rejoice."

"Titulus?" Jack asked.

"The sign the Romans nailed to the cross," Gary explained.

A commotion interrupted the conversation. The door burst open and three uniformed men rushed inside, guns drawn. Ahmed stood and greeted them in his usual gesture of friendship. He seemed as calm as if they were expected friends.

"Zaki Ahmed?" the accent seemed Hebrew.

"*Ken.*"

"*Ma nishma?*"

"*Beseder.*" Zaki turned to Gary. "They ask how I am and I say alright."

"These are your American friends?"

"You speak English. Good. These are my friends and they are tourists from America."

"Is that true?" the man spoke to no one in particular.

"We are from America, and we are tourists," Gary said.

"You are from America and you look like tourists, but you are not tourists. You are treasure hunters. No?" The man scanned the room as he spoke.

Footsteps echoed on the front terrazzo. A short balding man stepped into the room. Instead of a uniform, he wore a checkered shirt, a white tie and khaki trousers. The newcomer appeared to be about sixty years old. He flashed an ID as he entered and stepped directly toward Zaki.

"Inspector Rami Gurion, Israel Antiquity Authority, if you have forgotten my identity. At it again, Doctor Ahmed? How many times do I have to tell you all antiquities must be registered with the Jewish Department of Antiquities Authority?"

"Only once, Doctor Gurion. I register my find with you soon, but I show it to my friends from America first."

"Show or sell, Doctor Ahmed?"

"Show before I register, sometimes. But register before I sell? Always!" Zaki spoke apologetically and displayed an uncharacteristically submissive spirit. Gary had not seen Zaki so resigned. The cross search had come to an abrupt halt. Had Zaki given up? He might as well pack and head home. Celeste's smiling face eased his disappointment.

"I wanted to show my friends what I have found, but I patiently wait on you gentlemen to arrive. I want to register my find now that you are here."

Inspector Gurion turned to Gary and extended a hand. "Doctor Carter, I presume?"

"Yes." Gary was surprised the inspector knew his name.

"Please do not think we suspect you of any wrongdoing, but we must at all times protect our national interest from the unauthorized pillage of its antiquities. I'm sure you understand."

"Certainly." Gary felt a tinge of trepidation in his voice.

"Thank you for understanding, Doctor Carter." He turned to Zaki. "We will search the house and take any unregistered finds to our office for proper handling."

"I have no problem with that."

Inspector Gurion turned to Gary. "This does not mean Doctor Ahmed cannot have it back. He must file for such and then perhaps we can return it to him with proper forms." He turned again to Zaki. "Doctor Ahmed, do you have anything to declare?"

"Yes, Doctor Gurion. I have come across an unusual find. It is a very old wooden cross. I believe it to be the cross upon which *Mashiach* was crucified."

"Which *Mashiach*? We have had so many…*Mashiach sheker*… fakes. I will need a name to verify the date."

"*Yeshua*, the Christ."

"An unusual find indeed, Doctor Ahmed." The inspector sneered.

"I kindly request you document my find, give me proper verification of such and consider this meeting my official request for authorized possession of such artifact." Zaki continued with his uncharacteristic gentle mannerisms.

"Documenting this find should not take long, Doctor Ahmed." Gurion chuckled. "Stop by the office in a couple days and we will give you some form of documentation, whatever it is worth." He taunted Zaki.

"Thank you, sir." Zaki bowed and touched his forehead.

"You are forgetting something, Doctor Ahmed," Gurion barked. "Where is this cross of the *Mashiyah*?"

"Behind the double doors, gentlemen, you will find cross." Zaki motioned toward the doors.

One of the assistants opened the doors to reveal a wooden cross leaning against the wall. The inspector snapped pictures from different angles. Jack impatiently tapped the toe of his shoe against the Persian rug. Gary studied the face of Zaki who, for some reason, seemed to be annoyed at Jack's incessant tapping. *How strange!*

"Take it away," Gurion said to the officers. "Stop by the office, Doctor Ahmed. Like I said, you should not have trouble getting this one back."

"With papers?" Zaki asked.

"I am sure something less impressive than you would want." Gurion started toward the door. He turned. "It is obviously old, but so are the beams in dozens of old houses around Tiberias. After all, the city is quite old." He turned toward Gary. "Herod Antipas built the original city around twenty A.D. Do not fall for this one, gentlemen. Good day."

The officers filed out, lugging the cross. The door swung shut on a room of disappointment. Car doors slammed and engines faded in the distance.

Jack broke the silence. "That's the last we'll see of the cross."

"For sure," Rick said.

"Dad's gonna be mighty disappointed, after all he's invested."

"Not only your dad. So are Reverends Tillman and Small, and their followers, which I'm sure they're prepping for the greatest religious find ever," Gary said.

"Add me to the list," Rick said. "I'd hoped for an intriguing lecture when classes resume this fall."

"Oh you of little faith." Zaki shook his head. He pulled a knife from his pocket and snapped open the blade.

The room fell silent.

CHAPTER
TWENTY-SIX

Zaki stepped to the center of the room where the sun beamed through the skylight. Miniature dust particles waltzed across the shaft of light, each vying for stardom before drifting off into oblivion. He clasped his hands together and cleared his throat for attention.

"Act three coming up, my friends." He pushed aside the leather sofa and motioned for them to step aside as he grabbed the corner of the Persian rug and pulled it back. With the point of the knife he gingerly poked at the grouting between the ceramic tiles. "You made me anxious with your foot tapping, Mr. Metz."

"Sorry."

"It is okay, now." The knife sunk silently into what looked like grout but obviously wasn't. "Like you say in America, my friends, bingo!"

He pulled away the fake grout and removed the tiles, revealing a trapdoor. "There were three crosses that crucifixion day, my friends. I find one, but I think I may need three, so I make sure I have three. One stolen from my shop yesterday, you saw second taken away moments ago; both fake. You are about to see third, not fake, but authentic cross upon which Christ our Lord died."

CHAPTER
TWENTY-SEVEN

They entered from the parking lot onto the second floor of the Alexander Silberman Building. The life sciences' building was situated near the center of the Edmond J. Safra Campus of The Hebrew University of Jerusalem. They found the receptionist for The Center for Genomic Technologies.

"Doctors Ahmed and Carter to see Professor Kohen, please."

"Yes, Doctor Ahmed. He is expecting you."

A door opened and a smiling, gray-haired man appeared.

"Zaki, my friend." They greeted with a kiss on each cheek. "You are Doctor Carter? Albert Kohen." He gave Gary a cordial handshake.

"Yes, thank you for allowing us the use of the lab, Doctor Kohen."

"My pleasure to help out my old friend, Zaki. This way, gentlemen." He motioned toward a door and together they walked to the lab.

"I will leave you to your task. If you have need of anything, please do not hesitate to ask. I will be in my study." With a slight bow, Doctor Kohen exited the room and closed the door behind him.

Gary stood in the middle of the room and turned slowly to survey the lab. It was similar to what he was accustomed to at the American university. He made a lap around the room and finally positioned himself at a long table lined with a half dozen computers, monitors and microscopes. He donned rubber gloves and retrieved five manila envelopes from his Coach briefcase. From each of these he removed a four-inch by two-inch box and arranged them in a meaningful order. From each box he withdrew a small Ziploc baggie and set each in front of the appropriate box. He retrieved a container of sterilized tweezers and removed a small sliver of wood from one of the plastic bags and laid it gingerly on a Petri dish. He repeated this process, each time with fresh tweezers and a fresh dish, until all the contents of the plastic bags were placed in individual dishes. He then sprayed each from a container labeled *Fluorescent*.

Zaki watched in silence.

"Can you turn off the overhead lights, please?"

"No problem." Zaki hastened to the far wall and switched off the lights.

One by one, Gary slid the Petri dishes under an ultraviolet light. "Take a look."

Zaki stared at the dishes under the ultraviolet light. The small slivers in three of the dishes radiated in the dark. "What does it mean?"

"The three you see glowing have traces of blood. Real, genuine, human blood."

Gary set aside the two Petri dishes that didn't glow under the ultraviolet light. He placed each of the three remaining contents into individual small glass containers filled with a clear solution; these he labeled.

The day before, at Zaki's house in Tiberias, Gary had turned the kitchen table into a lab. He had carefully tapped into the cross and removed samples from underneath the hardened sap. Surprisingly, after almost twenty centuries, the wooden cross had remained preserved. Perhaps its owner hid it for a while, and the sudden plunder of the city by the Romans could have left it unidentified and thus insignificant, eventually forgotten by the ensuing absence of people in the area. Finally an earthquake sealed it into oblivion. After Gary had retrieved samples for testing, Zaki had rewrapped the cross—which was in three pieces: the crossbeam, the upright beam and the titulus—in Cellophane and placed it back in the space beneath the floor of his house. Once Gary saw the cross and gently touched its rustic surface, he didn't want to leave it in Tiberias, but it seemed safer in its hiding place in Tiberias than anywhere else, at least for the time being. He worked long into the evening, and they arrived late in Jerusalem.

Even though tired, Gary felt invigorated in the modern lab graciously furnished by the university. He continuously talked to Zaki as he worked. "It's the blood of a male. I've isolated that by the chromosomes—it's a Y chromosome. The next phase of the experiment is to isolate DNA. The solution I'm using is a fancy detergent that will wash away the red blood cells—which do not carry DNA—leaving only white blood cells which contain the DNA."

Gary placed the small glass vials of solution containing the blood samples inside a centrifuge machine, closed the lid and pressed the switch. The machine whined almost instantly.

"The machine spins at about thirteen hundred rpm's. In a couple minutes this action will explode the white blood cells causing them to release the DNA."

Gary barely finished his explanation before the machine stopped, and he removed the containers. Zaki paced as Gary moved to another table and hunkered over the vials and instruments. He explained each course of action as he used a pipette to collect less than a drop of the solution, which he placed in thimble-sized containers. He positioned these small containers inside another machine, which cooled and heated the solutions in a three-phase cycle.

"The university uses a system manufactured by Applied Biosystems. Their thermal cycler will separate the double helix. The two single strands will join into a longer single strand. During a process called PCR—which stands for polymerase chain reaction—we'll increase the amount of chemicals. This will amplify the DNA exponentially until we have a long continuous strand of DNA to analyze. I'll race the processed DNA down a narrow tube which reads it and feeds the information into a computer."

Gary created a mold from the liquid, which he placed inside an ultraviolet light transilluminator and closed the hood to shield from external light sources. With a digitized camera, he snapped hundreds of pictures of the specimens under the powerful lens of the high-tech camera, which fed its readings into a computer. He observed, documented and waited patiently while the instruments worked.

He rubbed the back of his neck, massaging his cramping muscles.

Zaki sat beside him. "Tired, my friend?"

"Tired but energized. Now we must simply wait for the analysis."

"How long?"

"Not long."

A series of lines appeared on the monitor. Zaki jumped to his feet.

"Now we're getting somewhere." Gary smiled. "The mystery of two millenniums isn't far away."

A printer clicked on. As images of endless rows of coded messages spewed from the printer Gary offered no explanations and Zaki asked no questions.

"Yes...yes...we're getting somewhere." Gary studied the printouts. He wiped the glistening drops of perspiration from his brow and upper-lip as he studied each page and compared each with the others.

"My next step involves comparing the DNA we've collected from the cross with the international databank of DNA profiles. We do this in order to get matches." Gary paused from his work and tilted his chair backwards, eyes closed.

"Can I get you something to eat?" Zaki asked.

"I'm fine. How did Jesus say it? 'I have meat to eat you know not of.'"

"I understand, my friend. It is how I feel when I sense I am close to finding some artifact of significance."

The daunting task required patience; Gary was blessed in that area. He studied the data, comparing. At eight o'clock in the evening, he pushed his chair away from the table, swiveled the chair around a couple times, thrust his fists into the air and screamed, "Yes! Yes! Yes!"

"Yes?" Zaki asked.

Gary pointed his finger at Zaki. "You, my friend, are going to be famous!"

Tears streamed down Zaki's cheeks. "Say it to me, Gary. Tell me it is His blood. Tell me you have seen the actual blood that washed away our sins."

"As John the Baptist proclaimed, 'Behold the lamb of God who takes away the sins of the world,' Zaki Ahmed, let me proclaim behold the blood of Christ that washes white like snow." Gary leaped to his feet and embraced Zaki, who sobbed uncontrollably.

A dozen voices screamed inside Gary's head. They celebrated with grandiose proclamations, highfiving each other over the greatest archaeological discovery since King Tut, and perhaps the greatest discovery ever. He envisioned a book that would outdistance Indiana native Lew Wallace's *Ben Hur*. He imagined an action-packed movie dwarfing Indiana Jones' *Lost Ark* and *Holy Grail*, but his would be filmed from legitimacy instead of legend. The search for the actual cross of Christ had produced more than drama. It was reality, and he was in the forefront of it all.

"I will tell you now," Zaki said.

"Tell me what?"

"The meaning to *Ani veAtah Neshane et HaOlam.*"

"Yes, I want to know. I had forgotten the words."

"You and I will change the world."

CHAPTER
TWENTY-EIGHT

"*What will you do with it if you really find the cross of Christ?*"
Celeste had asked the question, but it seemed irrelevant at the time. Her question now echoed in his memory, prodding his conscience. He avoided the question and returned to celebration.

Doctor Kohen opened the door and walked slowly toward them.

"What have you found, my friends?"

"It is wonderful news. Doctor Carter will explain to you."

Gary was convinced his research was accurate, but he knew others would be skeptical. Now came the tough part: presenting your results in a convincing manner. "You're familiar with the prophet's writings, 'Unto us a child is born—'"

"'A son is given...the government shall be upon His shoulders....' Yes, I am quite familiar with Isaiah's writings."

"Do you agree the prophet was speaking of the Messiah, a God visitation in some human form?"

"A theophany?"

"More. Much more. I'm speaking of the baby in a manger story, God in human form...the Incarnation."

"Being of Jewish faith, I do not believe the man *Yeshua*, Jesus as you call him, was *Mashiach*. We still look for the Anointed One. He will come someday, just as the prophet said."

"Putting our religious differences aside for a moment, let me ask a scientific question. If the prophet Isaiah envisioned God would become incarnate, and God did come to dwell with us as a man, what would the blood of the incarnate God look like when compared to humans?"

"Doctor Carter, you have asked a philosophical question and therefore I will give you a philosophical answer. When the God of Torah created Adam, He made Adam in His own image. God said 'It is good.' Why? Because Adam was flawless, that is why. So, if God should become incarnate in man, He would be patterned after the original Adam, not Adam the transgressor."

Doctor Kohen's quick response surprised Gary. He answered as if the question had already been posed to him in the classroom and he'd already considered his answer.

"You propose the incarnate God would be without human flaws," Gary asked.

"Yes."

"Then take a look for yourself, and see the perfection of God." Gary pointed toward the monitor. "I present to you the first and only flawless DNA strand I've ever seen. It's either Adam's blood before the fall, or else, it's the blood of God incarnate."

"Surely it is only speculation, Doctor Carter. Philosophical speculation." He studied the information on the screen.

"During my graduate work it began as a hypothesis that the DNA of the Jewish Messiah would be the most perfect known DNA strand. I believe my theory is now scientifically based. I've run the test with the most modern techniques known to man. See for yourself, or better still, redo the tests and make your own discovery."

"It cannot be the blood of Adam, for that is an impossibility. And where and how could you find the blood of God? What did you say to Him? 'Here, God, hold out your hand. I need to prick your finger.'"

Doctor Kohen studied Gary's work. He mumbled in a language Gary assumed to be Hebrew, as he deliberately surveyed the computer printouts, page after page. Zaki stood in silence, his hands clasped as if in a prayerful position.

Gary offered no further argument as Doctor Kohen studied the images on the printouts. The room grew quiet. *Will Doctor Kohen be honest or will tradition win out?*

Doctor Kohen stood, shuffled the papers neatly together and gently placed them on the counter.

"Well, Doctor Kohen, what do you think?" Gary asked.

"Where did you get this DNA pattern?"

"From a carbon-14 dated, first century, blood-stained, wooden cross."

"This cannot be." Doctor Kohen again turned his attention to the images on the monitors. As he studied the results, he spoke slowly and calculatingly. "If someone has somehow manipulated these images, they are bordering on blasphemy. I would not walk in their shoes. On the other hand, if what I am seeing is true, perhaps my people did crucify *Mashiach*. If this image is the actual blood of *Yeshua*, then Mary, His mother, was one of my ancestors."

Doctor Kohen took off his lab coat, tossed it on a chair and started toward the door.

"You can turn out the lights, gentlemen. I'm going home to read again the prophecy of Isaiah. I must have missed something from his ancient writings. And I must retrace the lineage of Mary. *Shalom.*"

"What do you mean?" Zaki asked.

"Doctor Carter will explain it to you."

CHAPTER TWENTY-NINE

Gary touched the brass mezuzah with his fingertips. *Hear, O Israel: The LORD our God is one LORD: And thou shalt love the LORD thy God with all thine heart, and with all thy soul, and with all thy might.* That Scripture was the common strand among the Jewish people during the Diaspora, riveting them together throughout dispersions totaling hundreds of years. *How incredible that the rabbi's family returned from Diaspora after nineteen hundred years, still inspired by Torah.*

He pressed the doorbell and the door opened almost immediately. Rabbi Arav's huge frame filled the doorway, his arms outstretched in a gesture of welcome. He stepped toward Gary and embraced him like a father his repentant prodigal.

"Welcome to my home. I am glad you have come. But your friends, where are they?"

"They felt like an imposition, Rabbi. Plus, they wanted to do some souvenir shopping."

"Ah, but they are always welcome, too. But I understand gifts from the Holy Land are special. Come in and let me introduce you to my family, and then we will enjoy the Shabbat meal together."

"Thank you, Rabbi Arav. I'm very pleased to be here."

"Please, my friend, call me Joseph."

"You must call me Gary."

Gary stepped inside the dimly lit home. Numerous candles flickered from settings around the living room, casting shadows on the walls. A lovely, petite woman laid aside a book and stood from the chaise lounge where she'd been reading. Two young lads sat across the room playing chess. They, too, stood, and snapped to attention.

"Now, Gary, meet my family. First, my wife Rachael."

"Pleased to meet you, Mrs. Arav. Thank you for allowing me to visit."

"You are most welcome, Doctor Carter. Please call me Rachael." She extended her hand in friendship. Gary, unaccustomed to Jewish protocol, hesitated, then took her hand and gently held it for a second.

"I hope you, as they say in America, have brought your appetite with you."

"Yes, I'm quite hungry."

Gary suspected Rachael to be much younger than Joseph. Her jet-black hair reminded him of the hair tone of Native Americans. In his profession, these were details he observed. She was small in stature standing beside Joseph. Still, her voice carried a resonance of personal strength and her appearance radiated strong character and genuine charm. Gary immediately felt at ease in her presence.

"These are our sons, Yakov and Efraim," Rachael said.

"Pleased to meet you. Which is which?" Gary asked.

"I am Yakov." The taller lad stepped forward and extended his hand to Gary.

"You must be a teenager, Yakov."

"Twelve, sir."

"Let me guess, about the eighth grade."

Yakov hesitated at the question. "I am not sure, sir."

"In America he would be in prep school. My sons have made me very proud, in a humble way, of course. They have both excelled in their studies."

"You must be Efraim."

"Yes, sir."

"I'm not going to guess your age nor grade." Gary smiled as he shook Efraim's extended hand.

"Nine years old, sir."

"Efraim is also advanced in his subjects." Joseph placed a hand gently on Efraim's shoulder. "The Shabbat dinner is waiting. Efraim, show our guest where he can wash his hands."

Gary returned and Rachael directed him to the chair at the opposite end of the table from where Joseph sat. Two Shabbat candles adorned the center of the table. The table setting of china and crystal reflected the candlelight onto their faces. *Kristallnacht.* Gary studied Jewish history at the university. Jews could never forget the debauchery of Nazi Germany and the night referred to in history as *Kristallnacht*, when violent gangs broke out the windows of Jewish merchants. *How can humans be so cruel to another just because they interpret Scripture differently? It is more than that. It is because they don't practice the Scripture they defend—love your enemy.*

"You understand the Shabbat meal is prepared before the Sabbath begins," Rachael said. "Cholent…you call it beef stew…is not my best recipe, but it passes the rules against working on the Sabbath, for rewarming the meal is not considered working."

"I'm not totally familiar with the details of the Sabbath, but I like beef stew." Gary chuckled and was pleased they reflected his humor.

"I am glad." Rachael draped a white scarf over her head and lit the candles. "*Barukh atah Adonai eloheinu melekh ha-olam, asher kidshanu b'mitzvotav, v'tzivanu lehadlik ner shel Shabbat.*" She blew out the match and sat down.

A covered dish sat before Joseph. He stood and uncovered the dish, which revealed two loaves of braided bread sprinkled with sesame seeds.

"The bread is called *challah*. It represents the manna that fell from heaven during our fathers' wilderness wandering." Joseph lifted the bread over his head and prayed. "Blessed are You, Lord, our God, King of the Universe, who brings forth bread from the earth. Thank you for our guest from America. Bless his stay in Israel with peace and joy. Amen."

He sat down, broke and sliced the bread and passed the pieces around the table.

"Perhaps you wonder why we still observe *Shabbat*, being Christian. It is not to deny our Christian faith, nor even to affirm ourselves as being Jewish. It is to appreciate God's Word. In observing Shabbat, we recognize the Old Covenant was, as the Christian writer of Hebrews noted, 'a shadow of good things to come, and not the very image of the things.' We look now in retrospect at the Old Covenant and can observe Shabbat with keen understanding and sincere appreciation. Yakov, would you mind telling Doctor Carter what the two candles represent?"

"Not at all, Father. The two candles represent two commandments regarding the Sabbath. One is zachor: to remember. The other is shamor: to observe. We are to remember our Lord gives us six days to earn our bread, and we are to dedicate the seventh to Him. Not only the seventh day, we are to live each day in fellowship with him. As the Prophet *Yeshayahu*—"

"That is the Jewish pronunciation for Isaiah," Joseph explained.

"The prophet of the Old Covenant expressed that the New Covenant would usher in a continual fellowship with the Lord, or continual Sabbath: 'This is the rest wherewith ye may cause the weary to rest; and this is the refreshing...'" Yakov seemed pleased with his explanation.

"And the second candle?" Gary asked.

"Oh, yes, sorry. The second candle reminds us we are to observe the commandments of the Scripture and obey the Lord our God."

"Thank you, Yakov, for sharing that with me. It's so true. In the States many Christians spend the Lord's Day, Sunday of course for us, scurrying about trying to squeeze out of the day all we can, with a couple hours set aside for the Lord. And there are too many 'Sunday only' Christians, giving little time or thought to Christ the other six days."

Rachael ladled the stew first onto Gary's plate, then Joseph's. Efraim held his spoon in one hand and a knife in the other.

"Hungry?" she asked.

"Very. I thought the rabbi was long-winded today. Did you not?"

"It is not for us to judge the time it takes someone to deliver his heart." Rachael spoke firmly but in a loving manner.

Gary smiled at Joseph.

"He does not speak of me. I am not the synagogue rabbi. But true, the rabbi was a bit long-winded."

"What is a Jewish service like?"

"The services at the synagogue are similar to those in our Christian service: prayer, hymns and a sermon. We even have baptisms, though it is a ritual cleansing that must be observed again and again, unlike the Christian baptism that represents Christ dying for our sins 'once and for all.' Tomorrow we will attend our Christian service, but sad to say, we are not free to share our faith openly and remain in favor with the Jewish community. This is a heavy burden we bear. We long for God to give us a door of opportunity to share our Christian faith with our people."

They talked on through the meal. Rachael insisted Gary have seconds. Yakov and Efraim smiled with delight when he graciously refused and their mother pushed the bowl of remaining stew toward them. Joseph pushed his chair back from the table.

Gary glanced at the clock on the mantle. *Have I overstayed my welcome? Is it impolite to eat and run? How do you exit a Shabbat meal?*

Joseph raised his face upward and recited the *birkat ha-mazon*—grace.

CHAPTER
THIRTY

"I should go. Thank you for a lovely evening. How do you say it: *Shabbat Shalom veShavua tov?*"

"Yes, and a peaceful *Shabbat* and a good week to you. The hour is still early. We must talk. After all, what more can we Jews do on the Sabbath?" Joseph laughed.

Yakov and Efraim resumed their game of chess, Rachael returned to her reading and Joseph and Gary retreated to the back veranda where they sipped strong tea and nibbled on dates.

"You seem quite happy," Joseph said.

"I am."

"Things go well for you in Jerusalem, yes?"

"Yes, very well. I know you think Zaki…Doctor Ahmed…is a bit eccentric, but he has made an incredible discovery."

"Zaki Ahmed drinks sanguine juice for breakfast."

Gary smiled.

"I should not have said that about Zaki. He is my friend, my Christian brother, but he has substituted the loss of his family with grandiosity. He told you what happened to his family?"

"Yes."

"It is very sad, but you must not become caught up in—"

"He has found the cross of Christ."

Joseph did not respond. Gary had seen the look before when he suggested his dissertation to his professor: *The Preservation of the Kohanim Bloodline Throughout the Jewish Diaspora and the Presumed Uniqueness of Christ's DNA.* The professor scoffed at the idea, but Gary insisted it was worthy of academic consideration, especially the research of the Kohanim bloodline. He theorized that God's DNA in Christ would override human imperfection. He surmised the DNA derived from Mary would have been a replica of known Jewish ancestry, but free of flaws, for God's DNA would have dominated over the mutated and recessive genes of Mary. The two genomes within each cell of Christ's body would have a perfect set of instructions, similar to mankind's known DNA, but unparalleled in perfection by any particular family lineage. For his thesis he'd build the double helix of Christ, creating a perfect strand from God's DNA. From cataloged DNA samples of Jewish descendants, he'd establish the possibility of Mary's DNA, and he'd unite the two and chart the complete road map of Christ's DNA. He'd replicate the DNA of the only perfect human being since Adam and Eve enjoyed the paradise of Eden.

"It is only an archaeologist's fantasy."

"I believe it's Christ's cross."

"Why would you believe such?"

"A number of reasons."

"Such as?"

"The titulus is still with the cross and the wording is just as the Scripture records. 'Jesus of Nazareth, King of the Jews.' In three languages: Hebrew, Greek and Latin. The print was faded but still legible, written in black letters upon the wooden plaque and coated with white gypsum."

"Easy to forge."

"It could be a forgery. That's my job—to separate romanticism from reality."

"You mean fake from genuine."

"The carbon-14 test is accurate."

"There were many crosses from the Roman era."

"The cross has a date carved into the wood, along with a message, written in the Aramaic language, that described the sympathies of the possessor of the cross."

"What date."

"Three thousand seven hundred eighty-nine."

"Using the Jewish calendar?"

"Right, which puts the date written on the cross at about the time of Christ's death, compared to our Gregorian calendar. Whether the cross is fake or not, it passes the date test for the time of Christ's crucifixion."

"Where did Zaki find the cross?"

"Bethsaida."

"Bethsaida? Why would he believe a cross found in Bethsaida was the cross used to crucify Christ in Jerusalem?"

"Because the big fisherman lived there. Are you familiar with the dig at Bethsaida?"

"I am. Bethsaida, along with Chorazin and Capernaum, belong to what is called the Evangelical Triangle. Most of Jesus' ministry took place within this twelve-mile triangle. Jesus judged these cities for their lack of positive response to his miracles. They were rather hard-hearted, and all three cities ended in ruin. First, the Romans quelled a rebellion in sixty-seven CE, literally destroying Bethsaida. An earthquake affected the ruins in three hundred sixty-three CE. Christian pilgrims searched in vain for this important New Testament city. An American archaeologist, Edward Robinson, discovered the supposed ruins in nineteen hundred thirty-eight. This area is the Golan and wasn't really accessible to modern archaeologists until after the Six Day War of sixty-seven. More recently, a Consortium of the Bethsaida Excavations Project has been formed."

"Yes. I am somewhat familiar with that. The University of Nebraska at Omaha is involved in the project. That location is actually where Doctor Ahmed found the cross."

"I still am not convinced."

"There is a statement carved on the crossbeam in Aramaic: 'On this tree he bore our sins in his own body.' That's very similar to a verse of Scripture from the New Testament: 'Who his own self bore our sins in his own body on the tree...'"

"From the writings of the Apostle Peter."

"Yes."

"A statement similar to Scripture engraved on the wood could also prove the particular cross was used after the writing of the New

Testament, by a minimum of thirty years and a maximum of…almost two thousand. The evidence could disprove its authenticity."

"I did a DNA test."

"How could that support evidence it was the cross of Christ? Would you not have to compare it with some know object of Christ?"

"Yes."

"What?"

There was blood encased on the cross. It's inconceivable what I found when I tested the blood, for it was unlike anything I've ever seen. The DNA was perfect, absolutely flawless. You're familiar with DNA?"

"I read about it. It is difficult to understand. In Torah as I search for God, I know what I search for, but I would not know what to look for under the microscope if I searched for evidence of God."

"Would you be offended if I simplify it for you?"

"Of course not. I would be grateful."

"The language of DNA is passed on from parents to children since Adam. So, in many ways we are all similar. Like the fingerprint, the DNA shows patterns unique to individuals, even to entire families. Only identical twins, or clones, are identical. The DNA shows differences, and it also shows similarities, so much so that an unidentified child can be traced to its biological parents. Also, it can show abnormalities and potential health risks, which is why some are morally opposed to genetic fingerprinting. In a stretch of the imagination, genetic testing could be used to deny health insurance, identify high-risk clients, or worse, abort a life in the womb. Are you with me so far?"

"I am in the same room, but you talk like a science fiction writer." Joseph laughed his hearty laugh.

"The genetic fingerprint is a simple, linear, written language that identifies the individual. It determines what that person is and from where that person comes. The physical events of the body for a lifetime are coded into the single cell at conception. Only by genetic alteration—an accidentally mutated gene or purposefully altered gene—can that person be anything else. The same is true for the defects—the potential for disease lying within the sequence of the code can be disastrous. There is already coded into a person's body the diseases that will eventually cause the person harm, or even death. Perhaps one day the field of genetics will be the answer to prevent much suffering by combating the disease, such as cancer, before it gets a grip in a person's body. I have said all this to point out something very special about the blood of Christ. My assumption about the DNA of Christ is His paternal strand of DNA—paternal being from God, not Joseph—would have been absolutely perfect. No DNA I have ever seen has been flawless—until today. There is always an average amount of expected flaws in any DNA sample. There was an unusually small amount of imperfections in the blood from the cross. I consider it perfect, just like I anticipated Christ's DNA to be."

"Can such be true?"

"Would it be otherwise?"

"No, I don't doubt God's perfection. I believe that with all my heart. I ask, can it be true you have actually seen the very blood Christ spilled to cover our sins?"

"Yes! And not only cover our sins, but able to heal all our diseases. By His stripes we are healed."

"How, from a scientific perspective instead of a theological one, do you suppose the blood of Christ heals our bodies? Is there any scientific explanation to that?"

"I believe so, though I don't believe it generally happens apart from faith. In each set of chromosomes, one from the father and one from the mother, if a mutation is present, or for some reason occurs in one of the genes, the good gene will compensate. If both are bad, then the unfortunate person will be affected accordingly with disease or abnormality. In a spiritual sense, through faith, when the perfect blood of Christ comes alongside the afflicted individual, the mutated genes are compensated for and the person is healed.

"The idea sheds light on much of Scripture. In the Old Covenant, it was a perfect sacrificial lamb, one without blemishes, brought to the altar. From a Christian perspective, I believe the Jewish sacrificial system was a type of Christ who was to come. I can therefore believe Christ's blood was perfect, untainted by the worldly strain of sin. That blood can, and has, washed away all our iniquities. And I now better understand how it can heal our diseases.

"I am puzzled by something I discovered that I thought you could help me understand." Gary paused in contemplation.

135

"What is that, my friend?"

"Since Christ's mother was of the tribe of Judah I expected the DNA she passed along to Christ to be of pure Davidic origin, with identifiable strains matching the known DNA pattern of the descendants of Judah. What I found surprised me."

"Oh, what was that?"

"Christ's blood possessed the Davidic pattern, but I also found strong matches of another known origin, which confused me."

"Not Jewish?" Joseph seemed ready to challenge the entire project.

"It was Jewish alright, a well-known Jewish origin."

"Whose?"

"*Kohanim.*"

"As in *Aharon HaKohen*? The descendants of Aaron the Jewish priest?"

"Yes. I was already aware the descendants of the Jewish priesthood are one of the purest preserved lineages, passed from father to son for over three thousand years, without interruption for more than a hundred generations. With such a direct lineage back to Aaron, it's easy to trace, but I wasn't expecting it to turn up in the DNA of Christ."

"You expected the DNA of Judah only, no?"

"Absolutely. So why did I find strong matches of the *Kohanim* family? Doctor Kohen at the university was certainly surprised."

"Rightly so. The Kohen name is a direct descendant of Aaron." Joseph closed his eyes as if in meditation. For a long while, he didn't speak, then he suddenly clapped his hands together loudly. "She was Elizabeth's cousin."

"What does that mean?" Gary was startled by Joseph's sudden outburst, and still puzzled.

"Elizabeth, mother of John the Baptist, and Mary, Christ's mother, were cousins. That made Jesus and John cousins. Right?"

"Yes." Gary was still confused.

"Elizabeth's husband, Zacharias, was in the temple doing his duties as a priest when the angel appeared unto him and told him to name his son John, or as we Jews would say, *Yochanan*, favored by *Yahweh*. John the baptizer was also a priest, just like his father, though he never assumed his place in the temple. The remnant of the

Kohanim still know their assigned week to serve in the temple, even though the temple was destroyed almost two millenniums ago. Elizabeth, the wife of Zacharias, was of the lineage of the priesthood. This is recorded in the gospel. Elizabeth was also Mary's relative, making her a relative of Christ, and thus some offspring of the tribe of Judah. Could not Mary as easily have had *Kohen* blood—intermarriage between the Davidic lineage and *Kohanim* lineage?"

"The Bible refers to Christ as a priest, so that could be the explanation." Gary felt somewhat relieved by the explanation.

"But the Book of Hebrews describes Christ's priesthood as being after that of Melchizedek, not after the biological lineage of the Aaronic priesthood."

"That shoots holes in the concept." Gary's bewilderment returned.

"Not necessarily. Christ's position as high priest was indeed after Melchizedek's order, a direct anointing from God, not man. His position as king came directly from the Davidic lineage, also a direct anointing from God after God rejected Saul and his heirs as kings."

"As for the *Kohanim* order, perhaps it was just a coincidence that Mary carried the gene," Gary said.

"Coincidence? Not with God. King, after the lineage of David; priest, after the order of Melchizedek; and now servant after the order of *Kohanin*. The Scripture also says, 'Christ made himself of no reputation and took upon Him the form of a servant?' *Yeshayahu* prophesied, 'Behold my servant, whom I uphold; mine elect, in whom my soul delighteth; I have put my spirit upon Him: He shall bring forth judgment to the Gentiles.' No, it is not coincidence. It is the wisdom of God. Christ fulfilled three roles—king, priest and servant. How incredible!"

A siren wailed in the distance.

"Hakol beseder b'Eli haseder."

"How does that translate?" Gary asked.

"Everything is in order within the chaos. God is still in control."

The conversation silenced. They gazed into the starlit sky, with patterns unchanged since creation. Gary reflected upon that wintry night of a distant past, in a small town but a few miles to the east. He envisioned the single star that stood sentry over the stable where a young child lay, and a virgin mother pondered the miraculous and peered into the misty eyes of the keeper of the universe.

A shooting star streaked across the horizon, and for a brief moment, the scene reflected the peace Jerusalem longed for——and Messiah had come to give. Peace eluded Gary. Celeste's question echoed again in his mind: *What will you do with it if you really find the cross of Christ?* He was sure he'd found it. He wasn't sure what he'd do with it.

CHAPTER
THIRTY-ONE

Celeste stepped from the door of the plane, carry-on in tow, and trailed the crowd up the sky ramp toward the terminal. She followed the arrows that marked the way to a clamoring throng waiting to enter Israel. With passport and entry papers in hand, she chose what she hoped to be the shortest line and anxiously waited her turn.

She cleared customs and apprehensively stepped inside the main terminal of Ben Gurion International. Strangers in unfamiliar garbs stared at her as she walked slowly past the crowd of families, friends and business associates waiting to greet the arriving passengers. Some held signs for identification. She scanned the audience as if by some fortunate coincidence she'd recognize a name.

"Mrs. Carter?" The voice from the crowd surprised her.

She looked in the direction of the voice and observed a young man holding a sign showing her name. He looked to be in his late twenties, with dark wavy hair and a smile that dispelled her anxiety. She smiled and he immediately stepped toward.

"Mrs. Carter?"

"Yes."

He instantly relieved her of the carry-on. "I will carry this for you?"

"Thank you."

"Your husband sent me."

She was grateful for the kindness and for a friendly face among strangers. He led her through the maze of roped paths and people lining the hallway.

"How did Gary know I was coming?"

"Your friend from America called Doctor Carter—"

"Officer Davis?"

"Yes, he called Doctor Carter and Doctor Carter sent me to pick you up and take you to the hotel."

"So Gary knows I'm here? I'm surprised he didn't—"

"He sends his kindest apologies, but his work is too demanding for him to come and get you. Welcome to Israel, Mrs. Carter."

"Thank you."

"Any more luggage?"

"No. I left in a hurry. I really hadn't planned to come."

"You miss your husband, I am sure?"

"Very much so. I'm sorry, I didn't ask your name."

"No, my apologies for not introducing myself. I am Asaph."

"I'm pleased to meet you Asaph. Thank you for picking me up."

"No problem. I have a vehicle waiting outside for us."

She felt some trepidation but walked alongside Asaph who gently guided her through the crowds of people and toward ground transportation. *Gary must really be into his work to send a stranger to pick me up instead of coming. He's generally more sensitive of my female apprehensions. Oh, well, I'll have to wait and hear from him his reasoning, which I'm sure will make sense. What would I have done if he hadn't sent someone. I never even considered that when I made my spur-of-the-moment decision to come to Israel. Whatever possessed me?*

"This way, Mrs. Carter." Asaph led her through double doors into the bright Israeli sunlight. A wave of heat accosted her nostrils and penetrated her lungs. She held her hand over her nose and breathed shallow gasps of oxygen trying to adjust to the pungent heat. She blinked against the bright sunlight and fumbled in her purse for sunglasses.

"Just ahead." Asaph continued to direct her.

A chauffeur sprang from the driver's seat of a black limo with tinted windows, parked alongside the curb. He hastened to open the passenger door. Celeste paused and looked at Asaph.

"Our transportation?" *And I doubted Gary's concern for me.*

"Your husband must love you much, Mrs. Carter. He spared no expense to rescue you from tiring Israeli traffic."

"Rescue me?" Celeste frowned.

"Perhaps that is the wrong word. Escort is maybe a better word. He is much excited about seeing you."

"I wanted to surprise him."

"You have. He was very surprised to hear you came. But pleased."

"I hope so."

Asaph sat opposite Celeste in the back of the limo and occasionally tossed her a reassuring smile. She took a Kleenex from her purse and gently dabbed perspiration from her face.

"You will get accustomed to the heat."

"I hope so. I didn't imagine how hot it would be. How far is it to Jerusalem?"

"About sixty kilometers, or about forty miles."

"Is Gary at the hotel?"

"No. He is working on his project. We will let him know you have arrived."

"Thank you. You've been so kind." She reciprocated his smile. "I can't believe I've come to Israel on such an impulse, with no planning whatsoever. I feel somewhat foolish—"

"Bakah Hotel, sir?" The chauffeur called to Asaph through a small open window in the wall that separated them.

"Yes, David."

"Bakaah?"

"You were expecting King David. They've moved from King David. I should have told you that before. I hope you are not distressed by my oversight."

"Just surprised."

"Have you not spoken to Doctor Carter since he arrived in Israel?"

"No."

"Then you had no way of knowing they changed hotels."

"Correct."

"I am sure he would have called to share his change of hotels, but once he knew you were coming he did not bother to call since he planned to have someone pick you up at the airport."

"How did you recognize me at the airport?"

Asaph did not immediately respond to her question. She sensed for a split second he averted eye contact as he peered out the window of the limo, which glided past a caravan of coaches loaded with tourists. A dozen cameras pressed against the tinted windows of the buses as excited tourists snapped pictures.

Asaph's warm smile returned. "I recognized you from a picture your husband gave me to identify you."

"What picture is that?"

Asaph took a small photograph from his shirt pocket and handed it to Celeste. She recognized the photograph immediately and tried to suppress her astonishment. The photo was a picture of her taken at the table in the restaurant at the Lazarus Mall in Columbus—only yesterday.

Asaph's facial expression immediately revealed he recognized his mistake.

CHAPTER
THIRTY-TWO

Asaph escorted Celeste across the small hotel lobby. *Something is terribly wrong.* Her mind raced, calculating options. *How can I get to Gary? My cell phone.* Her elation was short lived. *I hope the battery is okay. I must conserve power for the right time.* She glanced around the hotel for a policeman, anyone she could confide in. She wanted to scream out for help, but Asaph had intuitively guessed her musings.

"You may endanger your husband's life if you do not work in harmony with our plan."

Asaph firmly took her arm and nodded toward the stairway. Once on the second floor, he guided her to the end of the hallway where he knocked on the high arched, oak door. A slim, dark-eyed man, maybe twenty years old, with wiry brown hair, opened the door. He spoke to Asaph but avoided eye contact with Celeste. The man stepped aside for her to enter. She hesitated, so Asaph squeezed her arm firmly at the elbow and nudged her inside. She scanned the dimly lit room. Another young man, with a red and white checkered turban, sat in an overstuffed leather chair near the far wall. The chauffeur caught up with them.

"That room is yours." Asaph motioned to a room off the main area. He walked her to the room and quickly closed the door behind her. She surveyed the room, which seemed about eight feet wide, hardly larger than her walk-in closet at home. She placed her carry-on and purse onto the bed. She turned and was stunned Asaph stood inside the room, leaning against the door, staring intently at her. She recoiled in fear and fell awkwardly backward onto the bed. He held up an assuring hand, but offered no assistance.

"My apologies for startling you, but we must talk. Do you mind?"

She stood to face him. "Talk about what?" She flushed in anger and fear.

Asaph gestured for trust. He held up his hands submissively. His dark complexion contrasted with his white cotton shirt. His calm mannerisms and her ambiguous emotions weakened her resolve.

"It is okay that you are concerned. We are on your side. I am a Mossad agent. So are the others—Israeli secret police. They are young but well trained."

"I'm familiar with Mossad, but what's this all about? I have not asked for your help. Why am I being held against my will?" Anger returned, along with increased determination.

"Please, Mrs. Carter. Your husband is in much danger. We have been assigned to protect him and that assignment spills over into protecting you."

"From whom? From what? Where is Gary? Why is he in danger?" Celeste's anger quickly relinquished to concern.

"He has found an item of much controversy in the non-Christian community. We are trying to be diplomatic about this matter, but he refuses to reveal the whereabouts of the item, or to relinquish the item to proper authorities."

"You're talking about a cross?"

"Yes. Your husband is not aware of the dangerous situation he has gotten himself into. When we discovered you were coming, we realized the additional danger your presence in Israel posed, primarily the possibility of terrorists' activities, perhaps kidnapping for ransom..."

"This isn't a kidnapping?"

"You must be understanding, Mrs. Carter. We had to protect you from the powers that are warring against your husband. We also felt while we are protecting you from the enemy, you could be of assistance to us in convincing Doctor Carter to cooperate with the proper authorities. We need your help. Your husband needs your help."

"Can I go to him?"

"That would not be prudent right now."

"Why?"

"Let's just say the timing is not so."

"Am I a prisoner here?"

"Of course not, Mrs. Carter."

"How did you get the picture of me?"

"We have ways."

"Is Officer Scott working for you?"

"Scott? No, but we realized his association to you."

Celeste decided not to answer.

"Let us help you, and in helping you we will do our job."

"I'm hungry. Can I get something to eat?"

"We will have something sent up. What would you like?"

"I'd like to leave!"

"That is not possible right now."

"When?"

"Soon."

"Can I call Gary?"

"Later. The timing is delicate. The enemy monitors his phone, so if you call they may realize you are here."

"Who is the enemy?"

"That is complex, and it is essential they not know you are in Israel just yet."

"Why?"

"If they know you are here they may try to kidnap you to get to your husband. That is why we protect you. If Doctor Carter knows you are here he will try and come to you. If he does that, he will be exposed to the enemy, who are waiting, and they will capture him. Maybe they will torture or even kill him. Terrorists have no sentiments of goodwill toward those who oppose them."

"Why would they harm Gary?"

"They have found cause to consider your husband an enemy of their religion. He is a target of their extremism. We do not want anything to happen to your husband, Mrs. Carter. That is the justification for our unorthodox method toward you."

Celeste toyed nervously with her wedding ring as she considered the events leading up to this conversation. Asaph walked to the window and peered out, waiting. Silent. Calm.

"Why did you lie to me about the picture?"

Asaph turned abruptly. "What do you mean?" His posture stiffened slightly.

"That picture was taken after I last saw Gary. He couldn't have had it."

Asaph relaxed his ridged posture. He feigned an expression of regret and slowly stepped toward her, stopping within arm's reach. "I am sorry about that. I do not like to misrepresent our agency with deception. Please forgive me. We must sometimes stretch the truth a bit, especially in protecting the innocent."

Celeste didn't answer.

"We did not kidnap you and bring you to Israel, but once you arrived here we are obligated to do everything within our power to protect you. I will leave you now to your thoughts. What would you like to eat?"

"I'm not familiar with Israeli cuisine. Order whatever you think I will like. Maybe a pasta of some kind."

"I like ribs and sauerkraut. Would that be okay with you?"

"Beef?"

"Beef? Yes, of course, beef ribs."

I want to believe him. He seems such a nice young man to be mixed up in... espionage...or whatever he's into. He doesn't seem to even carry a gun. Perhaps my suspicions are unfounded.

"Beef ribs will be fine."

Asaph displayed his very pleasant smile.

CHAPTER
THIRTY-THREE

It was a minute past eight when Gary and Zaki stepped through the door of Doctor Rami Gurion's office.

"*Boker tov*," a secretary greeted them rather aloof.

"Good morning to you, Ms. Sara. This is Doctor Carter from the United States. He is here in Israel for a couple weeks doing genetic research. You certainly look pleasant today."

"Thank you." Her coolness melted under the warm rays of Zaki's charming voice. "How may I help you?"

"We need to see Doctor Gurion."

"I am not showing an appointment." She took back control of the conversation. "Doctor Gurion is rather busy today." She opened her appointment book in a manner that said take a number and wait for days. "I can check to see when he may be available to meet with you, if you like."

They were about to be turned out into the Judean heat by a frosty Jewish secretary who spoke perfect English. "Where did you learn English, Ms. Sara? Your accent and diction are perfect. Sounds Midwestern."

"Indiana University. Four year exchange student."

"No way! I'm from Indianapolis. Graduated from IU Med School."

"Really?"

"Really. This is my first visit to your inspiring country. I'm working on a project with Doctor Ahmed. We met Doctor Gurion just the other day at Tiberius. He instructed us to stop by, but we should've called you for an appointment. Are you visiting the States anytime soon?"

"Nothing planned right now, but I'd like to take a holiday back in the States someday."

"When you come for a visit, you must stop in and see my wife and me."

"I'd feel like an imposition."

"Not at all. Just keep it in mind. Here's my business card. I'm not sure if I'll have time to stop back."

"How kind of you. Before you leave, let me double check Doctor Gurion's schedule." She ruffled the pages of the appointment book.

The wall has fallen. Gary smiled at her as if they were fraternity buddies.

A minute later, after Sara just happened to remember a canceled appointment, Doctor Gurion led them into his office. Sara followed with steaming tea, cold rolls and an assortment of cheeses.

Shelves lined three of the four walls of Doctor Gurion's office. Various shapes, sizes and colors of relics covered the furniture, shelves and floor. Stacks of magazines and folders cluttered his desk and credenza. He lifted a one-legged figurine of black stone from one of the only two chairs except his own and made a place for them to sit.

"Basalt?" Zaki asked.

"Yes. We need to repair it. Found it at *et-Tell* at the Bethsaida dig. You are a Christian, Doctor Carter?

"Yes."

"I find it interesting we found more idols in the city where *Yeshua* ministered the most than we found anywhere else."

"That's interesting but not surprising. I believe it was one of your own Jewish writers who penned, 'Where sin doth abound grace doth much more abound.'"

"If you are referring to the writings of Paul, I am afraid we do not claim him." Doctor Gurion chuckled. "Actually, we found another city under the first century Bethsaida. We believe it to be a city of the Geshurites. Perhaps their capital."

"Conquered by King David?" Zaki asked.

"Yes. If you call marrying the king's daughter conquering the empire." Doctor Gurion laughed again. "I suppose the question is who conquered whom?"

"The offspring was not so loyal, no," Zaki added.

"No is right, for sure," Doctor Gurion replied.

"Who was the offspring?" Gary asked.

"Absalom. Absalom's mother was the daughter of the king of Bethsaida, or the ancient city under Bethsaida. King David married Maachah, the daughter of King Talmai, and he was very pleased with the peace-pact that went with the prenuptial arrangements. The city was well fortified and offered protection from David's northern enemies. Are you a student of the New Testament, Doctor Carter?"

"Yes, somewhat. I mean I have studied...read the New Testament." Doctor Gurion's question surprised him.

"Then you realize some of the apostles of *Yeshua* were from Bethsaida: Peter, Andrew and Philip. Maybe some others. Fishermen, were they not?"

"Yes," Gary said.

"We excavated a fisherman's house, with all types of fishing gear. Could have been Simon Peter's house. You think?" Doctor Gurion asked.

"I suppose so." *Is that a subtle hint he knows more about Zaki's discovery than we realize? He's not going to give the cross back.*

"Now, gentlemen, what can I do for you?"

"The relic you confiscated," Zaki spoke slowly and softly, "is of interest to Doctor Carter. We hope to get it back, with papers of authority to allow shipment out of the country."

"You speak of the cross?"

"Yes."

"One of the many used in Jerusalem during Roman occupation, perhaps."

Yes. One of many."

He's recognized its authenticity. Gary could hardly breathe. His worst fear had happened. *Unbelievers will control the future of the cross.*

"I will need to fill out some information forms to authorize its departure from Israel."

I can't believe this. Adrenaline surged and his body slightly trembled. *I dare not look at Doctor Gurion or he may notice. He's sending the greatest discovery of Jewish antiquity to America. Is this legal? Should I argue for the cross' genuineness?*

"Will it take long? Doctor Carter is leaving in a few days."

"No. I can expedite this." Doctor Gurion pulled a file from the stack on his desk and opened it. "In anticipation of your request, I have already started the process. I need a little more info. Where did you find the cross?"

"In northern Galilee."

"More specific please."

"The Golan area," Zaki answered.

Here we go again. Gary detected concern on Zaki's face.

"Date you found it?"

"Eighties."

"You have kept it stored all these years?"

"The cross had no meaning to me then."

"It does now? Why?"

"I've become a student of the New Testament."

"And?"

"I wonder what happened to the cross of the Christ."

"Interesting, especially for an Arab."

"I have become a Christian."

"Even more interesting. Still, I consider your find to be of no further interest to the Israeli Antiquities Authority. It is common knowledge the Romans plundered that area late in the first uprising. I think it could have come from a crucifixion from the rebellion."

I can't believe this is happening. Is tradition that blind?

"I assumed it was from a crucifixion." Apprehension faded from Zaki's face.

"We can only speculate," Doctor Gurion said. "Anyway, I am not particularly fond of displaying more Roman conquests of our people. Further, I doubt a Roman cross would have survived all these years. I suspect it is from a much later pageant of the Christian Easter. That is what I have filled in as a description of the relic. Not of much historical value, nor monetary. I will sign the papers for you now."

"This includes exportation approval?"

"For America?"

"Yes."

"Why America, Doctor Ahmed?"

"In Israel it is a relic of pageantry and legend. In America it may be of historical magnitude…"

"Worth some money?" Doctor Gurion asked.

"Perhaps," Zaki said wryly.

Doctor Gurion signed the papers, stamped each and handed a copy to Zaki. "These papers make it legal to ship the cross to America. Best wishes in your endeavor."

Gary glanced at Zaki. *Doctor Gurion has fallen for the cross switch. He doesn't have a clue Zaki has the real cross in hiding. And if he did he still doesn't believe it could be real.*

"Thank you." Zaki touched his forehead and bowed slightly.

"Whenever you are ready, simply call Sara. She will arrange for you to pick up your relic. Until then, you have my assurance of its safekeeping. It has been a pleasure meeting you, Doctor Carter. Perhaps I can visit you in your Indiana someday. Maybe search for Indian artifacts."

"Yes. It would be my pleasure."

"I can assure you, Doctor Carter, the pleasure will be mine. I very much would like to visit America."

CHAPTER
THIRTY-FOUR

The doorknob to Celeste's room slowly turned. She lunged upright in bed, startled. She'd fallen asleep atop the covers—fully clothed. A chill swept down her spine. Asaph entered.

"You will come with me, Mrs. Carter."

"What time is it?"

"Morning."

"I slept through the night? I guess I didn't realize how tired I was. Where are we going?"

"Into the front room. No reason to be alarmed. We must make contact with your husband. You will make the phone call to him now. I am sure he will be thrilled to hear your lovely voice once again."

She followed him into the main room where he motioned for her to sit in a chair vacated by the wiry-haired young man. She almost fell into the chair, somewhat groggy from a combination of lack of food and jet lag. Asaph handed her a handwritten note, which she scanned.

"Are you ill, Mrs. Carter?" Asaph asked pleasantly.

"I'm fine, thank you," she responded softly, knowing her face displayed the disappointment she felt from reading the note.

"It is delicate what you say to your husband. Many ears may be listening. Practice the note and then you will make the call…please." His please resembled an afterthought.

Celeste's hands trembled as she studied the note.

Asaph broke the awkward silence. "It is critical for your husband's safety you remain calm, Mrs. Carter. If he suspects something is amiss, he may panic and run. If he refuses to turn the relic over to the proper authorities, his enemies will make things very bad for him. We are trying to protect your husband from harm." Asaph sounded compassionate.

Celeste looked at Asaph but didn't speak. She stared into his eyes; he returned her gaze. *Can I trust him.* She turned her attention to the paper she held loosely in her trembling hand and perused the script again:

Gary. I need to talk to you about the cross.
I don't think you should keep it.
Why not turn the cross over to the authorities.
A government official by the name of Asaph called wanting to know where you are storing the cross. I told him probably at the hotel. Is that correct?
He said he needs to meet with you today. Is that possible?
Please, Gary, let them have the cross and come on home. I miss you very much.

Celeste paused from reading the script. "This is too vague. Gary will have additional questions."

"You must answer them all according to the tone of this script. Make him believe you."

"What if he doesn't?" Her voice cracked, she feared revealing signs of her desperation.

"You are a female. You are his wife. Make it work, Mrs. Carter."

Celeste didn't look up. She stared blankly at the note.

"For the sake of your husband's safety, make the call so convincing it will work." Asaph spoke in such a contrastingly gentle manner compared to the previous demand.

Celeste slowly lifted her head. "I'll try."

"Thank you, Mrs. Carter." He quickly punched the phone numbers. Celeste could hear the phone ringing; Asaph handed the receiver to her. With shaky hands she held it tightly to her ear.

"*Shalom.* King David."

So Gary is still King David. "Hello. This is Mrs. Gary Carter. My husband is staying at your hotel. Would you ring him for me, please?"

"Of course, Mrs. Carter. One moment, please."

Celeste scanned the room. Though portraying sparse interest, they were much aware of her presence. The wiry-haired one toyed with an open knife he nonchalantly tossed into the air and caught by the handle. He seemed to have a chip. The chauffeur and turbaned man halfheartedly played cards at the table, tossing glances her way as if she was a novelty. She had seen the look before during a college field trip to a prison. She felt faint and realized she was taking shallow breaths. *Breathe slowly and deeply.*

"Mrs. Carter?"

"Yes."

"Your husband does not answer. Shall I leave him a message?"

Celeste hesitated. She glanced at Asaph, and mouthed, "Shall I leave a message?"

Asaph shook his head.

"No. I'll surprise him later, thank you."

She held the phone to her ear until it went dead before she slowly hung it up. She had wanted so very much to hear Gary's voice.

"Gary is out," she said.

"We shall try later." Asaph smiled at her. "You did well, Mrs. Carter. Very well."

"Thank you," she managed to whisper.

"Now I need you to do something for my associates."

Celeste swallowed her fear. "What is that?"

"They would much like some tea."

Celeste nodded and stepped into the kitchenette. She grabbed the sink for stability as her knees buckled. She glanced out the window and saw a uniformed male with a machine gun slung over his shoulder. *Friend or foe?* She turned the hot water faucet and let the water cascade across her hands until the heat seemed unbearable. Tears blurred her vision. Fear subdued her gnawing hunger pains.

CHAPTER
THIRTY-FIVE

The phone rang as Gary entered. He tossed his key onto the bed, rushed across the room and grabbed the receiver. "Hello." Only a dial tone answered. He immediately dialed the front desk.

"*Shalom.*"

"This is Gary Carter."

"Yes, Doctor Carter. How may I assist you?"

"Did someone just try and phone me?"

"Yes, but she wanted to surprise you."

"She? Who?"

"Mrs. Carter."

"Celeste Carter?"

"If Celeste is your wife, then yes."

"Did she leave a message?"

"No, only she would try later. Like I said, she hoped to surprise you. I hope I have not spoiled things."

"No…not at all. Thank you and *shalom.*"

"*Bevakasha.* You are welcome, Doctor Carter. *Shalom*"

Gary retrieved his cell phone dialed Celeste's cell number; the connection seemed too slow. *Why haven't I phoned Celeste sooner? She had to call me first. How embarrassing!*

"Hi. This is Celeste. Try again later or leave me a message. I'll get back with you. Really! I will! Just leave a message!"

He smiled, but he wanted more than voice mail; he wanted to hear her say, "Everything is fine, and I'm having a great time in Ohio."

"Celeste, this is Gary. Hi, babe. Sorry I missed your call. What's up? We've located the cross, and I've run the DNA test. You won't believe it. I can hardly believe it, and I did the testing. It...the cross Doctor Ahmed found...has to be the cross on which our Lord died. The test doesn't lie. We've gotten approval from the Israeli Antiquities Authority to ship the cross to America, but we have had some slight problems. I'll explain in detail later. Send up a prayer. I can't wait to see you. Hope you're having fun shopping, relaxing and stuff. Love ya bunches. Oh, and greet your mother for me. Better still, give her a hug for me. *Shalom* from Israel. Wish you were here. *L'hitra'ot*...see you soon."

Gary pressed the end button and quickly dialed his agent. By the sound of Addington's voice he realized his error.

"Hello."

"Hey, Bob. I'm sorry about the call. I'm still in Israel. Forgot about the time difference."

"It's okay."

You got anything new?"

"The same offers I mentioned before. I know you want a larger advance, but the best I can get is twenty-five thousand."

"When they find out the latest addition to the manuscript, they'll give a hundred thousand."

"What kind of addition?"

"I don't have to speculate on the DNA of Christ anymore."

"How's that?"

"I've found the real cross."

"Run that by me one more time. We must have a bad connection. Or else I'm dreaming."

"You heard me right. I've found the original cross."

"How can you tell?"

"It had encased blood that tested as nothing short of the DNA of Christ."

"How long before you can get something to me?"

"I'll be home in a few days. It'll take me a couple weeks to sort through my journal and put together a new proposal. The rewrite will take a couple months. I think we should up the ante and broaden our search of publishers."

"I think you're right. I'll put out some feelers and get back with you when you get stateside."

"Thanks."

"Say hello to Celeste for me."

"Will do. She's at her mom's in Ohio. Having a great time, I'm sure."

CHAPTER
THIRTY-SIX

Café Hillel's relaxed atmosphere and world-class coffee was the perfect place to celebrate. Though Zaki and Joseph were polarized in various concepts, Gary hoped to narrow the divide and create a bond between his two new friends.

"Your friends love to shop," Joseph said. "I am sorry I do not get to see them again."

"Shop and eat," Gary said. "By the way, what am I eating?" Gary smiled.

"*Felafel, kabab* and *shwarma*," Joseph said. "Do you like it?"

"I do. But I must admit I'm missing McDonald's. Sorry."

They laughed.

No one seemed in a hurry, which seemed to be Café Hillel's mantra. Terrorists shattered the peaceful atmosphere of Café Hillel in September of 2003 when seven people were killed and fifty wounded. The chain survived and thrives, its red and black color scheme visible throughout Jerusalem and the world. The atmosphere was especially peaceful today. Local shoppers and workers contrasted the myriad of tourists that crowded the stone streets and weaved around the tables and chairs lining the sidewalk. A few of the passersby greeted Joseph, especially Jewish orthodox men in black hats with locks of hair flowing at the temples. Other than the scorching heat, it was a pleasant day in the Jewish section of Old Jerusalem.

"How do you say 'I love Israel' in Hebrew?" Gary asked.

"*Ani Ohev et Israel*," Joseph said.

"*Ani O...*"

"*Ohev...*"

"*Ani Ohev et Israel*." Gary felt like a child who had read a complete sentence for the first time.

"Very good!" Zaki said.

"How is it both of you, coming from competitive religions—that reject Christ as God—have embraced Christianity?"

"You speak of Christology as if it is difficult to understand," Joseph said.

"Some religions view the Christian faith as tritheistic instead of monotheistic" Gary explained.

"The faith of the descendants of Abraham is first, and foremost, the teaching of monotheism. The Lord is one. This is true in Christianity, Judaism and Islam, for we all trace our faith to the God of our father, Abraham." Joseph stroked his beard contemplatively.

"From a Jewish perspective, how can Jesus be God?" Gary asked Joseph pointedly.

"Emmanuel. Simply put, Emmanuel."

"Emmanuel? That's it?" Gary asked.

"Gentiles came from a background of polytheism, with multiple gods and goddesses. In attempting to clarify the descriptive terms for the only true God, they work the sacred Scripture backward from the new covenant to the old, trying to fit Christ into age-old monotheism. We, Ahmed and I, come from a background of monotheism. There is but one God, the God of Father Abraham. Our struggle was to accept Jesus Christ as Messiah. Once we accepted Christ as Messiah, all was settled. Since there is only one God, and the man Christ Jesus was God incarnate, Jesus is God. Emmanuel means God with us. Simple. No multiplicity of gods, no dividing of deity, no family of gods and no confusion as to whom we pray. We simply believe there is no one beside the one true God. Though as a Jew I may address God by his Old Testament name, Jehovah, as a Christian, I call upon him by his saving name, *Yeshua*, or Jesus, as you say in English."

"You make it sound so simple." Gary smiled.

"Why make it difficult?"

"Is that a Jewish thing?" Gary asked.

"Monotheism?"

"No. Answering a question with a question. Jesus did it. You do it."

They laughed.

"Many non-Christian faiths struggle with how Jesus, being a man, can be God," Gary said.

"That is a good question for mythology. It is a poor question for theology," Joseph said.

"What do you mean?"

"In theology a man can never become God, but God can become a man. In the Holy Scripture, God took a visible form so he could commune with mankind. That is how He walked in the garden with Adam and Eve. He visited Abraham in person before destroying Sodom. He was the fourth man in the furnace to deliver the three Hebrew children. In the manger, *Adonai Elohim,* the Lord God of Israel, became a man, so He, though sinless, could pay our debt of sin by sacrificing Himself on the tree. To become human like us, God needed a womb. He chose a Jewish virgin, and nine months later God entered the world as a baby, held and suckled by Mary. His deity did not prevent, nor diminish, his humanity. His humanity did not prevent, nor diminish, his deity. He was fully God. Still, he was fully man, from conception. That is Christian monotheism.

"In Christ, God was still the 'I am' of the Old Testament. Therefore, *Yeshua* could say 'before Abraham was, I am.' The prophet *Yeshayahu* wrote, 'Behold, a virgin shall be with child, and shall bring forth a son, and they shall call his name Emmanuel, which being interpreted is, God with us.' The angel told Joseph to call his name *Yeshua*, which is interpreted Jehovah is Savior. You see? It is simple. God is no longer far away, He is with us in Christ."

"Complicated by man," Gary said.

"Yes, but truth prevails." Joseph sipped long and slow from his cup. "Truth will prevail."

Two Israeli soldiers carrying automatic weapons walked slowly toward them. A sense of guilt gnawed at Gary. He and Zaki had not been completely honest with Doctor Gurion about the cross. *Have we stretched the truth too thin? Does Gurion know?*

The soldiers took the table beside them.

CHAPTER
THIRTY-SEVEN

"**D**octor Carter!" The shout came from the crowded street. Gary glanced in the direction of the voice. Reverend John Tillman pushed his way through the crowd toward him, waving.

"What a pleasant surprise." Gary greeted him. "Reverend Tillman, these are my friends here in Jerusalem: Doctor Zaki Ahmed and—"

"I've already met Doctor Ahmed at a luncheon some days back. He wouldn't sell me his cross, because he had promised it to you, nor would he show it to me." Tillman offered a conciliatory laugh and shook hands with Zaki.

"And this is Rabbi Joseph Arav."

"How lucky you are, gentlemen, to live in the City of God."

"Blessed," Joseph countered.

"Yes, blessed. Pleased to meet you, Rabbi Arav." Tillman extended his hand. They exchanged pleasantries and Tillman quickly resumed his conversation with Gary. "How are things going with the cross search?"

"I have exciting news that will interest you."

"What is that?"

"The cross Zaki found is the cross of Christ." Gary motioned for Tillman to join them at the table. "Coffee?"

"No, thank you. How can you be so sure about the cross?"

"You're familiar with DNA research?"

"Of course."

"On the cross Zaki found, there is blood, preserved through the ages, coated and sealed by the pine sap that oozed from the nail holes in the cross. I ran a DNA test on the blood, and I'm convinced it's Christ's blood."

"How can you tell without a comparable?" Tillman was more knowledgeable then Gary expected.

"Jesus was the second Adam. Was He not?"

"You are catching on, Gary," Zaki said.

"How's that?"

"Answering a question with a question."

They all laughed, except Tillman, who seemed unsure why they were laughing.

"It's an inside joke," Gary explained.

"I see." Tillman remained straight faced. "To your question, yes, Paul, in his New Testament writings, called Christ the second Adam."

"The first Adam received life from the breath of God. We can only presume the DNA of Adam came directly from God, created in God's own image. Perfect. Do you agree?"

"Right," Tillman answered with little commitment.

"Well, the second Adam—Christ—received His DNA from God when the Holy Spirit overshadowed Mary and caused her to conceive. Right?" Gary deliberately made his case.

"I suppose one could explain it that way." Tillman seemed unsure of the direction the conversation led.

"The first Adam was made in the image of God, perfect in all aspects. The second Adam was conceived by God, therefore likewise perfect."

"But unlike Adam of Eden, the second Adam had a mother, giving Christ human characteristics," Tillman said.

"True, and a very good point, but God's DNA would override any imperfections Mary's genes may have contributed. For the most part, the blood encased on the cross contained an absolutely perfect strand of DNA, unlike anything I've ever analyzed. Still, it contained known Jewish ancestry. I believe this flawless strand of DNA, is the blood of Christ, making the wooden beams the actual cross of Christ."

A commuter train interrupted the conversation. As passengers unloaded, an argument ensued on the street. The soldiers walked briskly toward the crowd and entered into a heated discussion with the group, causing further commotion, but the crowd slowly dispersed. The soldiers cautiously walked on.

"Where is the cross now?" Tillman asked.

"One is…it's still at the Israeli Antiquities Authority. They're storing it until we call for it. They don't believe it's authentic." *Did Tillman pick up on my slip of tongue?*

"Who's your contact there?"

"Doctor Gurion."

"Oh, I know Doctor Gurion very well. He has spoken to several of my tour groups. I've purchased quite a few antiquities from him. Nice fellow. I'm hoping to bring him to the States soon and have him speak on my program. Like I said before, I'm interested in acquiring the cross. Let's stay in touch." Tillman straightened a silk scarf around his neck, excused himself and continued along the street.

"Interesting fellow," Zaki said.

"Quite," Gary said.

"Does he have a Christian TV program in America?" Joseph asked.

"Not just one. He owns a conglomerate."

Joseph turned to Zaki. "What are you going to do with the cross, Brother Zaki?"

"Gary is interested in taking it to America."

"For public display? To sell to Reverend Tillman?" Joseph directed his question to Gary.

"I'm not sure. I have some interested parties willing to buy it. It's obvious you just met one of them."

"And what would men like Reverend Tillman do with the cross?"

Joseph's taut facial muscles and elevated body language expressed his concern for the future of the cross.

"Most would more than likely put the cross on public display. Make it available for all to see. Do you object?"

The two soldiers returned, crossed the street and walked toward the café. The open display of automatic weapons unnerved Gary. He was unaccustomed to such a show of armed force. The soldiers sat at the table beside them.

"Would you like to get your picture with the soldiers?" Zaki asked.

"No thanks." Gary smiled and shook his head dismissively.

"They do not mind. Tourism is big business in Jerusalem. Soldiers enforce peace but also make tourists, like you, safe and happy. Anyway, I would like picture to remember our time spent together: a Muslim by birth, a Jewish rabbi by profession and a fundamentalist from America, all dining together in *Yerushalayim*, united by one common denominator, *Yeshua*, the Christ."

Joseph removed his camera from his backpack and held it toward the soldiers. He spoke to them in Hebrew. "From America!" he added. One of the soldiers smiled and took the camera. Joseph motioned for the other to join them in the picture.

"Cheese," the soldier coached as he snapped pictures.

"*Toda*," Joseph said.

"*Bevakasha*. You welcome. I speak little English."

"Thank you," Gary said. "Toda."

"You welcome." The soldiers smiled.

"What is your name?" Gary asked as the soldiers eagerly shook his hand. They continued to smile but didn't answer.

"He was correct when he said he speaks little English." Joseph laughed.

"*Eich korim lecha?*"

"Ah... *shmi* Aaron...and Jacob."

The soldiers retreated to their seats, obviously pleased to have helped. Another train stopped and passengers emerged, shopping bags and backpacks full. The soldiers eyed the crowd.

"You asked if I objected to the display of the cross," Joseph said as the train pulled away. "I love the message of the cross, but I am concerned people might worship the relic instead of the Redeemer, that they revere the cross, but not the Christ."

"Revere maybe, but not worship," Gary said.

"Let me explain my position further." Joseph continued in a compassionate yet abrupt manner. "Do you remember the Old Testament account of the fiery serpents sent to punish the rebellious Hebrews?"

"During the Exodus wandering?"

"Yes, that is what I refer to. The situation was so perilous God instructed *Moshe* to set up a brass serpent. Whoever looked upon the brazen serpent, after being bitten by the poisonous serpents, was healed. We do not necessarily know why God instructed *Moshe* to set up a brazen serpent on a pole, but the act of obedience saved countless numbers of lives. After the fact, some eight hundred years later, the Israelites still had that same brazen serpent. They kept it around all those years, first as an instrument of God's mercy, then as a relic of remembrance but later as an item of worship. In time, it became a key part of their idolatry. My concern for such a relic as the actual cross is similar. A billion pilgrims would venerate the cross, bowing before it instead of worshiping the Savior—a subtle form of idolatry. That is my concern, especially if the cross falls into the wrong hands."

"A justifiable concern," Gary said.

"We Jews had our temple. Over time it became the proof of our religion, while our God waited afar off, wanting a relationship instead of ritual. We were too consumed with our sacrificial system of worship that we forsook our relationship with God. God warned us through the prophets, but as long as we had our temple to point to, we justified our lifestyle, no matter how unspiritual. We equated having the temple with having God. Finally, God gave insight to the prophet *Yeshayahu* regarding our worship." Joseph stopped abruptly, pulled a small Bible from his coat pocket and thumbed through the pages. "Yes, here it is. 'To what purpose is the multitude of your sacrifices unto me? saith the LORD: I am full of the burnt offerings of rams, and the fat of fed beasts; and I delight not in the blood of bullocks, or of lambs, or of goats. Your new moons and your appointed feasts my soul hateth: they are a trouble unto me; I am weary to bear them.'"

"You're suggesting your people placed too much emphasis on the temple sacrifices and too little attention on the condition of their heart?" Gary asked.

"Absolutely! God allowed our temple to crumble into ruin, in hopes we might see the God of the temple rising from the ashes. We did not, for we rebuilt the temple and repeated our errors. It, too, crumbled, about forty years after Christ's crucifixion. The disenchanting smoke from our loss still blinded us from seeing God, especially Christ. We wept over the loss of familiar surroundings, as if God and the temple were a package deal. We did not yet realize the temple in which God wanted to dwell was our hearts. So we mourned our loss of the temple but did not open our hearts to Him. Now, after fifteen hundred years, we are blessed to pray at the Western Wall, near the sight of the ancient temple. For years it was the closest we could get to the ancient site of the temple. We called it our 'Wailing Wall,' for there we stood and cried, longing for the days of Zion's bliss. Have you visited the wall?"

"Not yet."

"You must experience it. We no longer call it our 'Wailing Wall,' for since June seven, nineteen sixty-seven we won back control of our holy city. We now call it the 'Western Wall.' We come here every Friday night to celebrate our victories, but are we really victors? Or are we victims of our own folly, thinking, since we now have the city of God, we automatically have the God of the city. Do these walls contain God? Or does the battle for supremacy of this city keep Him out?"

"For your people and mine as well," Zaki added.

"We continue to emphasize stones and places and relics. We Jews have our wall near where the Holy of Holies once sat. The Muslims have the Temple Mount, where purportedly their prophet ascended. The Christian community claims the sights of the Crucifixion, burial and ascension. What more do we need? By the throngs we make pilgrimages to indulge in tradition. Do we truly find God in these places, or do we merely find things that represent the God we once had among us? I fear the cross on display would become just another distraction from the Savior, and from the salvation Christ purchased for us and offers to us freely. It will usurp the personal relationship Christ offers to us. It will revive the Christian pilgrimages, and the Christ within the heart will play second violin....is that how you say it?"

"Second fiddle." Gary smiled.

"Yes, second fiddle. Thank you. Why expend time and energy in prayer to communicate with an invisible God when you can kiss a symbol of God you wear around your neck? Why spend time reading the Scripture to find God's favor when you can place a sacred relic around your neck or on the dashboard of your car? You see what I mean?" Joseph asked.

"Yes. Still, there may be some benefit in displaying the cross that wouldn't usurp worship of Christ."

"Like what?"

"I've heard of an organization that buys the freedom of men and women who've been sold into slavery. We could display the cross and use the proceeds to carry on this ministry of mercy. What better way to use the cross than to set men and women free from slavery?"

Joseph hesitated. "Freedom from slavery is still incomplete. Have you not heard the story of the two young Moravian men who sold themselves into slavery in order to take Christ to slaves who were forbidden any other opportunity to hear the gospel? Those in bondage need freedom from sin more than freedom from chains. Else they, too, may join in worship of the cross. It would be a good deed, Gary, but they need the message of the Savior more than freedom."

"Your point is well taken. The decision will be up to Zaki."

"You give us much to think about, Joseph," Zaki said. "We will consider what you have shared before we make a final decision about the future of Christ's cross.

"Good. That is all I ask."

CHAPTER THIRTY-EIGHT

Celeste had to take the risk; time was running out, and so was Asaph's patience. She turned the shower on full force and tip-toed across the bedroom to the door. The sound seemed amplified as she slowly engaged the lock; she waited breathlessly listening for footsteps. There were none, only muffled voices as the men chatted.

Her options were limited. *Soon Asaph will have me making another call, but he's lying about almost everything. He lied about Gary changing hotels. They're not protecting me; I'm a hostage. It's the cross Asaph wants, for whatever reason. Once Gary turns the cross over to him, I'm certain they'll dispose of me. I'm more than their leverage. I'm also a witness to their scheme. A witness that will need to be silenced. I must warn Gary to guard the cross instead of giving it over to them. As long as he has the cross that will buy me some time, hopefully enough time for Gary or anyone to rescue me. In the meantime, I must attempt to escape.*

The battery was low on her iPhone. She'd turned it off to conserve energy. The charger was in Ohio; she'd forgotten it in her haste. She must attempt to reach Gary. All she needed was a little battery life. She grimaced as she pressed the OFF/ON button. Her emotions leaped gleefully when the phone came to life with its factory in-stalled musical charm. Celeste pressed a pillow over the phone to muffle the sound. She listened for footsteps. Nothing.

Her phone showed two messages: one voice mail and one text message. The battery indicator showed red. She quickly located the text message.

Celeste, read II Cor. 11:14, u r n my prayers, pastor

Celeste reached for her purse and took out a pen and pad and hurriedly scribbled the Scripture reference to read later. She retrieved the voice message and held the phone tightly to her ear to muffle the sound. In so doing, she engaged the speakerphone. *Celeste, this is Gary,* echoed throughout the room. She pushed mute and listened for footsteps. She heard what sounded like a chair scoot back from the table and footsteps coming toward her door. Her heart beat violently, pulsating in her temples, and she breathed short, shallow gasps of air.

"Mrs. Carter?"

It was Asaph. She didn't respond. He tapped lightly. "Mrs. Carter, are you okay?" She stood still, holding her breath, staring at the door. The knob moved.

"Mrs. Carter, I need to speak with you."

"Who is it?"

"Asaph."

"Sorry, but I have my shower running. I'm preparing to bathe. Could whatever it is you need wait a few minutes, please." She tried not to sound as desperate as she felt. *Did my "please" come out too distressed?*

"Okay," he said after a pensive pause.

"Thank you," she managed to say in the most pleasant voice she could muster up.

His footsteps retreated.

Celeste turned off the mute and retrieved Gary's message again. She put her head underneath the blanket and listened intently to Gary's excited voice. She quickly typed a message to Gary and pushed send. The phone blinked once and went dead. Her heart sank. She tossed the phone into her purse and rushed to the shower.

CHAPTER
THIRTY-NINE

Doctor Rami Gurion sat at his desk engrossed in paper work, the part of his job he least enjoyed. His sunburnt forehead and dirty fingernails showed evidence of what he most enjoyed: digging in Israeli dirt. He gingerly pushed his glasses atop his forehead and rubbed away the blurred vision. He leaned his chair backward in a relaxed position and closed his eyes. The telephone call startled him. It was another unwanted task. He hesitated.

"Hello."

"A Reverend Tillman on line one. Do you want to take it?"

"Sure. Thanks, Sara."

"*Shalom*, Reverend Tillman. How are you?"

"Good. And you?"

"Never been better. What can I do for you?"

"You can come to America and appear on my program."

"I'd love that."

"I'll have my assistant make the arrangements. But there's something else of more urgency that your help will be most appreciated."

"What would that be?"

"It's come to my attention you may have a certain relic that might be of interest to me. Could we meet sometime today and discuss it?"

"Certainly, Reverend. How about here at my office...this evening...six o'clock."

"I'll be there."

The phone went silent. Doctor Gurion pressed the intercom button.

"Yes?"

"Sara. I'm meeting Reverend Tillman at six. Before you leave prepare another set of authorization papers for the cross for Reverend John Tillman. Make arrangements for shipment to the United States."

"So is Doctor Carter...from the States...not getting the cross?"

"A change of plans."

"Anything else, sir?"

"Yes. Get Zaki Ahmed on the phone for me."

"Right away, sir."

"Thank you, Sara."

"My pleasure, sir."

CHAPTER
FORTY

A s Gary stepped out of the elevator to the café his iPhone dinged, indicating a text message. *It's Celeste.* Gary opened the message.

> *darling, in israel, held against will by 4 men, hotel*
> *b---??, i'm ok, forced 2 make call 2u, whatever i say,*
> *don't give up x, let this msg. supersede all others, 2*
> *verify consider something only u & i know, "no" :)*
> *2-14-02, luv u xoxo*

He quickly dialed her phone. The call went immediately to voice mail.

"Celeste. This is Gary. Got your message. What's going on? Call me."

He bumped into a lady carrying a poodle as he turned back toward the elevator. He rushed past the closing door, which automatically opened back up. He looked around the elevator into the stares of half a dozen sullen guests.

"Sorry." He managed an apologetic smile. No one responded verbally, but their countenances spoke volumes. He'd forgotten to push his floor button and did so just as the elevator passed it. It stopped one floor up and he dashed out the door, down the hallway and slammed open the door to the stifling stairwell. He descended one flight, crashed open the door to the hallway and rushed toward Rick's room. That was where he'd last seen Rick and Jack. He pounded on the door. No one answered. He fumbled for the extra room key, but the door opened just as he inserted the key.

"Gary! What in the world..." He brushed past Jack and grabbed a phone book. He thumbed frantically through the yellow pages, back and forth.

"Will someone please help me?" He screamed in desperation as he flung the phone book onto the floor and wrenched locks of his hair with both hands to deaden the pain of his soul.

"Gary!" Rick grasped his shoulders. "What's going on?"

"They have Celeste."

"Who has Celeste?" Rick asked firmly but passionately.

"Four men...I don't know...thieves...demons...terrorists. I don't know. They want the cross."

"How do you know this?" Jack asked.

Gary handed Jack his phone. "It's a text message from Celeste."

"We'll work this out, but we need you to get hold of yourself. What's the date and time, Metz?"

"It just came through a few minutes ago."

"Read it."

Jack read the message, stumbling over a couple words.

"Read it again," Rick said.

Jack read slowly.

"She says she's okay?" Rick interrupted.

"Held against her will. That doesn't sound okay," Gary barked.

"At least up until a couple minutes ago, she was okay. We have to believe that for now. We'll find her. What's the hotel name?"

"B. Just the letter B with three dashes and two question marks."

"Have you received any calls from her?" Rick asked.

"Yesterday. I missed it just as I came back to the room. I called the front desk and the clerk said my wife called but wouldn't leave a message. Said she wanted to surprise me instead. I assumed she was in Ohio, but evidently her surprise was in coming to Israel."

"Nothing else?" Rick lightly probed.

"I called her back on her cell, but she didn't answer. I left a voice message." Gary paused. Silence filled the room except for Gary's heavy breathing.

"What did you say?" Rick's gentle interrogation continued.

Gary hesitated. He closed his eyes contemplatively. "We'd found the cross…had authenticated it…received exportation papers…mentioned having some problems…the usual miss you stuff."

"Evidently she got the message, because she said no matter what she says on the phone 'don't give up the cross.' She mustn't feel her life is in danger or she wouldn't have texted 'no matter what I say, don't give up the cross,'" Rick said.

"What does 'no' and the date mean, Gary?" Jack asked. His ever-present grin seemed amplified.

"It's really nothing to keep secret…I, Celeste and I just haven't shared it with anyone."

"But it is important for this message. What?"

"The date is Valentine's Day two thousand two. It's the day I proposed to Celeste…"

"I thought you proposed on Easter Sunday," Rick said.

"That was the second time. She turned me down the first time. That's the mystery to 'no.' The date is meaningless other than to verify the message is definitely from Celeste. The message isn't a hoax. Only Celeste and I know those dates represent her turning down my proposal."

"We have to figure out the hotel," Rick said.

"Shouldn't we go ahead and call the police?" Gary asked.

"Let's figure out the hotel first and call the police on our way to the hotel."

"Good idea," Jack returned Gary's phone.

Gary studied the text message. *B---??* "There probably isn't but one motel that starts with a B and has three more letters. But what do the question marks mean?"

Rick snatched the phone book from the floor. "Let's ask the desk clerk for help." He started for the door.

Gary hesitated. "Celeste may call again, so I need to be in my room. Rick, you go to the front desk and ask about all the motels that begin with the letter B. Jack, you stay here and call Zaki so we don't tie up the phone line in my room. Get him here a.s.a.p. We'll need him to go with us for directions. I'll send Celeste a text message explaining our game plan. Join me in my room as soon as you've finished your jobs."

*****

"*Shalom*, David," Rick greeted the clerk.

"*Shalom*, Mr. Hogg. How may I help you this beautiful morning?"

"I'm needing to know a hotel beginning with the letter B."

"Please, Mr. Hogg, is something wrong with our service that you want to move? Give us a chance to work with you first. I can assure…"

"No, David, it's not that at all. Gary's…a friend of ours is staying at a hotel that begins with the letter B. We didn't get the complete name. We'd like to have our friend move here to King David and be with us."

"Oh, very well. We would be pleased and honored. Let me check my file."

David clicked the mouse to his computer and scrolled down the page. "Here it is, Mr. Hogg. Belmont. Would you like that I write down the address and phone number for you."

"Yes, please."

"No problem." He scribbled the information on a hotel notepad and handed it to Rick.

"Thank you." Rick scanned the paper. Is this the only hotel in Jerusalem beginning with B?"

"The only one I have on file, Mr. Hogg. It's a very good hotel, more like a country inn, but we will be most pleased your friend comes to King David. Not to boast, but your friend will like King David much better."

"I'm sure."

*****

The phone rang. Gary leaped to his feet and grabbed the receiver. "Hello!"

"This is David at the front desk. Is this Doctor Carter?"

"Yes."

"I have someone on the line for you. Please hold while I put her call through.

"Gary?"

"Celeste. How…where are you?"

"This is not Celeste." Gary's heart sank.

"I'm sorry. Who is this?"

"This is Kathleen."

"Oh, hello, Kathleen…Mom. Have you heard from Celeste?"

"That's why I'm calling. I haven't heard from her since she left for Israel. Didn't you know she was coming?"

"Well, I do now…actually just a short while ago I found out."

"Is she with you?"

"No, not yet."

"Why not?"

"There's a slight problem. Celeste called…" It was important that he convey the message gently without shading the truth of the danger Celeste was in. "I'll stay in touch Kathleen…Mom. I'll call you every few hours until we locate her. In the meantime would you mind calling our pastor and a few friends and have them send up a pray. It can be frightening traveling alone in a foreign country. You understand what I mean?"

"Yes. I've already called your pastor."

"Good. I'll call you soon. Love ya, Mom."

"I love you, Gary. Good-bye."

"Good-bye."

CHAPTER
FORTY-ONE

"What do you mean the cross has been taken, Doctor Gurion?" Zaki spoke firmly into his cell phone.

"Just that. The cross has been stolen. Someone took the cross from our storage room. We will do our best to get it back for you, but sometimes these things just happen. Our security department is working diligently on finding the thief and retrieving your cross. In the meantime, you must be patient with us and trust our expertise in this matter."

"While I am patient, the cross slips across the border into Jordan or Syria, no?"

"No relic as big as a cross slips out of this country without documentation, Doctor Ahmed. My name must be on such documentation. You need not worry. The cross will turn up, soon I am sure."

"I am holding you responsible, Doctor Gurion."

"I am a responsible person, Doctor Ahmed. I do not need a lecture from an amateur like yourself. *Shalom.*"

"*Shalom.*"

Zaki smiled, for the plan was working better than he imagined. He had his own set of export papers from the antiquities ministry. Now the antiquities ministry thought they'd given, or sold, the cross to another. Only his friends knew of the third cross, the real cross, and how the crosses had been switched. Perhaps the enemy would now leave him alone. He checked his cell phone and realized he'd a missed call. He scrolled through the system to retrieve the message and listened intently to the shocking news left by Jack Metz. Guilt surged through his spirit like a stiletto to the heart. After all, he was responsible for the Americans being in Israel. His grandiose scheme was suddenly unraveling even while he spun it. His idea was simply to get the cross out of the country and into the hands of a responsible person. He felt he had found such a person in Gary Carter. He had no inclination men would stoop to such low degrees, especially to obtain such an honorable relic as the cross. He never imagined Gary's wife would be an object of their debauchery. He knew how it felt to lose a wife. A lump formed in his throat. He grabbed his keys, hit the light switch and headed for a taxi.

CHAPTER
FORTY-TWO

Celeste sat by the window drying her long, brunette hair with a towel; the sunrays broke the chill of the air-conditioned room and warmed her spirit. *The weather is so beautiful. If only I could be with Gary.*

She didn't hear the door open but sensed a presence. She turned and grimaced to see Asaph standing just inside the room. Startled, she drew the belt to her robe tighter around her waist.

"I frighten you, no?"

"I didn't expect…I didn't hear you knock," she said curtly.

"May I come in?"

"It seems, sir, you're already in."

"I mean, Mrs. Carter, may we talk?"

"If you wish."

"I do not want to harm you but I am getting very annoyed with your husband's lack of cooperation…"

"What does that have to do with me?"

"You are my bartering tool. Since my superiors are becoming very impatient, I must use my tool."

"Just who are you working for? Certainly not the Mossad."

"Would you like to meet him?"

"Him? One person?" Celeste hesitated. Her mind raced. Pastor Johnson's text message spoke of a demon disguised as an angel of light. Asaph's light was definitely diminishing; the disguise disintegrating. "Yes, I'd like to meet your superior."

"Perhaps someday soon you shall meet him. Until then, you must cooperate with me." He no longer cloaked his contempt.

"Why do you want the cross?"

"I am a bounty hunter. I do not hunt what I want but what my customers desire. I care little for the cross. I am among the scorners. 'Come down from the cross and we will believe?' That would have been me, if I had been there."

"Christ couldn't come down."

"That is why I do not believe. He was an impostor that got caught in his scheme."

"No, that isn't true."

"Then why—if he was truly who he said He was—did he not show his power by one more miracle instead of dying like another criminal on a Roman cross? He was no miracle worker; he was an charlatan."

"He had the power to come down from the cross, but He couldn't do so because of us."

"Us? We were not there."

"All of mankind past, present and future were there symbolically. If Christ had escaped the cross, our debt of sin would not have been paid, and we would have to pay the debt through eternal damnation. It was His love for us that held Him to the cross, not the nails."

"My client does not want Christ's love. Rather, he wants the cross upon which Christ died."

"What about you, Asaph. Don't you want His love?"

"I prefer the reward I will receive for retrieving the cross, not what you propose Christ offers through his death on the cross."

"But—"

Asaph held up his hand compellingly to silence her. He quickly turned and exited the room, pulling the door shut.

CHAPTER
FORTY-THREE

Gary snatched up the phone. "Hello?"

"Is this Doctor Gary Carter?"

"Yes."

"Please listen carefully, Doctor Carter."

"Who is this?"

"It is not important who I am. It is only important that you listen carefully and follow my instructions."

"I am listening."

"Very good. I had hoped to covertly get from you an item of much interest to me."

"Do you have my wife?"

"I asked you to listen, Doctor Carter. I am running out of time. Therefore, we, I and my organization, must resort to more overt means."

"Who is your organization?"

"That is no concern of yours, and yes, we have your beautiful wife, Celeste."

"Can I speak with her?"

"When the time is right. She was brave to follow you to Israel, but courage alone is not enough for her to be able to see you again, if you do not obey my demand. You have something we want. We have someone you want. Today only we will make a deal with you. Tomorrow will be too late for your wife."

"You're wanting the cross?"

"Yes. Give us the cross and we will give you back your wife. If you fail to deliver us the cross, we will eventually have to take it by force, and the consequences will be paid for by the life of your wife. Do you understand."

"Yes."

"One more thing. Absolutely no police. Do I make myself clear?"

"Yes."

"Have the cross ready for delivery today. We will be in touch with details."

"How do I know—"

The caller hung up. Gary fell backward into a chair, staring at the phone he clutched as if it was the only connection that linked him to Celeste.

CHAPTER
FORTY-FOUR

Celeste was hungry, scared and angry, but in no particular order. She was hungry because her captors seemed to exist without food and evidently assumed she could also. She was scared because she was completely cut off from everyone who cared about her, especially Gary. She was angry because she'd been duped into going with a complete stranger who consistently lied to her and continued to hold her against her will. Pastor Johnson's text message offered some consolation, for she sensed he was aware something was wrong and he was praying for her.

She paced and stewed over her predicament, fighting her female impulse to cry. *Asaph would laugh at my tears.* At least two of them guarded the room at all times. Her cell phone was dead. She stopped pacing and starred out the window. *Evidently my message didn't reach Gary or else he would have rescued me by now. I must get to him.* An unexpected adrenaline rush kicked in and an emotional syndrome of fight/flight surged. Her body shuddered uncontrollably. She clasped her hands together in an attempt to control the trembling. She felt instantly sick at her stomach.

She was desperate enough to fight back and too angry to consider the consequences.

She paced again. *Surprise the enemy with a frontal assault. Sail directly into the waves. Fear nothing but fear itself. I can do all things through Christ. Never give up.* She stopped and scanned the room for a weapon. *Pillows? Towels? Waste can? Nothing. A tool?* She eyed the bed sheets.

During graduate school she audited a class in search and rescue. The instructor showed a film of a daring rescue where climbers used an accident victim's bedding to create a rope and sling with which they lowered his body from a mountain ledge. The memory gave her an idea.

She walked to the window and cautiously released the latch. Gradually, to resemble normal activity, she slid the window open, occasionally stopping and purposefully walking around the room to make her presence obvious. She quietly knotted the sheets together to make a rope and tied one end to the bed rail. She lowered the makeshift rope out the window. As she feared, the rope dangled way too short. *Perhaps someone will see it and call for help.* She allowed the braided sheet to dangle from the ledge, but her room faced the back entrance and no one was in sight. *I can't shout for help, or Asaph's thugs will hear. What would they do to me before rescuers could get here?* She wrenched at the thought. Up to this point, her captors had only lied to her. And starved her. *What lies beyond their manipulative masks of deception?* She didn't want to find out. She desperately wanted to escape.

Celeste looked around the room for nothing in particular but hoping an object would spark an idea. Her suitcase sat on a stand. "My sewing kit. Scissors." she mouthed silently. *Why didn't I think of that before? I can cut the sheets into smaller strips.*

She grabbed the suitcase and dug through her garments for the kit. It was gone. They'd searched her luggage. *When? It had to be during the night while I was asleep.* Just the thought made her angrier still. *How did I get it through airport security?* The thought would have been sobering otherwise, but under her circumstances it seemed a minor oversight. *Why didn't Asaph take my phone? Because I clung to my purse like it was a lifeline.* "I must escape...I will escape," she muttered firmly through gritted teeth.

She flung the suitcase onto the bed but quickly regretted doing so. A voice called out from the other room.

"Mrs. Carter, are you well?"

Breathe slowly. One, two, three. "Yes, I'm fine, thank you. When may I have something to eat?"

"Asaph is out. He will bring food soon I am sure."

"Thank you."

"No problem."

"Yes, no problem." She made a face at him toward the closed door. *Good, Asaph is gone. I must escape before he returns.*

Celeste hurriedly returned to her dilemma. *How do I lengthen the rope? I can tear the sheets into strips? No, they will hear the ripping.* She paced the room thinking and looking. *Nothing more to use.* She peered down from her second-story room and shook her head in rebellion against what seemed her only escape route. The length of her makeshift rope was long enough only if she dropped the final several feet, but the landing was rough enough to break a leg if she dropped onto the broken masonry blocks strewn along the base of the building. *I could toss my mattress onto the pavement to break my fall. It'll never fit through the small window.* She stuck her head out the window and looked about for any overlooked options. A balcony protruded from the hotel slightly above and to her right. That gave her an idea.

CHAPTER
FORTY-FIVE

Gary toyed nervously with his Mont Blanc, twirling it like a baton between his fingers as he paced the hotel room. He glanced often at the telephone resting on the end table. "How long has it been?"

"You've asked that same question five times in the last ten minutes." Rick sat by the window in a high back, wooden chair he tilted on the back legs. "It's almost one. A quarter till to be exact."

Jack sprawled on the sofa, napping. A car magazine rested on his chest.

"I can't stand this waiting!" Gary's outburst awakened Jack and startled Rick, who toppled backwards in his chair.

"We have no other options except to call the police or raid the hotel ourselves."

"Without Zaki to guide us, no room number and without weapons?" Rick picked himself up from the floor.

"Why doesn't she call or text message? I can't believe I've gotten her into this. How long does it take Zaki to get here?"

"That's probably Zaki." Rick rushed to the door. Zaki, pale and subdued, walked directly to Gary, placed his hands on his shoulders and pulled him tight to his chest.

"I'm sorry, my American friends, for getting you into all this."

"Thank you, but we came of our own freewill," Gary said. He explained to Zaki as best he could the details of Celeste's kidnapping. "We're waiting for the kidnappers to call with instructions."

The room grew awkwardly quiet except for the rhythmic ticking of the bedside clock and Gary's pacing. The phone rang. Gary grabbed it.

"Hello!" Gary paused. "I'm sorry, Kathleen. I meant to call you, but I don't really have anything to report."

Gary fiddled with the cord as he listened. "Yes, I noticed your incoming call on my cell, but I'm trying to keep the line open in case Celeste calls."

He switched the phone to his other ear. "Yes. Your call is important...you're right. I...ah...did get a text message from Celeste that she is here in Jerusalem, but the hotel name is unclear. We're trying to locate her." Gary listened. He vacillated from apology to acceptance of the reprimand he was receiving, to anxiety over the telephone line being tied up.

"I expect her to call any minute. I'll let you know."

He held the receiver away from his ear and extended it into the air. Kathleen Brown was indeed upset, not only at not knowing Celeste's whereabouts, but also from being uninformed by her son-in-law.

"I'll stay in touch...I love you, too...I'll tell her as soon as she calls...okay. Bye."

Gary managed to smile as he hung up the phone. "Celeste takes after her father." The lighthearted gesture relieved the apprehension in the room.

"Gary, we have to call the police." Rick sighed. "This thing has gone on too long."

"I agree with Mr. Hogg," Zaki said.

Gary hesitated as he contemplated the idea. "You're probably right. Let's draw up a game plan. First of all, per the demand of the kidnappers, can we retrieve the cross from the Antiquities Authority at a moment's notice?"

"What do you mean?" Zaki asked.

"That is what they want...the cross. They'll trade Celeste for the cross. Since we can't retrieve the real cross quick enough from Bethsaida, we'll have to use the fake cross and hope it works."

"I did not know they wanted the cross today or else I would have already told you the fake cross at the antiquities office has been stolen, or else sold."

"This can't be happening." Gary starred at Zaki in disbelief.

"If the kidnappers hear of this, it is not good. They will not realize we still have the real cross nor will they believe such a story. We must call the police immediately. We have lost our leverage to bargain with these people. If they think we no longer have the cross, they will dispose of your wife like she is a dead dog."

"Ahmed's right," Rick said. "We have to act fast, but we must be proactive or we'll do something stupid, and we can't afford to do that. I suggest we rendezvous with the police at the Belmont. We can call them on our way to make sure we're there when they arrive. We'll bring them up to date on the facts and hope they don't arrest us for withholding evidence."

"Let's go." Gary headed for the door.

"Let's pray first." Zaki stopped him.

"Sorry, guys. You're right, Zaki. Lead us in prayer, please."

Zaki extended both hands in a gesture of forming a prayer circle. The others clasped hands and bowed their heads as Zaki prayed.

As they exited King David Gary stopped at the front desk. "If Celeste calls while we're out, tell her we're on our way."

"No problem, Mr. Carter."

"Would you mind looking up the number of the local police department for me?"

"No problem." He thumbed through a phone book, scribbled the number on hotel stationary and handed it to Gary.

"There must be a problem, no? May I help in some way?"

"The best thing you can do is take the call from my wife. Thank you for your concern. *Shalom*."

A pleasant aroma emanated from an assortment of plants that adorned the foyer. Surprisingly the fragrance resurrected recitations of the love songs of Solomon whose poetry could have originated from the terrace of his palace, built for a thousand wives, somewhere on one of the mounts of Jerusalem. Solomon's references to flowers made sense in light of the myriad of pleasant perfumes filling the air. *A thousand wives does not make sense.* Only one of Solomon's wives captured his heart. *O thou fairest among women... I am the rose of Sharon, and the lily of the valleys. As the lily among thorns, so is my love among the daughters...I am my beloved's, and my beloved is mine: he feedeth among the lilies.* He and Celeste had read and analyzed the Scriptures together, sometimes laughing at the descriptive terms. *My beloved is unto me as a cluster of camphire in the vineyards of Engedi.* How bizarre he recalled them at this moment! *Make haste, my beloved, and be thou like to a roe....* Gary related to this verse. It made sense.

"*Shalom,* Doctor Carter." The desk clerk smiled.

For Gary, life was everything but peace. *Is it too late to prioritize?* He would give his life if he could reverse his decisions of the last few days. One seldom, if ever, gets the chance. You live with the circumstances. *How can I live without her?*

CHAPTER
FORTY-SIX

Jack drove and Zaki gave directions. Zaki initiated the call to the police department.

"Shalom. Israeli Shoter."

"Ata medaber Anglit?"

"*Ken.* Yes, I speak English little. How may I help you?"

"Good." Zaki handed the phone to Gary.

"This is Doctor Gary Carter. There has been a kidnapping. It's my wife. They are holding her at the Belmont Hotel. Do you know where that is?"

"Yes."

"Can some officers meet me there?"

"Are you at the Belmont now?"

"No. We're almost there."

"Who are 'we,' sir?"

"Me and some…three friends. Can some officers please meet us there?"

"Yes. I will call for someone now. Will you stay on the line, please?"

"Yes."

Gary stared out the window, silently praying.

As they sped toward the outskirts of Jerusalem, Zaki chattered. "Belmont is lovely country inn about fifteen minutes' drive from

190

Jerusalem. The inn is situated in Judean hills on grounds of Kibbutz Tzuba. It is quiet place, but like so many places in Israel, ploys of evil men rob us of peace. Someday, perhaps soon, our Prince of Peace will return to our land. That is why we request, 'Pray for the peace of Yerushalayim.'"

Zaki talks nonstop when he is nervous. I think I know what he felt like when he received news about the bombing.

"Doctor Carter?" Gary held up his hand in a gesture for silence from the others.

"Yes."

"Some officers are on their way to the hotel Belmont. They will meet you there."

"Thank you, sir."

"No problem, Doctor Carter."

Jack drove fast. He made sharp turns with slight deceleration. Gary and Rick hung on in the backseat, bouncing from side to side and off each other as they sped into the Judean countryside. Blaring horns didn't intimidate Metz. It was as if they challenged the view of the finish line, with no holds barred, as if nothing but crossing the finish line first mattered. For once in his life Gary did not mind Metz' driving. They entered the ground of the kibbutz ahead of the police. Jack slowed as they approached the inn. The grounds comprised a series of buildings that looked more like an apartment complex back in the States. The four exited the car and entered the office. The desk clerk showed concern as they hastily entered.

"*Shalom.*" He gave a sideways glance as if looking for the nearest exit.

"*Shalom. Ata medaber Anglit,*" Zaki asked.

"A little."

"Please, one of you explain what has happened." Zaki turned away and walked swiftly to the outside.

"We are American citizens looking for a friend who has been abducted. You understand?" Rick assumed the lead.

"Yes." The clerk seemed to relax a bit. "You Americans...friend of you be abducted?"

"*Yesh lecha...*ah...guests...four men and a woman?" Rick held up four fingers on his right hand and one with his left to help the clerk understand."

191

"Ani lo Mevin." The clerk shook his head indicating he didn't understand.

"We need Zaki," Rick said.

The sound of a siren interrupted the conversation. A miniature, black police vehicle, lights flashing, pulled cautiously onto the grounds. Two officers exited the vehicle and approached warily.

"Ata medaber Anglit?" Rick asked.

"Yes, I speak English. Officer Goldstein, and this is my assistant, Officer Jacobson."

"Shalom," Officer Jacobson responded cautiously.

"How may we help you?" Officer Goldstein asked.

"I'm the one who called for assistance. We are American citizens. My wife is missing…kidnapped, I fear."

Gary explained to the policemen as best he could the situation. The officers listened with apprehension. Goldstein asked the usual interrogative questions: description of the missing person, nationality, when they arrived, when they planned to leave, any communication with the kidnappers and their last communication with Celeste. He seemed somewhat unsure of the necessary procedures, since the missing person was an American citizen. He excused himself and walked to the cruiser. Gary assumed he was calling a superior. Officer Jacobson obviously couldn't speak English, as he made no attempt to communicate with them, even while his superior was away. He spoke in Hebrew in a rather calming manner with the desk clerk who was obviously disturbed at the excitement, escalated by his inability to understand what was happening.

"We may need to involve the American Embassy," Officer Goldstein explained when he got off the phone. "Do you have your passports?"

"Mine's at the hotel," Gary said.

"You're not a guest here?"

"No. We're at King David."

"I left mine at the hotel also," Jack said.

"Here's mine." Rick pulled his from his ever-present leather travel bag attached to his belt in the front. The officer took the passport and flipped through the pages, studying it like he might find some clues. He paused at the photo and gave Rick a quick glance.

"Seems to be in order." He handed it back to Rick, whose demeanor mirrored western disdain for such intrusions of privacy, but he didn't comment.

An unmarked car arrived, identified only by a flashing light temporarily mounted on the roof of the driver's side, followed by half a dozen patrol cars. A man in a pin-striped navy blue suit and sanguine red tie emerged from the lead car, unwrapping a stick of gum, which he popped into his mouth. An assistant followed closely; his brown and white, checkered bowtie hung sideways against the lapel of his tweed sports coat, and the front pocket of his coat revealed a multi-colored assortment of ink pens. He donned a detective hat, straight out of the fifties' gangster era, pulled down over his eyes. His penny loafers made a flopping sound as he took quick short mother-may-I steps beside his superior. He clutched a pen and clipboard as if he were doing a shower check at a youth camp. Gary couldn't help but smile, even under the circumstances. The additional policemen fanned out across the grounds, machine-guns in hand, assuming protective positions.

The two newly-arrived detectives directed their attention to Officer Goldstein, one shouting in Hebrew interrogatory demands—obvious from his gesticulation—before he flashed his ID.

"Inspector Abraham Harris from Jerusalem Special Investigation Division. My assistant, Officer Perez."

"Doctor Gary Carter, U.S. citizen. These are my friends, also from America...and a friend from Jerusalem."

"Certain protocol we have to follow, Doctor Carter. You understand, I am sure. We have informed your embassy. They are sending someone over.

"How long," Gary asked.

"Not sure. How long, Perez?"

"Hopefully within the hour, sir." Perez checked his watch.

"We may not have an hour," Gary lamented.

CHAPTER
FORTY-SEVEN

"We feel the least attention we draw to this, the better. You expressed to Officer Goldstein you don't think the abduction is by a terrorist organization. Why?" Inspector Harris chewed incessantly on gum.

"It's a lot to explain, sir, but as I've already said, the bottom line is I'm here to authenticate a relic of antiquity. There are a few individuals who want the item. Some of them are here in Jerusalem. I believe one of them has kidnapped my wife as a ransom tool."

"Who are these...people you speak of?"

Gary hesitated and cleared his throat.

Rick answered for him, "A couple televangelists from the States, some individuals we've encountered, but we don't know their identity, and some thugs here in Jerusalem who beat up our friend..."

"What's your name, sir?" Harris interrupted.

"Professor Richard Hogg, University of Cincinnati, history prof...friend of Doctor Carter."

"He has his passport, sir," Officer Goldstein commented. Rick held out the passport but Inspector Harris waved it away.

"Who are you?" Harris pointed at Jack.

"Jack Metz, temporary chauffeur, also from the States." Jack had his ever-present mischievous grin. Harris gave Jack a quick wipe-that-smile-off-your-face glance and turned to his assistant. "You getting this all down, Perez?"

"Yes, sir." Harris' assistant worked feverously jotting down information as they spoke.

"You speak of a relic. Did you find the relic here in Jerusalem?" Harris directed his question to Gary.

"No. In fact, I didn't find the relic. Rather, I was called on to attempt to authenticate the relic for its owner. It was actually found in Galilee."

"Then we have a bargaining tool to win Mrs. Carter's freedom."

"Had a bargaining tool," Zaki spoke up.

"And your name, sir?" Harris asked.

"Zaki Ahmed. The relic belongs to me."

"You are Jewish?"

"No. Arab."

Harris stared at Zaki. "What do you mean had a bargaining tool?"

"Someone took it from Antiquities Authority last night. I just found out today."

"Do the kidnappers know?"

"We do not think so, sir."

"Let us keep our fingers crossed," Harris answered. "We must assume they, whoever they might be, do not know the relic is missing."

Officer Jacobson, who had gone to the clerk at the front desk, returned with some scribbles on a notepad.

"What have you got?" Harris asked impatiently.

"The inn has sixty-four suites in a series of buildings and is booked solid with tour groups with the exception of one building. They have isolated a suite in that building that does meet the description. They are nationals, maybe four men, and have occupied it for a couple days."

"And a woman?" Gary asked.

"Not confirmed."

"Let's take a look." Inspector Harris started toward the building at a fast gait. "We are going in," he said to the entourage following at his heels. He then brandished a small handheld radio and barked instructions in Hebrew. The radio squawked and others responded.

"We have the compound surrounded." He turned to Gary, who walked quickly beside him. "I will need you to stay back when we reach the building they're occupying. I will call you if I need you."

With an inn worker who spoke little English acting as guide, the group moved rapidly across the grounds. The inn worker talked nervously in broken English. "Is lovely place indeed, no? Each apartment with kitchenette…air cool…very comfortable. Wonderful place for holiday. We no usually have anything like this to happen. Safe place."

The worker stopped abruptly beside a green hedge that acted as a privacy fence and pointed toward a two-story building.

"That the building?" Harris asked.

"Yes. They in suite on right side." He seemed proud of his English and pleased to accommodate them.

"Does the outside door lead directly into the suite?"

"Yes."

"Stay here," Harris ordered.

Rick and Jack closed in beside Gary. They remained silent. Rick firmly gripped Gary's shoulder. Six policemen rounded the hedge and hurried across the lawn to the building. An officer stood guard at each of the house's front corners. Two more huddled at the door. Harris waved two officers toward the rear of the building. Harris and his assistant sprinted across the lawn to the front door.

"*Israeli Shoter! Liftoha delet!*" Harris pounded on the door.

"What's he saying?" Gary asked the hotel worker who remained with them behind the green hedge.

"He identify police and demand door open." The worker crouched lower behind a hedge.

After a moment, with no response from within the apartment, one of the officers kicked in the door and rushed inside, followed by the others. A commotion erupted inside the building. Shouts echoed throughout the apartment. A window raised and a man leaped through the opening, landed on his head and tumbled across the grass. Officers quickly subdued him. Gary started toward the building, but Jack held him back with a firm grip around his shoulders. Rick stepped in front of him. After a good five minutes––that seemed like an hour––the ruckus ceased.

Three men emerged in handcuffs, escorted by officers, and were forced to sit on the grass with the one who jumped through the window. Inspector Harris and Perez finally exited the building. Harris raised a calming hand toward Gary.

"Wrong inn I am afraid, Doctor Carter. No sign of Mrs. Carter, or any female being in the apartment. I am sorry. It is not a dry run. Contraband. We will question them about your wife, but I am confident they are not connected with her abduction. I am curious as to why you felt so sure it to be this hotel?"

"Celeste sent me a text message. She didn't seem to know the name, only it started with the letter B. Our hotel clerk thought Belmont was the only hotel in or near Jerusalem beginning with the letter B."

"Really? Any info available?" Harris turned to Perez, who quickly typed a few commands into his pocket-sized computer.

"Yehuda Street, sir." Perez snapped the computer shut.

"You are right," Harris shouted. "The Little House in Bakah. Let's go."

CHAPTER
FORTY-EIGHT

Celeste worked quietly, but determinedly, with a fingernail file, unscrewing the chrome coated towel rack from the bathroom wall. She smiled in satisfaction when the metal bar fell into her hand. She hurriedly wrapped a towel around the rack and tied it securely with narrow strips of white bedding to silence the clanging it might make. Any unusual noise would warn her captors of her attempt to escape. Still, haste was likewise obvious. Satisfied with her job, she nervously knotted the end of the makeshift rope onto the middle of the metal bar and rushed to the opened window.

Peering out the second floor window, she surveyed the lot below. No one stirred. She leaned out the window and tossed the metal bar up and to her right, toward the protruding balcony. It landed on the concrete railing, bounced, teetered, fell backwards toward the ground and bounced silently off the side of the building as it swung freely. Celeste's grimace quickly turned to a smile that expressed the approval of her foresight to wrap the metal bar with the towel. She pulled in the homemade rope, hand over hand, careful to keep it from snagging on protrusions from the building. Leaning as far out the window as seemed prudent, she swung the knotted sheet back and forth, like a pendulum, slowly letting out more length, as if fly fishing, and flung it with all her strength toward the balcony. It cleared the railing and landed on the floor, bounced and made more noise than Celeste anticipated. Now came the real challenge. She tugged on the braided rope, causing the bar to rise and drop onto the concrete balcony. Her intentions were to get the bar to fall between the balcony balusters and act as an anchor. She would then cling to the rope, swing toward the balcony and climb the wall to the balcony. Then she would escape through the room above hers. To her dismay the bar refused to catch hold between the balusters.

Time and again she repeated the process until her upper body ached. She paused and looked across the lot as her tired arms and shoulders rested. *In another time and under different circumstances, this would be such a unique place to vacation.* The smell of apricots and oranges, and a mingling of the fragrances of a dozen native flowers from the garden below, wafted upward upon the breeze. She slowly inhaled the bouquet of aromas. Across the way she saw the alluring shops and could hear the many and varied voices coming from the streets. She assumed their identities: local shoppers, vendors, children on their way home and tourists, perhaps some from the States. No one within an earshot had a clue about her predicament. If she were to be rescued, she'd have to do it herself.

A dark Mercedes sedan, immaculately clean, with its mirrored chrome reflecting the bright sun, and its tinted windows protecting the anonymity of its occupants, pulled slowly onto the lot and stopped thirty yards directly in front of Celeste's second floor window. The back door opened and a man in a dark suit clambered out. His back was to her, but Celeste could tell it was Asaph. She froze. The makeshift rope dangled from the window as revealing as a skull and crossbones hoisted up the mast of a pirate ship. Asaph paused while the chauffeur hustled to retrieve something from the trunk. They cradled shopping bags as they walked from the car toward the building. Asaph looked upward and locked eyes with Celeste. He flung the bag in the air toward her as if it were a weapon and sprinted toward the hotel entrance.

CHAPTER
FORTY-NINE

Their rental car—sandwiched between two police cruisers with lights flashing and sirens blaring—strained to keep up. Gary's cell phone rang. Celeste's mother. He tried to assure her things were okay.

"I'm on my way to meet Celeste right now."

"Are those sirens I hear? Is something wrong? Is Celeste okay?"

"It's always noisy here in Jerusalem, Mom. Couple of police cars headed somewhere. I'll have Celeste call when I reach her motel."

The conversation ended brusquely when the lead cruiser suddenly stopped. Jack slammed on the brakes and veered right onto the sidewalk to avoid plowing into the lead car and being rear ended by the escort. Gary scrambled to retrieve his cell phone, which he'd dropped from the abrupt stop.

Inspector Harris raced back to their car. "Sorry gentlemen," he yelled. "We've had another bombing. I have to respond. You can drive on to Bakah but wait for me in the parking lot. I will be there as soon as I can, or else I will send someone to help. Got to go."

Without waiting for a response, he dashed to his car, which did a U-turn and sped away, followed by the other cruisers.

The four sat for a moment in stunned silence. The engine had died and steam billowed from under the hood.

"I can't believe this. I can't believe this!" Gary repeated the phrase again and again as he repeatedly banged the back of the seat with his forehead.

"That is how I felt when I received news of the bombing that killed my family. The police cannot stop senseless killing as long as men's heart's are full of hatred."

Zaki's chatter awakened the need for composure within Gary; he had no time to feel sorry for himself. He realized the need for calm, yet urgency. "We have to find her. Let's go it alone, if necessary."

Jack cranked the engine. The car refused to start. The battery weakened. Jack turned off the ignition, climbed out of the car and opened the hood. Steam shot outward. Gary fidgeted as Rick studied his map.

"Where are we, Zaki?" Gary asked.

"Yehuda Street is just up the way. We're almost there. Just a few blocks straight ahead," Zaki said.

Gary leaped from the car. "Take the keys, Jack. Leave the car. Let's go."

A taxi pulled alongside them. "*Monit?*"

"*Ken!*" Rick opened the door and jumped in. The others climbed in.

"Your Hebrew is coming along, Professor Hogg." Zaki said.

"Thank you. I'm trying, but it's a tough language."

"*L'aan?*" the driver asked.

"*Ata medaber Anglit?*" Rick asked.

"Yes. A little. To where you go?"

"Bakah…Yehuda Street."

"A Little House in Bakah. I know place. I take you there safe."

CHAPTER
FIFTY

With his heart hammering like the pistons of a racing machine, Asaph rushed through the garden of blooming flowers thriving under the shade of stately old pine trees. He hurried toward the front door of the beautiful ottoman-style renovated mansion. Above him loomed decorative arches and perfectly symmetrical columns. The setting summer sun reflected off lovely arched windows that fit well in the décor of Old Jerusalem. He flung open the front door of the hotel and flew past the front desk clerk who gave him a quizzical look as he hurriedly ascended the stairway two and three steps at a time.

Asaph pounded on the door to the suite as he fumbled with his key, cursing profusely. The door swung open and, without explanation, he brushed past his wiry-haired assistant who'd answered the door, sending hot coffee flying into the air and raining down upon them both. He burst through the door to Celeste's room. His prisoner was gone. In three strides, he crossed the room to the window and peered down. The makeshift rope dangled from the window, swinging in the breeze. He saw a purse. A slipper clung to a bush near the wall beneath the window. Its match lay a few feet away on the pavement of the parking lot.

"She cannot get far barefooted," he screamed, as he commanded the others to follow chase. They rushed out of the room, bumping into the chauffeur, and scrambled down the stairway, falling over each other in their haste. Asaph cursed them as he raced out the front door of the hotel.

CHAPTER
FIFTY-ONE

Celeste pressed herself against the wall. Her heart throbbed in her ears. When the commotion faded into the distance she slowly pulled back the curtain and stepped out of the shower. She walked to the bed and picked up her suitcase and extra purse. She propped her foot on the bed and fumbled with the laces to her white tennis shoe. Her hands trembled as her determined heart pounded in her chest.

The desk clerk glanced in her direction as she cautiously descended the hotel stairway to the front desk. Obviously confused by the recent tumult, he feigned a smile.

"Do you speak English?"

"Yes. How may I help you?"

"My name is Celeste Carter. I am an American citizen. The four men who just left your hotel have held me captive against my will."

"I shall call the police immediately, Ms. Carter."

"I would be grateful. First, may I use your phone to make a local call to my husband?"

"Certainly. I will make the call for you. What is the number?"

"King David Hotel. Ask for Doctor Gary Carter."

The clerk punched in the numbers and then poured coffee into a Styrofoam cup and handed it across the counter to Celeste."

"Thank you." She cradled the cup in trembling hands.

"No problem, Mrs. Carter...*Ken. Shalom.* Do you speak English?" He gave her a conciliatory smile. "Doctor Gary Carter's room." He held a hand over the mouthpiece. "We will find him. How long have you been…he has gone out, you say? I am calling for his wife from Bakah Hotel. When do you expect him?"

The desk clerk glanced distractedly beyond Celeste toward the front entrance. "Their desk clerk said to tell you Doctor Carter is on his way." He slowly lowered the receiver.

His darting eyes alarmed her. The sudden sound of scuffled footsteps on the terrazzo accentuated her already accelerated heartbeat. Heat from the street rushed into the foyer as the door burst open. The footsteps stopped abruptly. She sensed stares and perceived heavy breathing from lungs short on oxygen. She felt nauseous, her body instantly clammy.

"I will call the police, Mrs. Carter," the clerk whispered.

"Thank you," she mouthed.

She awkwardly turned to face her attackers. The bright Judean sun dipped partially behind the buildings across the street. Its focused beam radiated through the open doorway; the bright rays momentarily blinded her. She tried to blink away the spots that burned her retinas and clouded her vision. All she could see was a stunning prismatic sphere that, surprisingly, elicited pleasant memories etched over time from viewing ten thousand sunsets.

She raised a hand to shield her eyes from the glaring sunlight. The four men silhouetted in the enormous arched entryway. The brilliant sun produced a golden outline around them. She knew who they were, but in some defensive manner, she imagined a heavenly angel of light sent to rescue her. That's what she silently prayed for.

Celeste was a connoisseur of sunsets. She and Gary had driven four hours the second night of their honeymoon in Hawaii to see what locals boasted to be "the most majestic sunsets on earth." She stood on the beach, barefoot, playing with sand between her toes, waiting for the flaming orange ball to begin its rapid descent into the Pacific Ocean. Like the Times Square countdown on New Year's Eve, she counted aloud with childlike enthusiasm as the sun dropped into the ocean and out of sight. As Celeste stood transfixed by the natural phenomena, Gary snapped frames of her awestruck expressions. He captured a couple unique shots with her face framed in the fiery sphere and one with the sun resting upon her shoulders.

For a brief moment, Celeste longed for a view of the setting sun over the hills of Brown County back home in Indiana. She wished she could take her mother shopping one more time in Nashville, a quaint little artist community in Brown County, southwest of Indianapolis. The two of them would shop until they dropped, then relax in the rocking chairs on one of the many porches and watch a brilliant display of pink, lavender and orange as the sun reflected off the clouds while it slipped behind the lofty hills.

It was on one such shopping trip, as the sun dipped beneath the horizon, her mother explained her growing fondness for sunsets. "With twilight comes the realization life is slipping away too quickly, so one relishes every moment of the sunset, for it may well be one's last." They observed intently the variation of colors and the numerous formations of the distant clouds as the sun played peek-a-boo behind them. The awesome scene disappeared too quickly as the western horizon succumbed to the blanket of darkness drawn across the sky. All the pleasure was registered within the brain like the split-second frames of some memorable event captured upon film for future pleasure. Sunsets captured memories. Memories created scrapbooks that strengthened the twilight years of life.

One of the men stepped toward her. Her body stiffened as she clutched the handle of her carry-on and prepared to swing the makeshift weapon with all her might at the approaching intruder.

"Celeste."

She hesitated.

"Gary?"

He rushed to her and she collapsed into his embrace.

CHAPTER
FIFTY-TWO

They rendezvoused briefly at dusk; the dim lighting in the quarries underneath the ancient city concealed Goleth's physical features.

"I need a little more time," Asaph said.

"Does that mean you have failed in your mission?"

"I never fail."

"Then where is the cross?"

"I will get it."

"So, you have failed?"

"The cross is probably on its way to America. I will get it for you. I simply need more time."

"You are out of time."

"Then how do you expect to obtain the cross?"

"Time is on my side. It is my friend, the one thing I have plenty of. I no longer need your services."

"Then who will obtain the cross for you?"

"I have comrades in high places. If it takes until eternity, I will get it."

Before Asaph could respond, Goleth turned and vanished into the darkness of the cavern.

CHAPTER
FIFTY-THREE

In the lobby of King David, Zaki handed Gary a manila envelope. "Here are the authorization papers for exportation. I give you charge of the cross. Do with it as you like, but you must protect it. Do not let it fall into wrong hands."

"I imagine there'll be a similar container as ours on another flight," Gary said.

"Let us hope it is not same flight as yours. Authorities might get suspicious of two crosses of Christ."

Gary turned to Joseph, "You are the teacher of Torah. Tell me I shouldn't feel guilty for our deception of the Antiquities Authority by switching the crosses." Gary clasped Joseph's hand, pleased he came to see them off.

"You should not feel guilty, my friend. You did not switch the crosses. You merely played out the game others tried to manipulate to their advantage. In so doing, you protected the real cross from those who would exploit the object of our Lord's suffering, and they would do it solely for personal gain, not out of love for our Lord."

"What Joseph says is true. We did not switch crosses. The enemy kept stealing the wrong cross. We know the true cross is not safe here. It has too many enemies, and we have too few friends to protect it. As the cross was protected by providence these last two millenniums, once it has been found, it now needs someone like you to protect it from those who would certainly exploit it. They neither love the cross nor our Lord who hung on it. They love only what it can earn in gold."

"Do you think the fake cross was really stolen from the Antiquities Authority?" Gary asked.

"Perhaps. Perhaps not. I will not be surprised if it turns up in America with some religious organization," Zaki said.

"I'm sorry you have made no money for all your efforts in finding the cross."

"God will bless you, my brother, for not taking undo advantage of his suffering." Joseph placed an affirming hand on Zaki's shoulder.

"He already has." Zaki thumped his clenched fist against his chest. "It is a burden I can bear. The wooden cross was becoming too burdensome. My request is Gary finds a way to preserve Christ's cross for sake of posterity while keeping it from becoming idolatrous veneration. You are right, Joseph, it is not a cross, but savior who hung on a cross, that is to be worshiped. The cross does not seek to be worshiped. It wept sorely because it had to bear our Lord in such an agonizing way. Its tears cover and protect His blood for two millenniums, but the cross' hiding place is no longer safe. I believe you will know what is best way to protect cross."

"I'm not sure, but I'm working on a plan. I'll stay in touch on the progress." Gary embraced Zaki and Joseph.

"What about cost to store and maintain the cross. Where will you find that kind of money without openly displaying cross?" Zaki looked forlornly as he asked the question. "I do not have any resources to help."

"Don't worry, my friend. It will work out, somehow."

"Time to go." Jack pushed a luggage cart and chatted with a bellboy pushing another cart. The young man clutched a car magazine Jack had given him.

"Would you autograph, please?" the young man asked Jack.

"Of course. Hey, Hogg, you got a pen?" Rick retrieved a pen from his pocket and handed it to Jack who grinned as he winked at Rick. "Sure is fun being famous! This beats selling toilet plungers at the hardware store any day of the week. Don't you think?"

"Absolutely, but you should now carry your own pen, being famous and all."

"Keep it up and you're going to develop a sense of humor." Jack grinned.

"You think?" Rick revealed a slight smile.

They walked as a group through the King David lobby and to a waiting limo. Jack led the way; Rick walked between the rabbi and Zaki. Gary and Celeste, hand-in-hand, followed. As they stepped through the front doors of the hotel, a cheer went up from a group of well-wishers. They stood like security in a circle around the limo, friends of Joseph and Zaki, fellow Jewish Christians living in the City of God, holding hands and singing a melodious yet melancholic chorus.

"What is the song?" Jack asked.

"It is the Shema," Joseph said. "It was the chorus of the ages that held the hearts together though splintered as a people to the far reaches of the world. Wherever they went, no matter how meager their belongings, they always carried that song in their hearts. Though separated by millenniums and thousands of miles, this one song always kept them as one people."

Tears flowed.

Once the song was finished Joseph lifted his hands toward them and prayed: "*Barukh atah Adonai, eloheinu melekh ha-olam.* Blessed art Thou, Lord our God, King of the universe. The LORD bless thee, and keep thee: The LORD make his face shine upon thee, and be gracious unto thee: The LORD lift up his countenance upon thee, and give thee peace."

The Jewish group responded in unison, "*Barukh hu, u'varukh shemo.* Amen."

A long container rested atop the limo, fastened by rope. Gary had personally taken extreme cautions with the crating of the cross. It was now his responsibility, a burden he didn't relish, but it was a task he submitted to as being the will of God.

The four climbed into the limo and closed the doors. Gary rolled down his window and waved to the entourage standing on the sidewalk in front of the hotel. They waved back. The limo pulled away from the curb and turned toward the street. Gary leaned out the window and yelled to them, "*Ani Ohev et Israel.*"

"And we love America," they called back. "God bless America!"

The tinted window of the limo subdued the brilliance of the morning sun as they drove west toward the Mediterranean. Gary removed the papers from the manila envelope and studied their contents. He knew he held within his hands the opportunity to make millions of dollars. He closed his eyes and pondered the possibilities. His mind was set.

CHAPTER
FIFTY-FOUR

"I never before considered the high pitch whine of jet engines a pleasant sound," Celeste said.

"Nor I, but today it's musical." Gary occasionally glanced out the window at the workers loading the luggage; he cringed at the thumps from beneath their seating as workers tossed the baggage into place. "Careful please."

"What's wrong?"

"They're so rough with the luggage." His uneasiness wouldn't pass until the plane was airborne. His anxiety would return with a vengeance at stateside customs, even with the proper documentation in his briefcase, signed by Doctor Rami Gurion and stamped with an official Israeli Antiquities stamp.

Gary's cell phone rang. He glanced at the number. "Hey, Bob."

"Hello, Gary. How's the trip coming?"

"Just got on the plane to head home."

"Fill me in on some of the new ideas for the book."

Gary hesitated.

"You there?"

"I'm here, Bob. I don't exactly know how to say this, but I've been doing some thinking... soul search, I guess. I've decided not to do the book."

"You what?"

"I can't do it. At least not now, and I certainly can't do it for personal gain. Maybe later... as a way to raise money for the cross' preservation."

"You've already done a lot of work."

"I know. You've done a lot of work, too. I'm sorry for letting you down like this. I want you to withdraw all proposals to the publishers."

"It's your call. No hard feelings on my part."

"Thanks, Bob. I'll call when I get home and we'll discuss options, perhaps work together on another project."

"I hope so. Have a safe trip. Give my greeting to Celeste. I heard she was spending some time with her mom in Ohio."

"Yeah, she enjoys visiting her mom. I'll tell her you asked about her. Take care."

Celeste placed her hand gently on Gary's arm. "I'm proud of you. I know that was a difficult decision."

"I feel badly for Bob more so than for myself. He put a lot of time into this deal."

"Did he take it okay?"

"I think so."

"What are you going to do with the cross?"

"I'm not sure." Gary stared out the window as the Airbus began its taxi to the runway. Celeste gently squeezed his hand. He responded in turn.

Once airborne and given clearance, Gary turned on his new PowerBook and began typing. Celeste snuggled against him and fell asleep almost instantly, causing him difficulty in hitting the right keys.

A quiet settled throughout the plane as people settled in for the Atlantic crossing. Gary stared out the window at a distant plane. An hour passed before Celeste stirred.

"Did you nap?" she asked.

"Not sleepy."

"What are you typing?"

"A letter to Reverend Small. How does this sound?" He read to Celeste from the rough draft.

Cross Switch

Dear Reverend Small,

I have recently returned from Israel. My trip was filled with inspiration and excitement. I met with my contact in Jerusalem and performed work with him regarding a primitive cross he found. He is a fine Christian brother and I am sure you would love his compassion for Christ.

After thorough DNA testing on this particular cross, I found it to be of such uniqueness I am personally convinced it is the cross of Christ. However, after much consideration, my contact has decided to forgo selling the cross to anyone. His desire is to place the cross in protective keeping from both human intruders and the elements of deterioration. This decision was made after much consideration of prayer and spiritual counsel.

I know you expressed interest in purchasing the cross. However, this isn't possible, due to the owner's decision. There will be much immediate expense to place the cross in a secure environment. The ongoing cost of preserving the cross will be astronomical. It is therefore my pleasure to inform you your previous financial gift to this project will assure the cross of Christ will be in constant safekeeping. I have informed my accountant to establish a trust for the purpose of facilitating your gift to this project. You can be pleased you are a part of the ongoing preservation of the cross upon which our blessed Savior died.

I am indeed indebted to you for your help in this worthy cause. Your generous gift has made our weighty task bearable.

Sincerely,
Doctor Gary Carter

"What do you think?" Gary asked.

"He'll sue you."

"I don't think so."

"Why not?"

"A lawsuit would reveal too much personal information about his ministry."

"Is it ethical to keep the money without giving him something in return for it?"

"If I kept it for myself, it would be very unethical. For the cross project? Yes, I believe it is ethical. He set himself up for this and he'll have to suffer his loss."

"Don't you feel a tinge of guilt?"

"For not giving the money back to Reverend Small?"

"Yes. After all, it was, or still is, his money. Don't you agree?"

"No, I don't agree. It's from donations of thousands of caring Christians who assume his intentions are pure and ask for nothing in return. He gave it to me, no strings attached, if I remember correctly. When I consider what Zaki Ahmed has sacrificed financially by his decision to give the cross away, Reverend Small's contribution is mere pittance. I don't think Reverend Small has been squeaky clean in all the events the past few weeks, nor were his motives pure in giving the money in the first place."

"Half a million is a lot of money."

"Do you have any idea what it'll cost to keep the cross in a humidity-controlled atmosphere, encased in some sort of platinum container, protected from bugs and the elements and safe from thieves for the next few decades?"

"Not really."

"It'll take every dime the cross' trust fund generates and more. Reverend Small said for me to consider it a gift for my ministry. Well, my ministry now is to protect the cross. What little discomfort losing the money does to IBIMM's budget is small compared to Christ's death on the cross. For once the cross has cost Reverend Small instead of making him another mint."

"What will you tell Reverend Tillman?"

"That's an issue I don't think I'll have to worry about for a while."

"You think he bought the cross the Antiquities Authorities had?"

"I suspect so."

"How much money do you think he gave for it?"

"A lot. He's going to be awfully upset when he finds out the stain on the wood isn't blood."

"How do you know?"

"Zaki confessed. He faked the bloodstain."

"Will Reverend Tillman suspect you have the real cross?"

"I think so. That's why I have to put it into safe keeping immediately. I suspect he'll come after it when he realizes his is fake. He is a persistent man with the means to get what he wants. I also suspect he had something to do with your kidnapping. He knew too much about your activities, especially your going to Ohio to visit with your mother. I think he had you kidnapped as security to make sure he got the cross."

"He may be conniving and self centered, but I don't think he was involved with my kidnapping."

"Why not?"

"I can't put my finger on it. Call it woman's intuition, but I don't think it was Tillman's doing. The kidnappers were too...too inhuman. Never ate...never slept. The leader's eyes were like firebrands when he became angry. Plus, the text message from Pastor Johnson seemed to verify they were demons in disguise."

"Do you think they were a part of skull-face's forces?"

"I'm not sure, but I'm sure glad it's over."

"Will the spiritual warfare ever be over this side of heaven?"

Let's talk about something else."

"Like what?"

"Shopping."

"Where?"

"Circle Center."

"How long?"

"Days."

"Sounds wonderful."

215

CHAPTER
FIFTY-FIVE

Goleth's footsteps echoed throughout the chamber. He stopped a few feet short of the throne and knelt, waiting for Zatar's venomous outrage. It did not come.

Goleth broke the silence. "I have found the cross, Your Majesty."

"Found? I do not see it."

"I have found it but have not yet been able to obtain it. I will, Your Majesty. Soon."

"I have waited too long. While I sit here waiting, the story of the cross draws many away from me. Do you not understand? I must have the cross in order to destroy its influence."

"I will get it for you, Your Majesty. I need a little more time."

"No. You have failed me too long. Your time is up. I have a plan of my own."

"What is that, my lord?"

"You will see soon enough."

CHAPTER
FIFTY-SIX

They exited the plane and walked briskly up the ramp leading into the Indianapolis terminal. A salvo of cheers and the snapping of lenses startled them.

"What's this all about?" Celeste asked.

"Looks like a leak has sprung in our secret plan."

The wall of reporters made Gary uncomfortable. Celeste snuggled closer to his side.

"Doctor Carter, could we ask a few questions?" a reporter called out.

"I don't really know what to say. What kind of questions?"

"About the cross. Is it true you claim to have found the cross upon which the Romans crucified Jesus Christ?"

"Yes and no. A friend of mine, Zaki Ahmed, from Israel, found a cross. I did some DNA testing and found very strong evidence the cross is authentic."

"Authentic as in the cross Christ was crucified upon?" A reporter challenged Gary's inconclusive answer.

"Yes. I believe it is the cross of the Crucifixion."

"Where was the cross found?"

"In Galilee…northern Israel…the ruins of Bethsaida."

"Have you brought the cross with you?"

"Can we see it?"

217

"What are you going to do with it?

A bombardment of questions gushed from the sea of reporters. Gary held up his hand in a gesture for order.

"At a later time when we are more prepared and not so tired I will make a statement. I don't want to make any more statements at this time." Gary pushed his way through the crowd, with Celeste pressing close to his side.

"Are you going to sell the cross, Doctor Carter?"

The question stopped Gary in his tracks. He turned slowly in the direction of the voice. He recognized the face. The man stood head and shoulders above the crowd. It was the chauffeur, Brother Benjamin's chauffeur, the one who escorted him while he was in Orlando. Jamel Thomas.

"No." Gary's voice revealed his resentment for the insinuating question. "No, the cross isn't for sale."

"The cross has always been for sale, Doctor Carter." The accusing eyes of Thomas glared at him.

"What do you mean by that, sir?" a reporter asked, the attention suddenly turning away from Gary and focusing on the tall, dark stranger in the crowd.

Gary tried to walk away but the crowd surrounded them.

"I'm speaking of the commercialization of Christianity, from the archaic act of selling of indulgences to the present day selling of religious trinkets. If the monies used to purchase the millions of crosses that adorn the steeples of churches and decorate the dashboards of cars and hang around the necks of individuals would be given to charity, we could feed the starving of the world."

"That could be said about most anything we purchase," another reporter argued.

"The cross of Christ is different. It hails from a higher stratum of accountability," Thomas responded.

"So you're saying no one should profit financially from the relics of Christianity. Are you suggesting Doctor Carter should refuse personal profit from the cross?"

"I relinquish the floor to the qualified and highly esteemed, Doctor Carter." Thomas tossed a smug smile at Gary.

The reporters immediately turned their attention back to Gary. Celeste clung tightly to his arm. He patted her hand gently as he mentally braced himself to face the uncertain glasnost demands of the press.

"What are your plans, Doctor Carter?"

"I—"

"Do you have a buyer?"

"I—"

"Have you placed a value on the cross?"

Gary held up a hand for order. "One question at a time, please." As the reporters quieted, he searched his soul for the right answer, an answer he'd only recently accepted. He looked beyond the crowd into the steely and exigent eyes of the challenging Jamel Thomas. "I believe the gentleman is right in his evaluation. Mankind has profited from the cross of Christ in ways unintended by our Lord. No, I don't feel I, nor anyone, should prosper financially from the sale or display of the cross upon which our Lord Jesus Christ suffered. It's like selling pieces of the rope used for a lynching. The mob shouldn't profit."

"That seems to be a fitting sermon for now, but what are your long-range intentions? Are there offers on the table? What kind? How many?"

"I don't believe the cross can rightfully belong to any one individual, church or denomination. It belongs to no one, and it should receive no veneration. Some question whether or not it should even be the emblem that represents our Lord, because it's the emblem of death. Our Lord isn't dead. He has risen. Still, I can't discard the wood that may have been touched by the body of our Lord, and into which His blood seeped and which I believe to be identifiable through scientific means. Therefore, the man who found the cross, Doctor Zaki Ahmed, an Arab Christian who lives in Jerusalem, has asked me to protect the cross from future deterioration, but also from further veneration. I will attempt to fulfill his request. Thank you for your concern."

"Don't you have a book on this subject in the making, Doctor Carter? Won't you benefit from that?" Thomas evidently didn't believe Gary's sincerity.

"Had a book in the making. I recently asked my agent to withdraw all proposals." Gary grabbed Celeste's hand and hurried through the crowd toward the baggage claim. The mass of reporters followed them, shouting additional questions.

Gary appreciated his foresight to have a professional storage company retrieve the cross. He hastily collected their luggage and headed for a set of doors leading to ground transportation. They started to cross the street when a black limo pulled alongside them and blocked their access. The driver's door opened and Jamel Thomas stepped out.

"Not again," Celeste whispered.

"Doctor Carter?"

"Yes."

"I'm pleased with your comments about your intentions for the cross."

"I'm pleased you're pleased, Mr. Thomas. Thank you for saying so." Gary patted Celeste's hand and she relaxed her grip on his arm.

"It may interest you I no longer work for Reverend Small. I've moved my family to Indy and I'm working for a local limo service. Had to take a cut in pay, but some things are worth more than money. Could I give you a lift?"

The tinted windows blocked Gary's view of the inside of the limo. Celeste's grip tightened again on his arm. Her nails dug into his Israeli-tanned skin. He heard her heavy breathing and felt his own heart racing. He hesitated.

A couple loaded to the hilt pushed their luggage cart alongside the limo. "Is this limo taken?" A man in a flowery, Hawaiian shirt, khaki pants and sandals hastily unload his luggage onto the sidewalk.

"Where to, sir?" Thomas asked.

"Fishers."

"With delight." He opened the door for them.

Gary could only stare as Jamel Thomas loaded the luggage into the trunk of the limo.

"Maybe next time, Doctor Carter."

"Yes. Next time." Gary smiled.

CHAPTER
FIFTY-SEVEN

The dedication service for the new sanctuary drew a large crowd. Gary and Celeste sat close to one another in the similar section of the old church: right side, just behind the young people. The new facility was lovely, yet modestly decorated. A host of guests, including community leaders, out of town ministers and pastors from area churches crowded the platform, each awaiting their turn to offer congratulations. Proud parishioners and a multitude of visitors came to celebrate the occasion, and as dedications can go, the service became lengthy.

An elder was halfway through a historical monologue of the local congregation—its beginning under an old oak tree, the first building they purchased, former pastors and milestones they'd accomplished the past seventy-five years—when Gary leaned toward Celeste and whispered into her ear, "I spoke to Pastor Johnson about me helping in a Sunday school class."

Her eyes brightened. "That's wonderful. What class?"

"The educational director said there's an opening in college and career."

"Does that mean you'll be home on the weekends?"

"Yes."

"I'm glad."

221

The elder finished his documentary, folded his notes and sat down. The choir director, caught off guard by the abrupt ending, rushed from the foyer to the platform. The master of ceremonies asked for an expression of appreciation for the elder's fine presentation of the church's history. The congregation clapped.

"How do you like the way the stucco slightly protrudes from the wall forming a cross?" Gary asked Celeste.

"It's okay."

"I like it. Not too gaudy but still there as a reminder."

"Just above the baptismal seems rather fitting," she responded.

"Buried with Him in baptism. Appropriate, huh?"

"Certainly appropriate."

On the director's cue, the choir rose to sing. The stage lighting that spotlighted the ministers slowly dimmed and simultaneously brightened behind them where it illuminated the fifty-voice choir. A cerulean hue accented the navy blue crosses on their white robes. The stucco cross behind them blended perfectly on the towering wall, not overbearing, but present; not showy, but sending forth a subtle, yet certain, message of the cost of redemption. It exuded a silent invitation that there's still room. It was a constant reminder of Christ's proclamation, "And I, if I be lifted up from the earth, will draw all men unto me."

Celeste leaned close to Gary. "The dimensions of the cross seem a bit off, maybe a little wider than I imagined Christ's cross to have been."

"You think so?"

"Yes. You should have given Pastor Johnson the dimensions of the real cross. He could have shared it with the architect. Ours would be the only cross with the exact dimensions of the real cross. By the way, where is the real cross? I haven't seen it since we left Israel, and you haven't said a word about where you've stored it since we returned home." Celeste's elevated voice invited the attention of the young people in front of them. She smiled her charming and innocent smile at a couple of teenagers who'd turned around to stare.

Gary gave her a scolding glance for speaking so loudly. One of the teens winked his approval at Gary and smiled.

"Where did you store the cross?" she whispered insistently.

"Somewhere safe."

"Where?"

"If I tell you, it may put you in danger again. You'd have all kinds of explanations to make to the curious…not to mention the exploiters. If I don't tell, you can always plead innocence."

"So you're not going to tell me?"

"Maybe someday. In the meantime, you'll have to settle for what you call an ill-dimensioned stucco cross over our church baptistery. I think it's kind of a nice touch to an otherwise drab wall. Don't you think so?"

Celeste stared long and intently at the wider than usual stucco cross protruding from the wall, rising just behind the heads of the elevated choir. She never answered Gary's question.

www.ingramcontent.com/pod-product-compliance
Lightning Source LLC
Chambersburg PA
CBHW031359250626
47155CB00004B/1337